THREAD HERRINGS

Center Point
Large Print

Also by Lea Wait and available from
Center Point Large Print:

Twisted Threads
Threads of Evidence
Thread and Gone
Dangling by a Thread
Tightening the Threads

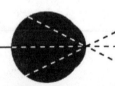

**This Large Print Book carries the
Seal of Approval of N.A.V.H.**

THREAD HERRINGS

A Mainely Needlepoint Mystery

LEA WAIT

CENTER POINT LARGE PRINT
THORNDIKE, MAINE

This Center Point Large Print edition
is published in the year 2019 by arrangement with
Kensington Publishing Corp.

The text of this Large Print edition is unabridged.
In other aspects, this book may vary
from the original edition.
Printed in the United States of America
on permanent paper.
Set in 16-point Times New Roman type.

ISBN: 978-1-64358-063-0

Library of Congress Cataloging-in-Publication Data

Names: Wait, Lea, author.
Title: Thread herrings : a mainely needlepoint mystery / Lea Wait.
Description: Large Print edition. | Thorndike, Maine : Center Point
    Large Print, 2019. | Series: Mainely needlepoint mystery series
Identifiers: LCCN 2018048017 | ISBN 9781643580630
    (hardcover : alk. paper)
Subjects: LCSH: Murder—Fiction. | Large type books. |
    GSAFD: Mystery fiction.
Classification: LCC PS3623.A42 T476 2019 | DDC 813/.6—dc23
LC record available at https://lccn.loc.gov/2018048017

THREAD
HERRINGS

CHAPTER 1

"Happy the maid who circling years
   improve
Her God the object of her warmest love
Whose cheerful hours in pleasant moments
The book the needle and the pen divide."

      —Stitched, with three alphabets,
    in 1794 by Lucy Davis, age thirteen,
      in Ipswich, Massachusetts.

"This is an adventure?" I grumbled, still half asleep, as I maneuvered my sweatered-parkaed-and-booted self into the passenger seat of the faded red van Sarah Byrne used for her antiques business. "The sun isn't even up. I couldn't read the thermometer outside my kitchen window clearly because it was covered with snow, but the temperature is somewhere near zero."

Sarah laughed. "Good morning, Angie! Aren't you the born Mainer who likes to take early morning walks?"

"Not in the dark. Not in a deep freeze. So . . . not in February." I managed to fasten my seatbelt after lengthening it to fit over all my cold weather attire. "And definitely not without coffee." I'd managed to get myself out from under my quilts

7

and feed Trixi, my six-month-old black kitten, but I hadn't had time to make coffee. "When I lived in Arizona I missed Maine winters and hated the heat. I'd forgotten about frozen noses and toes." I looked out at the dark world. "Although once the sun comes up all that snow and sparkling ice will be beautiful."

" 'It sifts from Leaden Sieves— / It powders all the Wood. / It fills with Alabaster Wool / The Wrinkles of the Road—' " said Sarah.

"Emily Dickinson quotation, right?" I wasn't even wide-awake yet, and Sarah was already spouting lines from her favorite poet.

"Emily always has something relevant to say," she said, smiling at me. "Don't worry. Coffee is doable. We'll stop at the Dunkin' Donuts up on Route 1. You'll have plenty of time to wake up before we get to Augusta."

"The auction doesn't start until nine o'clock," I complained. "Why did we have to leave at five-thirty?"

"The preview opens at seven, and it takes more than ninety minutes to get to Augusta," she reminded me. "You and Patrick went to Portland yesterday to check out art galleries, so we couldn't go to the preview then. We have to get to the auction house in time to register and claim seats and check out the lots being auctioned. Sales are always 'as is, where is.' Auctioneers sometimes miss details, and no auctioneer knows about all antiques. You can't totally depend on his or her word for anything during the sale."

"No returns?"

"Definitely not," said Sarah. "That's why we have to decide ahead of time what we want to bid on, and how much we're willing to spend on each item. It's easy to get carried away and spend too much if you haven't planned ahead."

"And you do this once or twice a week." I shook my head incredulously, hoping the motion would help keep my eyes open.

"This time of year I pick up inventory for next summer. Summer's when antique collectors and people furnishing their homes in 'authentic' period styles invade Maine with full wallets and open credit cards. I only open my shop 'by appointment or chance' in January and February."

I hadn't known anything about antiques (other than those I'd grown up with in my early nineteenth-century home) until I'd met Sarah. Some of her antiques were fascinating, and some strange. But she made a living from her shop, From Here and There, so she knew what she was doing. Months ago I'd said it might be fun to attend an auction; auctions were a Maine experience I'd missed.

This was the first one she'd thought I might be interested in. Several pieces of antique needlework were being sold, and, after all, the business I managed, Mainely Needlepoint, was all about needlework. Most of the time we did new custom work, but we also identified and restored older pieces.

"Did you and Patrick have fun in Portland yesterday?"

The heater in the van was beginning to make a difference. My nose was no longer frozen, and I pulled off my gloves. "We had a good day. Patrick's been on a painting binge for the past month. He still has trouble holding a brush because of his burn scars, but his occupational therapist says painting will improve his flexibility. Between his painting and opening his gallery on weekends, I haven't seen him much recently. I've been organizing the accounts for Mainely Needlepoint and contacting decorators we haven't worked with to try to add some commissioned projects. So when Patrick suggested I go with him to Portland to check out other galleries, I agreed. He's looking for galleries that might feature his art, and, at the same time, collecting names of artists to add to his gallery here in Haven Harbor." I was getting a crash course in art. Dating an artist and gallerist could do that.

"I'll bet you had a good lunch, too. Portland has great restaurants."

I nodded. "But not a long lunch. A lot of galleries are in Portland." My feet had hurt after walking all day in my L.L. Bean boots. They kept out snow and slush, but, despite my heaviest wool socks, they weren't comfortable for long city walks.

"Did Patrick find any artists whose work he liked?"

"A couple he's going to contact. And Clem—you remember Clem Walker?"

"That television reporter you went to high school with?" Sarah crinkled her nose. "Couldn't forget her. She was here at Christmas, along with her crew, filming people like Skye, who wanted a quiet holiday without publicity."

Patrick's mother, Skye West, was a well-known actress, and Clem and her camera crew had been pesky around the holidays. "She was, I'll admit. But she's an old friend, and she's helped me out a couple of times in the past year. Sometimes a reporter has to be a pest to get a story. Anyway, she called me a few times in January. She's dating Steve Jeffries, a sculptor from Biddeford, and she wanted Patrick to see his latest exhibit. She's hoping Patrick will take a couple of Steve's constructions for his gallery. Yesterday we saw some of his work."

"How was it?"

"Large. Interesting. Movable metal sculptures someone with a lot of money might install in his or her garden or in front of their business. Abstract, of course. Some were wind-sensitive, like giant pinwheels."

"Sounds big for Patrick's gallery."

"True. But he was intrigued by a couple of Steve's smaller pieces. In any case, art was yesterday. Today is antiques. I'll be excited as soon as I wake up."

Sarah pulled between mounds of plowed snow into the Dunkin' Donuts parking lot and joined the cars in the takeout line. "One large hot chocolate with whipped cream," she ordered, and then looked at me.

"My usual."

Sarah knew me well. "And one large coffee, black. Plus a small box of assorted donut holes." She winked at me. "Sugar for energy, right?"

A few minutes later we were back on our way, sipping and munching.

"We'll make good time," said Sarah. "I was afraid the roads would be icy, but so far they've been sanded."

Route 1 was clear of snow, although in the early morning darkness it was like driving through a white-walled tunnel.

The coast of Maine gets little snow most years, considerably less than western or northern Maine, or the White Mountains in New Hampshire. But this year had been different. We hadn't seen grass since Thanksgiving.

"Road crews are out twenty-four hours a day when they're needed."

"You're right," said Sarah. "I haven't missed

one auction this winter, or had one canceled. Everyone with a truck seems to have a plow attachment."

"Plowing is one of the winter jobs fishermen and landscapers and those in summer tourist industries count on," I agreed. "At least in years when there's snow."

"Most Mainers welcome snow." Sarah shook her head. "Open winters, when there's little snow, are devastating for people who work in winter tourist industries like skiing or snowboarding or snowmobiling."

"So . . . before we get to Augusta, fill me in. I know there are needlepointed pictures and samplers in the sale that we'll check out. What else do we have to do?"

"First, we register and get our bidding numbers," Sarah explained. "We'll have separate numbers, since I'm a dealer."

"What's the difference?" I asked, relishing a jelly-filled donut hole and trying to keep from dripping jelly on my parka.

"I don't have to pay sales tax, since what I'll buy will be for resale," Sarah explained. "You have to pay tax. We both have to pay the buyer's premium."

"What's that?"

"Fifteen to twenty percent added to the winning bid that goes to the auctioneer and his staff. So when you bid, remember, including taxes, you'll be paying twenty-five percent more for each item than you've bid."

"That's a lot," I commented.

"It can add up," Sarah agreed. "But unless there's a bidding war, auction prices are lower than retail. They have to be, or dealers wouldn't buy, and most of the bidders today will be dealers. And because dealers will only bid wholesale values, people like you, making personal purchases, can get bargains."

"I remember the mink coat you wore to Skye's Christmas party," I reminded her. "You got that really cheap."

"I did," she agreed. "Not everyone wants fur these days. But I don't think any fur coats will be in this auction. Most of the lots today, according to the flier, are furnishings from two estates near Augusta. Old Maine families."

"Why wouldn't the families keep their heirlooms?"

Sarah shrugged. "Sometimes multiple heirs can't agree on dividing an estate. Should they consider current value? Memories and sentiment? How can distributions be made equitable? So instead of arguing they put everything up at auction and bid against one another for whatever they want. And, of course, sometimes no one in the family wants anything, so it all ends up at auction. Technically, we're going to an estate sale. More typical auctions include items consigned by many different people."

"An estate auction doesn't sound like fun for the families involved."

"No," Sarah agreed. "But their loss may be our gain."

I shook my head. "I'm lucky I'm the only descendant in my family. Gram's already given me her house and a lot of the things in it." Gram had married Reverend Tom last June and moved down the street to the rectory, where Tom lived. They were happy, and, at twenty-eight, I'd unexpectedly found myself the owner of a large Haven Harbor house. I was still getting used to the challenges of home ownership. "What families are selling their estates at this auction?" Maybe I'd heard of one.

"The brochure didn't say. Consigners don't always want to be identified, because of family squabbles, or financial difficulties, or just because they want privacy. Every family's different." Sarah didn't need to say anything more. Her recent family experiences with inheritances had not been positive.

"Not knowing who the owners were makes it all a little mysterious," I added.

"Sellers at auctions are seldom identified. People downsizing; people who've cleaned out their attics or barns and found interesting items they don't want to keep. People who've inherited things their parents treasured, but that they don't want. 'Our own possession—though our own—

/ 'Tis well to hoard anew— / Remembering the Dimensions / Of Possibility.' Remember that collection of antique needleworking tools I bought last fall?"

"Of course. Gram loves the Limoges needle and thimble cases I gave her for Christmas."

"That collection had been handed down a couple of generations. Earlier owners had added to it, but the current owner removed a few items she was especially attached to, and then auctioned off the rest. That happens, especially when someone has amassed a large collection. No one in the family wants the whole collection, so it ends up at an auction house where it's bought by other collectors, or by dealers."

"So, what do we do after we register and get bidding numbers?" I asked, wiping sugar off my hands and lap and finishing my coffee. The sun wouldn't be up until almost seven, about the time we'd get to the auction house. But I finally felt awake.

"We put our coats on the seats we want, to reserve them, and we buy catalogs."

"Lists of everything to be sold?"

"Right. In the order they'll be sold. The list includes a brief description, and an estimate of the amount the auctioneer thinks the lot will go for. That's helpful, but don't feel confident or intimidated by the estimates. They can be wildly inaccurate," Sarah advised. "And remember, you're bidding not only against people in the room, but also those bidding by telephone or Internet, and those who've left bids before the auction starts. What each item is sold for depends more on who the bidders are on any given day than on the lot's value, although both are important. A mid-nineteenth-century iron bank in the shape of an elephant may be worth seventy-five dollars to an antique dealer. But if there are collectors of banks, or collectors of elephants, in the audience, it could go for hundreds. Dealers drop out of the bidding when it gets too high for them to resell at a profit, but collectors sometimes keep going way above retail prices."

It sounded complicated.

"And then we get to look at the items themselves?"

"Exactly," Sarah confirmed. "We'll both want to look at the samplers and other needleworked items, but after that we can wander. I want to check out the pine furniture they advertised and the folk art and antique toys. They sell well for me."

"I'll look at the jewelry," I mused. "You once told me jewelry can go below appraised value, and I only have one or two pieces that aren't costume jewelry. It would be fun to dream."

"Exactly what auctions are for," Sarah confirmed.

The van was heating up, or maybe I was, after

the coffee. "Sorry to have been so grumpy when you picked me up," I said. "I'm looking forward to this. My first auction! It's like a treasure hunt."

"You never know what you might find," Sarah agreed. "Just make sure to look carefully at anything you might bid on, so you don't have any surprises after you get it home."

CHAPTER 2

"We have nearly, if not quite, lost the art of embroidering in wool, in which our grandmothers so excelled. Tokens of their labor and skill remain in many an old country house, where coarse twilled calico, or perhaps a flimsy neutral fabric of neutral tint, has been transformed into a priceless heirloom, covered diagonally by foliage and birds in worsted embroidery."

—From *Peterson's Magazine*
(an American magazine for women),
April 1874.

The auction house parking lot was full. Most of the spots between piles of plowed snow were filled by trucks or vans; the occasional car was an exception. And, despite the month and weather, license plates were not only from Maine but also from New York, Connecticut, Massachusetts, Vermont, and even North Carolina.

"Dealers," Sarah pointed out. "The brochure was designed to be enticing. Two old families, items from the eighteenth and nineteenth centuries, and possibly before. That's catnip to an antique dealer."

We lined up at the registration desk. The other bidders ranged in age from twenties to, I suspected, eighties. Many seemed to know one another. Sarah gave the auctioneer's wife, who was registering bidders, her Maine resale certificate. All I had to do was fill out my contact information and a credit card number. ("There's a surcharge if you use the credit card. Paying by cash or check is preferred. The credit card is just backup," Sarah whispered.) Or, I figured, to be used if I took whatever I'd bought and headed out without paying. I was glad I'd brought my checkbook.

Sarah was number sixty-three, and I was sixty-four. Lucky numbers? I hoped.

My adrenaline (or was it the caffeine?) was flowing as we hung our coats on two seats in the third row, on an aisle.

"So we can get out easily if we want to buy coffee or use the ladies' room," Sarah explained. "From the third row we can see the items as well as anyone, but the runners won't be stepping on our feet."

"Runners?"

"The men and women who get the items from the display room, bring them to the auctioneer, and then walk them around to display them while the bidding is going on. If the items are small, the runner will then deliver them to the highest bidder."

I nodded, fascinated. This world had its own vocabulary.

The display room of the auction house was about the size of a high school basketball court, but with a lower ceiling. Paintings, prints, quilts, wall clocks, mounted deer, moose, and bear heads, and an assortment of household items like bed warmers, farm tools, and copper pans were hung on one wall. Rows of furniture, from potty chairs to beds to bureaus, dining room tables, desks, rocking horses, and butter churns, stood in rows in the middle of the room. Glass cases of jewelry, china, old guns, and small decorative items were along the back wall. Carpets and rugs filled one corner. The rest of the items, from kitchen tools to snuff boxes to dollhouses to writing boxes, were arranged on tables.

"See the boxes under the tables?" Sarah pointed as we wove our way through the crowd to the wall where the needlepointed items were hanging. "Those are box lots: books and kitchenware and tools and miscellaneous household items, none of which are too valuable. The boxes are sold as individual lots—you get whatever's in them. If you're lucky, a couple of good items are in each box. And sometimes a treasure escapes the auctioneer's eyes. That's why you'll see people going through the boxes carefully."

Everything in the room was tagged with a lot number.

All around us, people were examining the items. Some stood, looking slowly and carefully at lots they were interested in. Others were checking tape measures or magnifying glasses or reference books on antiques. Tables were being overturned, pictures removed from the walls, and catalogs checked. No one talked much, or, if they did, they spoke softly to a friend or partner.

"You don't want to advertise what you might be bidding on," Sarah explained quietly. "Dealers watch other dealers. If they know, for example, that Mrs. Jacques is an expert on porcelain, and that she's going to bid on, say, lot 454, they figure that lot must be good. They might bid against her because they trust her judgment. So she'll make a note in her catalog to remind herself to bid. After all, there may be six hundred lots in an auction, and she may only be interested in, say, forty-two. She may not even make that note until she's looking at another lot."

"Wow. I had no idea so much was involved in bidding."

"Dealers are competitive," Sarah assured me. "After all, this is how we make our living."

We'd almost gotten to the wall of framed paintings, prints, photographs, and, yes, needle-work.

Five pieces were tagged to be sold as separate lots. Sarah took one off the wall and turned it over. "The frame looks original," she said, pointing to the shading on the back and the four-sided nails that secured the backing. "It's a traditional Maine sampler, dated and signed."

Charity Providence, age eight, had stitched it. Her work was neat, but faded. The linen backing was tan, and, although, looking carefully, it appeared that she'd stitched her three alphabets in shades of blue, the threads were now grayed with age. Charity hadn't stitched a verse, but she'd included her location (Hallowell, Maine), the year (1800), a two-story house surrounded by what might be pine trees, and a border of strawberries.

"Nice," said Sarah. "A little too faded, unfortunately, for most collectors, but the stitching has held. Silk threads in samplers as old as this one have often rotted and broken. I suspect her family framed this shortly after she finished it, but in those days they didn't have glass that blocked the sun's rays. It might even have been hung near a window."

The sampler next to Charity's was a memorial sampler, stitched primarily in black threads, showing a man, a woman, two children, and a dog, all with bowed heads, mourning at a gravestone beneath a weeping willow tree. The two names on the gravestone were hard to read, but the last name was Providence.

"Is all the needlework from the Providence family?" I asked.

"I'd guess so," said Sarah. "Remember, everything in the auction is from two families. I don't know what the current name of the family is; the Providences may have daughtered out, but Providence was a family name in late eighteenth-century Maine."

I stopped. " 'Daughtered out?' "

"A generation that had no sons, only daughters. When the daughters married they took their husband's names, or they died single. In either case, the original family name ended. So whoever put these pieces up at auction may not have the last name Providence."

Daughtered out? I was the only child in my generation. If I married and took my husband's name, the Curtis name in our branch of the family would disappear. I decided on the spot that if I married I'd keep my last name.

The third piece on the wall was a genealogy piece. Not a family tree; more a listing, like recorded dates in a family Bible. Name, date of birth, and date of death. I counted twelve members of the Providence family, the last of whom died in 1838. "It looks as though several people worked on that piece, at different times," I said. Some names were stitched more neatly than others, and the threads marking the dates of death didn't match those of the birth dates.

"You're right," Sarah agreed. "The linen might have been kept in a drawer or desk, and taken out and added to when there was a birth or a death. See?" She pointed. "There's no way of knowing what the relationships of these people are other than by guessing based on their dates."

"Four children died before they were three," I added, looking closely at the dates.

"And see the listing for Verity? A child was born the day before she died. Probably she died in childbirth," Sarah said.

"Sad."

The fourth sampler was a more conventional one, very elaborate, with a verse, alphabets, numbers, a rural scene with sheep and dogs, and urns of flowers in each corner. The colors were brighter than those in the other samplers. "This one will go high," Sarah predicted, softly. "It's dated, 1802; it's from Maine, again: Hallowell. And it's well preserved."

It had been stitched by ten-year-old Amity Providence. Charity's younger sister? If we'd had more time I would have looked at the genealogical sampler again.

But there was a room full of other lots to check out.

"What about this one?" I asked, passing several oil paintings and pointing to another large needle-work. "It looks like a coat of arms."

"It does. Although about a third of the stitching is gone. I wonder if it was done here, or in England? Stitching coats of arms was more common there. Americans didn't have family crests or coats of arms."

The coat of arms *was* in poor condition. The glass protecting it was cracked, and dirt had sifted onto the embroidery. Threads were broken or missing in several places, so only part of the crest was clear, and the linen backing was torn in several places. Still, it fascinated me. "Is that an eagle?" I said, trying to make sense of what might have been part of a bird on the crest.

Sarah shook her head. "I'm not interested in it. No one wants someone else's coat of arms, and that one isn't in good enough condition to sell, anyway."

"It could be repaired," I suggested. "Gram is pretty good at that." I kept looking at the crest, wondering who'd stitched it, and when. Who'd been proud of a heritage that included a coat of arms? The other embroideries were from the late eighteenth and early nineteenth centuries. I wasn't an expert on American history, but I knew not a lot of Americans had bragged about their connections to nobility—especially English nobility—right after the American Revolution.

Or maybe the coat of arms was from another country? I didn't know enough to guess.

"Why bother trying to repair it?" Sarah asked. "It's not beautiful. It's in poor condition. Its only value might have been to the person it represented, and, if it's here, no one in his family wanted it."

"But don't coats of arms belong to families?" I asked.

"They were awarded to individuals, not families," Sarah corrected. "Embroidered coats of arms originally were worn over armor, so knights could be identified when they were in competitions or battles." She glanced at the embroidery in front of us. "I don't see any identifying name, either of the owner or the woman who stitched it. In any case, I need to look at the other lots." She made a couple of notes on her catalog. "I'll bid on the four other samplers," she said softly to me. "I'll have to think about how high to go. That last sampler may be a budget-killer."

"You go ahead. I'm going to wander and see what else is here," I said.

Sarah headed for the cases of china, which had no interest for me.

I took one more look at the coat of arms. I couldn't say exactly why, but it fascinated me. Was it cast aside as an embarrassment, which might explain its condition? And when had that been? Shortly after it was stitched? A hundred years ago? Two hundred?

Other prospective bidders were standing near me, waiting for me to move on. A middle-aged woman with short brown hair highlighted with blond took my place next to the coat of arms. "What about the samplers?" she said to the bearded man with her.

He shook his head. "Just old stuff. Where

would you hang them? I'd rather we used our share of the money to buy some good mahogany furniture, or maybe a gold-framed mirror."

"Josie's going to want the dining room table and chairs," she answered. "She's always wanted them. We don't want to try to outbid her on those. What about Grandmother's wedding ring china?"

"I don't care about china. You can't put that old stuff in the dishwasher anyway. What about the clock?" He pointed at a grandfather's clock nearby.

"It never kept the right time. Drove me crazy."

They moved on.

I didn't know who they were, but they must be connected to one of the families who'd owned these furnishings. If they, or Josie, whoever she was, had wanted them, why were they being auctioned off?

A small mystery, but not one that concerned me.

I walked past several watercolored seascapes, a large oil portrait of a ringleted little girl in a blue dress holding a doll by its arm, and several framed World War I posters. Three men were looking through a box of pictures—prints?—in a corner.

Who'd owned all these things? The parents or grandparents of that woman I'd heard talking about "Grandmother's china"?

Once, each of these things now lined up to

be sold had been chosen, had taken its place in a household, valued, and thought of with sentiment. Now, sadly, they were filling spaces in a large auction-house showroom, destined for antique shops, and, I hoped, for other homes where they'd be valued.

I almost laughed at myself for being so sentimental.

These were things, not people.

The farther I walked through the preview room the more I realized how little I knew about antiques, or about what people valued. One man was carefully examining a box of old photographs. If they weren't relatives, why would he be interested? Sarah would know. I didn't.

I admired an old, framed, Maine state flag that, the catalog said, had been flown over the statehouse in Augusta during World War II.

I didn't need any furniture, but I walked along the rows of pine, mahogany, cherry, and oak tables, bureaus, and desks. I liked the cherry pieces best, but, according to the auction catalog estimates, they'd all go too high for me. I tried to imagine eighteenth- or nineteenth-century men and women dining at the tables, or writing at the desks. I shivered, wondering who they'd been, and what their lives had been like. How they'd feel if they saw their possessions being auctioned off to strangers.

The vintage jewelry didn't interest me as

much as I'd hoped. "Would you like to see any of the pieces up close?" asked the auction house employee standing in back of the glass showcase.

I touched the gold angel I wore on a chain around my neck. Mama had given it to me for my first Communion, and it reminded me of her. It was only valuable to me.

I moved on to the earrings. "We have a number of small earrings in this sale," she pointed out. "What's your birthstone?"

"I was born in April," I said, knowing that probably prohibited my buying birthstone earrings.

"Diamond," said the woman, hovering over the earrings. "We have two pairs of diamond earrings." She picked them up and handed them to me.

"Is this silver?" I asked, looking at the tiny studs in my hand.

"Platinum," she corrected me.

The slightly larger pair of earrings was set in gold. The stones weren't large, but the gold reflected them. "I like these," I said. "But they're clip-ons. I have pierced ears."

"Any jeweler can change them for you," she assured me. "I suspect that pair was owned by a young woman. Older women tend to prefer larger stones."

I nodded, as though that made sense, and

handed them back to her. "Thank you for showing them to me."

She turned to the next potential bidder. I marked the lot number of the diamonds set in gold in my catalog. They were appraised at $4,000. Too high for me. And I didn't exactly live a diamond-earring lifestyle. But if I'd had more money I'd have been tempted.

China, crystal, hand-painted porcelain. Vases, teapots. A display case of swords, pistols, and rifles that I couldn't even get close to because of the crowd. A lot of people were interested in antique weapons.

Other things were fun to look at, but I didn't need a nineteenth-century dollhouse, or a cuckoo clock, or a mahogany writing case, or French marionettes. Who would want these things?

Part of the fun of the auction would be seeing who bought what, and for how much.

I drifted back to the wall where the embroideries were hung. Two women were looking closely at the sampler Sarah had predicted would go high. No one was paying attention to the coat of arms and family crest. I was pretty sure that was an eagle, or at least part of one. And a flag, although so many threads were missing I had no idea what country it represented.

Where was Sarah? I headed for the refreshment table and bought another cup of coffee. This was going to be an interesting day, but a long one.

CHAPTER 3

Epitaph inscribed upon a tablet in the Cloisters in Westminster Abbey, in London, England: "She was excellent with her needle."

—From *The Dictionary of Needlework: An Encyclopaedia of Artistic, Plain and Fancy Needlework* by Sophia Frances Anne Caulfeild and Blanche C. Saward, London: L. Upcott Gill, 1882.

"See anything you want to bid on?" Sarah asked as she sat next to me. I'd stopped looking fifteen minutes before, and was sipping coffee and watching other people finding their seats, consulting handwritten lists or auction catalogs, and sometimes checking what I assumed were notebooks listing either items they were looking for, or those they already had in stock.

"I saw a couple of possibilities," I said, not ready to admit anything. "It'll all depend on what they go for."

Sarah nodded. "Always. And then, there are moments when something you hadn't even considered bidding on is going for such a low price you can't resist it."

"How many auctions have you been to?" I asked, curiously.

"Hundreds, I guess. In Australia there weren't as many as here in New England. Now I get to thirty or forty a year."

"Wow." I'd had fun so far, and the action hadn't even started. But thirty or forty a year? I was pretty sure the fascination would wear off after a while.

Sarah checked her own notes and asked, "What's the highest lot number you're interested in?"

I glanced through my (short) list. "267."

"Good," she nodded. "My highest item is 301. We should be able to leave around noon or a little after."

"How many lots does the auctioneer sell an hour?" I asked as a tall, heavy-set, bearded man put a wooden gavel on the high desk in the front of the room.

"Depends on the auctioneer," Sarah answered. "Between sixty and a hundred at most auctions like this. At high-end art auctions, not as many."

"In one hour?"

She nodded. "You'll see."

"Everyone take their seat," the auctioneer bellowed. He didn't need the microphone on his desk. "Preview is closed. Runners, bring lots one through fifteen to the front." I had to listen closely; he spoke faster than anyone I'd ever heard. "Remember. All items will be sold where is as is. If you haven't examined an item ahead of time, don't bid on it. Small items will be delivered to you. Large items will be held with your number in the back of the hall. All items must be paid for before they're removed from the building, and all items must be removed today unless other arrangements have been made. All bidders must be registered and have numbers. Raise your numbers high when you bid. The auctioneer has the discretion to determine which bids are successful if more than one person bids at a time. Any disputed bids or claims should be referred to the Maine Board of Licensing of Auctioneers in Augusta."

He stopped and sipped from a large bottle of Poland Spring water. "Lot number one, to the front!"

A middle-aged woman with graying hair wearing a yellow "Augusta Auctions" T-shirt over her jeans walked quickly to the front of the room, holding a large, mounted owl. I'd missed that in the preview. How many other items had I missed? And who would buy an old stuffed owl?

Turned out the elderly man in the first row would. The runner handed him the owl and immediately a second runner appeared next to the auctioneer. Item after item came to the front, was described, and then was hammered down. Fast.

The woman I'd heard earlier talking about

her grandmother's wedding ring china bid on it, despite frowns from the man with her. She smiled triumphantly as several boxes were delivered to her seat just off the center aisle.

She also bid on a mahogany dressing table, but so did a redheaded woman four rows in back of her. They bid each other up and sent dirty looks toward each other. The redheaded woman was the successful bidder. I glanced at the catalog. She'd paid a thousand dollars over the estimate. She might be the Josie the couple had mentioned.

Sarah saw me checking. "Depends on how much bidders want something. Estimates can be high or low."

I nodded.

Sarah was the successful bidder on the first two embroideries we'd seen, Charity's sampler and the memorial sampler. I was surprised that the depressing depiction of the tombstone and mourners went for a higher price than the sampler.

"People collect mourning art and jewelry," Sarah whispered as we made space by our feet for the two framed pieces.

I didn't ask what mourning jewelry was. It sounded depressing.

The small platinum and diamond earrings went for $500: much less than I'd anticipated, but still over my budget. I didn't bid.

Sarah got the genealogical sampler.

But she'd been right about Amity's sampler, the most elaborate in the auction and in the best condition. Three people, including Sarah, bid to start. Then, when a woman in a red turtleneck dropped out, a serious-looking couple in the back started bidding. Sarah stopped at $2,000. Bidding . didn't.

"Wow," I said. "Sorry you didn't get it."

"Those people are with the Saco Museum," Sarah said, looking at the couple who'd bought it. "They have a great collection of Maine samplers. If I couldn't get it, I'm glad it went to them, and not to a dealer or private collector."

I refocused in time to see the coat of arms come up. At first, no one bid. "Going to pass!" the auctioneer said. By now I knew that meant that with no interest, he wasn't going to sell it. I took all my courage and raised my number. "One hundred dollars!" I called out, to my own (and Sarah's) surprise.

He nodded, glanced around the room, and then pointed back at me. "Sold, to the young lady in the third row."

I felt dazed as the runner dropped the large frame in my lap. Carefully I put it at my feet, as Sarah had put her framed items. I'd made my first auction purchase.

Sarah shook her head. "What are you going to do with that?" she asked.

"I don't know. But I liked it." Was fascinated

with it, actually. I could hardly wait to get home and take it out of the old frame so I could see it better.

Sarah bought six cups hand-painted with flowers, and a set of twelve Nancy Drew first editions. I'd seen items like that in her shop. She had customers for them.

The woman with the blond highlights bought three lots in a row: a set of chairs, an elaborately framed mirror, and a high-backed wicker chair. The redhead bought a mahogany dining room table, a sideboard, and some Chinese porcelain birds. If she was Josie, I was glad she'd gotten the dining room table she'd wanted.

The two women watched each other constantly. Both family members? Maybe. But, at least today, rivals.

A high mahogany bed covered with myth-ological carvings was next. It would need a large room. "Wealthy people in the nineteenth century and before had high beds, for warmth in the winter," Sarah said, quietly. "Hot air rises. Usually there's a step stool matching the bed to help people climb up."

Both the streaked-blond woman and the redhead raised their bidding paddles and left them up. The auctioneer moved from one to the other, increasing the bid with each move. The bidding got high enough that the room quieted as other buyers watched the competition. Then, when I was almost sure the redhead had won the bed, at $5,500, a tall, skinny man in a Bowdoin College sweatshirt yelled out, "Seven thousand."

The auctioneer hesitated only a moment before asking if anyone would bid $7,500.

Both women who'd been bidding against each other looked furious.

The bed was knocked down to the man in the back.

After that he outbid both the streaked blonde and the redhead several times. Both of them were looking angrier every minute.

I'd guessed the two women were related. Was that man a relative, too? Or maybe a dealer. He was spending a lot of money.

I was tempted again when the diamond earrings in gold that I'd liked went for only $400. Bidding was contagious. But I was a new business owner. Custom needlepoint was an interesting business, but time-consuming and not as dependable as a salaried profession. I had a lot of years ahead to buy diamond earrings. And now I knew auctions were a good place to look for heirloom jewelry.

Sarah bought a box of miscellaneous Santa Clauses from the 1940s and '50s, and a handsome nineteenth-century mahogany travel desk. (A box that opened to display a writing surface and space for pens and papers and blotters.)

All the items she'd been interested in had come up by a little before twelve-fifteen. As we stood in line to pay for our purchases, I heard another bidding war between the three people I'd been watching—this time for the grandfather clock. They'd all spent thousands today, no matter who ended up with the clock.

"Want to stop in Hallowell for lunch?" Sarah asked as we took our purchases to the van. "It's been a long time since we ate those donut holes this morning, and the Liberal Cup is a fun brewpub."

I agreed. Hallowell wasn't far, and I was happy to fill up on beer-battered clams, while Sarah ate an enormous veggie burger. We both ordered the Bug Lager, which was perfect with both our lunches.

A sign on the wall read: "Hallowell is a drinking town with an antiques problem."

What would Gram and Patrick think about my first auction purchase? Patrick might not be as intrigued by the embroidery as I was, but I hoped Gram would be interested in trying to restore it.

And, of course, Trixi would be fascinated with smells dating back a couple of hundred years.

I could hardly wait to get home and tell them both about my day.

CHAPTER 4

"Be sovereign grace the guardian of my
  youth,
May Heaven-born virtue in my breast
  preside,
While wisdom, honour, innocence and truth,
Attend my steps, and all my actions guide."

—Sampler stitched at the Westtown
School in West Chester, Pennsylvania,
in 1802 by Mary Lea of Wilmington,
Delaware. Mary died in 1810,
when she was twenty-three.

By the time Sarah dropped me at my house it
was after four, dark, and close to suppertime,
although I was comfortably full after our stop at
the brewpub.

Trixi, of course, was sure she was starving,
and immediately circled my feet, and then led
me to the kitchen, where her stainless steel food
bowl was shiny and empty. I gave her some more
dry food and half a can of her favorite salmon
paté cat food. Some days she ate better than I
did.

While she was gulping her supper, I covered
part of my (not cherry) dining room table with

an old blanket and put my auction purchase on it, facedown.

The glass was already broken, and by taking the frame off and removing the linen I could see more clearly what condition the stitching was in.

I carefully pulled out the handmade four-sided nails that held the wooden backing in place and lifted the wood off.

Below it was a piece of off-white wool, torn and stained from the wood and dampness. I suspected it had originally been padding to protect the embroidery from being stained by the wood. I lifted it off carefully, expecting to find the embroidered linen below it.

Instead, I found a piece of thick paper, folded into a packet. Maybe it identified the person who'd embroidered the coat of arms?

I unfolded it carefully. The paper cracked at several seams no matter how painstaking I was. Inside was a twelve-inch-long pale blue silk ribbon, embroidered in alternating yellow and red flowers, with a narrow lace edge and a small embroidered red heart at the end. It must have been there for years, hidden from sun and air. The colors were still bright, unlike the faded silk threads on the coat of arms.

I picked the ribbon up carefully and smoothed it out on the blanket.

Then I looked more carefully at the creased paper.

"Foundling Hospital," was printed on the top, with "October 26, 1757 at two o'clock" filled in by hand beneath the printed words. The script was elaborate, and the purple ink faded. A magnifying glass and a brighter light helped me read it. "Number 12876" was written below the date, and the rest of the form was also filled in. "A male Child about two weeks old. Has been baptized Charles."

No last name. Or Charles was his last name? Underneath a list of clothing Charles had brought with him (only a few items), it read "Let particulare Care be Taken off this Child as it will be call'd for again."

What did it all mean? I put down the paper and looked at the coat of arms. Sarah had been right. It was in poor condition.

But where was the Foundling Hospital? And how did a piece of paper from a foundling hospital end up tucked behind an embroidered coat of arms? Had it been hidden? By whom? Why?

Was it connected to the Providence family whose name was on the embroideries Sarah had purchased? The paper was dated 1757. That was forty years earlier than the samplers. Had it been in back of the coat of arms since 1757? Or had it been placed there much later, when the coat of arms was framed?

And how were the coat of arms and the Foundling Hospital paper connected to Maine?

My mind filled with questions.

I poured myself a glass of red wine and called Sarah. "I removed the back of that coat of arms I bought today. Behind the embroidery was a folded paper from a Foundling Hospital, a receipt for a baby named Charles, and an embroidered ribbon."

"Weird," Sarah agreed. "I can't imagine what that means, or how it got into the lot you purchased. Sounds like you have research to do."

"Were there any people named Charles listed on that genealogical sampler you bought?" I asked.

"I'll check. I don't remember. And, although not all the samplers are dated, the earliest birth listed on the family tree one is in the 1770s. After 1757, for sure. I would have remembered a date that early."

"Wow." I sat, looking at the paper and the ribbon and the coat of arms. "When I bought the coat of arms I'd hoped to find out who it represented. But now I have a whole other mystery!" I picked up Trixi, who was sniffing the treasures I'd spread on the dining room table.

"Have you Googled *foundling hospital?*" Sarah asked.

"No. But I will. Although there must have been foundling hospitals in lots of places."

"True. But the paper you found was in English, right?"

"So the hospital I'm looking for would have been in the United States. Or England."

"Or any of the British Isles, or Canada."

"Or Australia," I added.

"Not Australia," Sarah corrected. "Australia wasn't founded until 1788. And the convicts who settled it then wouldn't exactly have been equipped to establish a foundling hospital."

"Okay," I said. "But you'll check the genealogical sampler you have for dates and names?"

"I will. I'd check it right now, but I left my purchases from today downstairs in my shop, and I'm tired. I was about to take a shower and call it a night."

"Then, tomorrow. I don't think a day will make a difference considering the date we're talking about. And, Sarah—thanks for taking me with you today. I had fun. The world of antiques is more complicated than I'd imagined."

"Come with me any time," she said. "Next auction is in Bangor early next week."

"Not next week. But maybe some time. In the meantime, I have Mainely Needlepoint work to do, and a foundling hospital to find."

"I'll let you know if I find a Charles tomorrow," she promised. "Good night. And good luck!"

I carefully picked up the paper, ribbon, and embroidery and tucked them in a drawer in the dining room unreachable by kitten paws, moved to my living room, which doubled as the Mainely Needlepoint office, and turned on my computer. Sarah was right, of course. I should look online.

According to Samuel Johnson's dictionary, in 1757, a foundling was a "child exposed to chance, without a parent or owner." Interesting definition, especially the "owner" bit. I'd always thought the word *foundling* meant orphan. Maybe it did in some circumstances, but not all orphans were "exposed to chance."

My search quickly turned up two foundling hospitals in English-speaking countries: The New York Foundling Hospital and the London Foundling Hospital. The New York institution (still in service, I noted) was founded in 1869. Too late by over a hundred years to be the organization I was looking for.

The London Foundling Hospital, on the other hand, was founded in 1739. It, too, had survived until today, but with changed programs, and under the name the Thomas Coram Foundation for Children.

The paper I had was dated 1757. I kept reading, fascinated. When a baby was entrusted to the hospital, no records were kept of the mother's or father's name, but the child was registered with a number ("Number 12876" was written on my paper), and family members were encouraged to return and reclaim their child when they could. The parent kept half of a "token" left with the child that was kept with the registration paper, called a "billet," to identify the child if a parent came to reclaim him or her. Frequently these tokens were pieces of fabric torn from the child's clothing, or a ribbon (!), or embroidery.

Sadly, of the 16,282 children who were admitted to the London Foundling Hospital between 1741 and 1760 only 152 were reclaimed. Two-thirds of the infants admitted died, although the sources I read reminded readers that the infant mortality rate for all children born in London during those years was fifty percent.

Fifty percent. What was the mortality rate for the women who'd given them birth?

So it appeared that "Charles" had been entrusted to the London Foundling Hospital. Since all children there were renamed, his name would have only been known to his biological family, whoever they were. Had he been one of the few reclaimed? Or one who'd died?

But if he'd died, then how had his registration billet ended up tucked behind an embroidery more than three thousand miles across the sea from London?

I kept reading. During some years all infants left at the hospital were accepted, leading to incredible overcrowding. In other years, a limited number of babies were accepted every month, and the children to be accepted were determined by a lottery. A mother seeking to leave her infant had to reach into a bag holding black and white balls. If she withdrew a white ball her infant was accepted for admission. If she picked a black ball, her child was not accepted. There were many more black balls than white in the bag. My eyes filled. How painful it must have been to decide to relinquish an infant—and then have your child rejected. What would you do next?

Once a fatherless child myself, although luckily with Gram to take over after Mama died, I found it fascinating that it wasn't only mothers of illegitimate children who gave up their infants. (In many years the hospital only took in children two months old or younger.) At least a third of the babies' parents were married, forced by separation or hardship to hand over their babies. As I'd suspected, some of the mothers had died.

I sipped my wine and read further.

How lucky we were to live in the United States now. If a mother or father felt he or she had to give up their child now, adoptive parents were ready—and eager—to raise their child in a safe and comfortable home. Agencies ensured that. What heartbreakingly desperate circumstances parents and their babies had been in years ago.

But how could the billet for one of those poor babies end up hidden behind a coat of arms? Those infants must have been children of deep, bone-chilling poverty, not children whose fathers would have had a coat of arms. And what was the connection to Maine? In the late eighteenth century Maine had been the District of Maine, a part of Massachusetts referred to as "the Massachusetts wilderness."

Not a place a titled man with a coat of arms would be found.

One sentence on the London Foundling Hospital's website might explain it. From 1756 until 1801, despite the limits on the number of babies being accepted into the hospital, any child who came with a donation of one hundred pounds was guaranteed a place in the hospital, no questions asked. Seventy-five babies were admitted that way.

How much would that be today? Google had the answer. One hundred British pounds in 1757 was the equivalent of about $15,000 today.

Much more money than most families—certainly any poor families—would have had.

Had Charles been one of those special seventy-five babies?

I had no way of knowing.

But I had a lot more questions.

I'd turned off my computer, but not my imagination, and was climbing into bed when Patrick called.

"How was your day with Sarah at the auction?"

"Fascinating," I admitted. "And guess what I bought?" I explained about the embroideries Sarah and I had bid on, and the packet I'd found, and its apparent connection to the London Foundling Hospital.

"Curious," he agreed. "Are you going to do more research?"

"Absolutely," I said.

"Could someone at the Maine Historical Society Library help?" he suggested. "I just talked with Steve Jeffries. You remember, the sculptor?"

"Clem Walker's friend," I agreed.

"I'm going to drive to his studio in Biddeford tomorrow morning to see more of his work, and talk about his possibly having a show here in Haven Harbor. I could drop you in Portland at the Maine Historical Society and pick you up on my way home. We'd both have company on the drive."

I hesitated only a moment. I had work to do for Mainely Needlepoint. But I liked both the idea of spending time with Patrick and of checking out the MHS. "Sounds good. When are you leaving?"

"Pick you up about nine?"

"See you then!"

I curled up under my quilts. Packed snow blanketed the Haven Harbor Green across the street, but the night was clear, and moonlight reflected the silhouettes of trees and houses on land that wouldn't be green until summer.

Trixi curled up on the pillow next to me.

Some Mainers headed south in February. But they missed so much.

What would I discover tomorrow in Portland?

CHAPTER 5

"Embroidery is, at the date of this writing, the most popular of all kinds of [needle] work, both in dress and ornament, and it is a fortunate circumstance for many women that it is so, for hundreds have been kept in employment in the last two years who would have starved had not the fashion of elaborate ornament on every article of dress been revived."

—From *The Ladies Guide to Needle Work, Embroidery, Etc., being a Complete Guide to all kinds of Ladies' Fancy work*, by S. Annie Frost, New York: Adams & Bishop, Publishers, 1877. Note: The Panic of 1873 was the beginning of a financial depression that lasted from 1873 until at least 1879 in both the United States and Europe.

Trixi woke me at seven, when the sun rose. Winter days were short, and she didn't want to miss a minute of daylight. Especially when it was breakfast time.

I managed to take a hot shower alone, Trixi purring me on as she walked back and forth from the bathroom to the top of the stairs. Had I forgotten? Breakfast was in the kitchen.

I picked a blue sweater that more-or-less went with my blue and green plaid flannel shirt, found clean jeans and wool socks, and headed downstairs.

Trixi was gulping her dry food and I was brewing coffee when Sarah texted. **"One Charles on Providence list, but not born until 1824."**

A descendant of "my" Charles? But Charles was not an unusual name. There might be no connection.

I texted back. **"Send full list of names and dates? E-mail? Heading to MHS this a.m. with Patrick."**

"Will do," came back.

I scrambled a couple of eggs with Gruyère and pepper and toasted a muffin. I'd be in Portland today, but not for an elegant lunch.

I took my coffee mug to the living room, opened the drawer where I'd hidden the treasures from yesterday, and put the billet, the ribbon, and the coat of arms in a padded envelope. I wasn't sure whether the historical society library would be able to help, but with the list Sarah was going to e-mail me, I could show them all the information I had now.

I was about to turn on my computer when my phone rang. Dave Percy, one of the Mainely Needlepointers, was on the line. "Fast call,

Angie. My class starts in a few minutes. But when do you need the needlepoint cushion for the Drake family?"

"March first," I answered, without checking my files. "Any problem finishing it?"

"No. I'm fine. Just wanted to check. I'm setting up a field trip for my sophomore biology students, and it's eating up more time than I'd hoped. Got to go now!"

Haven Harbor High School was lucky to have Dave. He was probably the only biology teacher in the state who had his own poison garden, and emphasized botany as much as zoology in his classes. Plus, he was the man to call if I needed to know something about a plant. Or a poison. It had happened.

Sarah's e-mail came a few minutes later.

FAMILY REGISTER
Joshua Providence, born Dec. 12, 1772,
   died Nov. 10, 1814
Verity Providence, born May 26, 1773,
   died Jan. 2, 1797
Mary Providence, born April 24, 1791,
   died May 26, 1792
Amity Providence, born June 7, 1792,
   died Dec. 4, 1810
Elizabeth Providence, born March 2, 1794
Hannah Providence, born Sept. 3, 1795,
   died Oct. 6, 1795

**Hannah Providence, born Aug. 20, 1796,
died Aug. 21, 1796**

**Joseph Providence, born Jan. 1, 1797,
died Dec. 10, 1838**

**Sarah Providence, born July 15, 1800,
died Jan. 11, 1857**

**Charity Providence, born Aug. 29, 1793,
died June 10, 1824**

**George Providence, born July 4, 1821,
died Feb. 28, 1832**

**Charles Providence, born Nov. 28, 1824,
died March 1, 1832**

I'd hoped there would be more names and dates, although there were a dozen.

The last date listed was Sarah's death in 1857. Who'd filled in that date? It must have been someone who'd outlived him. Maybe Elizabeth, whose date of death wasn't listed.

Joshua and Verity might have been married. Verity had died the day after Joseph was born.

Had his older sisters helped raise him? Had Joshua remarried?

The historical society would have genealogical information.

But I didn't know if the Providence family was connected to the Charles named on the foundling hospital document, or to the coat of arms. The coat of arms might have had nothing to do with the other embroideries.

Or maybe it did.

I printed Sarah's list and added it and my few notes from last night to the padded envelope.

Patrick was right on time.

" 'Morning, lady," he said, kissing me lightly as I got into his car.

" 'Morning. So you've decided to have a showing of Steve Jeffries's sculptures?"

"Not officially. I haven't issued an invitation. First I want to see what he has in his studio. I like his work, but, although part of my gallery is two stories high, most isn't. I'm hoping he has some smaller works. If not, I'll offer to show one of his larger pieces. I'd have to plan the rest of the exhibit around it so other work wouldn't be overwhelmed by his."

"Clem will be pleased you're following up with Steve," I said. "I'm surprised she didn't call to thank us for looking at his work in that Portland gallery the other day."

"You deal with her. I'd rather deal with Steve directly. He seems like a nice enough guy. I know Clem's your friend, Angie, but she's a little pushy."

She had to be pushy to change from an over-weight brunette in high school to a slim blond television reporter ten years later. Not to speak of being a woman in the workplace. If she were a man would Patrick think she was pushy? "She didn't have an easy time of it growing up."

"Neither did you. And you're not pushy."

I wasn't going to get into a debate about what Clem or I were like years ago. Or the definition of a pushy woman. I changed the subject. "So, how long will you be at the gallery?"

"Don't know how many pieces he has to show me, or whether it would be worthwhile to take him to lunch. If I don't see a future relationship with him, I'll make my visit brief."

"You'll call when you know when you can pick me up?"

"Of course. I figure you'll have at least two hours in Portland. Biddeford is twenty-five minutes from there, but that gives you my hour traveling, plus an hour in Jeffries's gallery, to do research."

"I'm not even sure I know what I'm looking for."

"I'm sure someone there will help you. So you're trying to find out who this 'Charles' is?"

"Right. But I don't know if that's his first or last name, or even if he used that name after he left the Foundling Hospital—which I'm assuming he did, since the registration slip the hospital called a billet is now here in Maine. I'm also wondering whether the historical society would recognize the coat of arms I bought. It's faded, and a lot of threads are missing."

"They might know if any distinguished Englishmen settled in Maine. Was there a date on the embroidery?"

I shook my head. "No. I don't think there ever was one. Or, if there was, it was part of the threads that have broken or worn away."

"So how is Sarah? I haven't seen her in a while."

"She's fine. Attending a lot of auctions to buy inventory for her business."

"I assumed Maine winters would be long and dreary, but everyone seems at least as busy now as in the summer."

"True enough. I talked to Dave this morning; he's stitching a cushion for one of our customers, but he's also teaching, of course, and he's spending a lot of time arranging a field trip for his students."

"And how's your grandmother?"

"She and Tom have been working at the food bank several days a week, and they have the usual choir rehearsals and women's guild meetings and Sunday activities. I'll admit I haven't gotten to church for a couple of weeks. I need to do that or I'll be getting a gentle reminder soon."

"And your other needlepointers?"

"Ruth's writing up a storm; Captain Ob's carving a couple of signs for the gift shop downtown as well as stitching some 'Save the Cormorants' pillows to fill orders we've gotten. Word is spreading about those. Ob's wife, Anna, is doing some, too. Everyone's busy. When are you going to open your gallery full-time again?"

"I'm thinking the middle of March. But it might be April. So far I have new exhibits lined up for June and July. I'll be changing them each month then. Early spring most artists want to leave their work up for a couple of months."

"So more people have a chance to see it?"

"Exactly. And I've been busy with my own paintings, too."

"Every day I admire the painting you gave me for Christmas. It's hanging in my living room, where I can see it while I work."

"And your needlepoint cushion looks perfect on my couch."

Portland was over an hour away. We chatted along the way, admiring the sun glinting on ice-covered tree branches along the highway. Crinkled, cracked ice glistened on the banks of rivers we crossed on our way south, and ice floes drifted slowly toward the sea. The New Meadows River was frozen hard enough so a dozen ice-fishing hutches were scattered along it.

"What are they fishing for?" Patrick asked.

"I don't know. I was never into ice fishing," I answered. "A few friends used to do it, but most of their families had huts on frozen lakes farther inland, or north. They caught trout in the winter, I remember. One of Gram's friends brought us a couple one year."

A long time ago.

"Could they be fishing for herring?"

"I suppose," I said. "In rivers. But most herring schools are in the Gulf of Maine in summer. They migrate to warmer feeding grounds in winter." I looked at him. "Why did you think they were fishing for herring?"

"Seems to me I've seen signs for herring for sale."

I smiled. "Herring's used for lobster bait. And, of course, they're sardines."

He frowned. "Okay. Got me on that one. How can a herring be a sardine?"

I shrugged. "I don't know. I just know herring canned in Maine and New Brunswick is called sardines."

"So, you're saying that when I'm eating sardines, I'm eating lobster bait?"

"That you are." I grinned.

"That's wicked weird," Patrick pronounced.

I shook my head, amused. I suspected the word "wicked" hadn't been in his vocabulary applied to anything but witches until he moved to Maine.

Patrick dropped me off in front of the Maine Historical Society's building on Congress Street. "I'll call as soon as I know when I can pick you up," he promised.

The historical society library was set back from the street. I opened the door cautiously. A whole library full of historical information about Maine and Maine people was intimidating. Would I even know the right questions to ask?

File cabinets, bookcases, and tables filled the room. In the back several people were seated at desks.

I took a deep breath and walked over to an oak desk where a young man wearing a turtleneck under his suit jacket was sitting. Strangely, a basket of white gloves was on the corner of his desk.

"May I help you?" he asked, looking at the padded envelope I was carrying.

"I hope so," I said. "I'm trying to find out about a coat of arms that might be connected to a family in Maine, maybe in the late eighteenth century."

"Coat of arms?" He looked at me. "I don't know a lot about them. They're connected to individuals, not families, although after the death of an owner they can be handed down. But only one person at any time can officially use a specific coat of arms." He looked at me quizzically. "They're not exactly common in Maine."

"I know." I paused. "I bought an embroidery at an auction in Augusta yesterday. It's a coat of arms of some sort with no name, or date. I think it's late eighteenth century because of other embroideries found with it. I'd like to find out who it belonged to."

"That won't be easy to do, at least for me." He paused. "Coats of arms aren't something we have a lot of information about. We do have genealogical information here. Sometimes we can help people tracing their Maine roots, and sometimes not. If we don't have records here, I'd suggest you check the town or towns where the family might have lived. Churches, town halls, library archives, or graveyard associations may have local historical information."

"Graveyard associations?"

"Some towns have organizations that record burials, historically and today, and keep graves cleaned off. In Maine that's not always simple, since there are so many small family graveyards."

Interesting, but not a help. "So there's no place I could find out who the coat of arms I bought belonged to?"

"Not in Maine. The only place I can think of that you could go would be the College of Arms in England. They're the official authority for coats of arms for the United Kingdom and parts of the Commonwealth."

I wrote that down as he continued.

"I've never contacted them, but an antiques dealer I know did several years ago. Like you, he'd bought a coat of arms and wanted to establish its provenance."

"Were they able to help him?"

The librarian shook his head. "I don't know. I

do remember him saying they charged a lot for their search services."

Not good news. I turned to leave.

"If your coat of arms is from the eighteenth century, it might have something to do with the patents."

I turned back. " 'The patents'?"

"Land grants. In the 1630s the British crown gave what they called 'patents,' or rights to land, to ten people. The patents included most of what is now Maine, plus some of Canada, New Hampshire, and Vermont."

I frowned. "I don't remember learning that in school." Or maybe I'd forgotten it. In school I'd found history boring. I was beginning to see how it was not only interesting, but sometimes had direct connections to people and events today.

"Your teachers might not have covered it. Patent ownerships were complicated and vague, and most of the owners didn't establish settlements, or, if they did, the settlements didn't last. Most people who immigrated to New England in the seventeenth and eighteenth centuries didn't acknowledge that, officially, someone back in England owned the land where they were building their homes, farms, and villages. Some might not even have known. In other places, colonial settlers were afraid the English proprietors would make them tenant farmers, as they'd done to farmers in Scotland and Ireland. To complicate matters, the patents overlapped, since they were based on incorrect maps and written in England, and also conflicted with deeds of land Abenakis and Micmacs and Passamaquoddies had sold. By the middle of the seventeenth century the Massachusetts Bay Colony had bought out several of the early patent holders, and Maine became known as the District of Maine."

That was complicated. No wonder I didn't know about it. "Okay. But what has all that to do with coats of arms?"

"Some of the men originally granted patents, like Ferdinando Gorges, had coats of arms. Of course, he died in 1647, so that was earlier than the period you're researching. But I'd guess other patent owners, or their sons or grandsons, also had coats of arms. A few came to Maine in the seventeen hundreds, hoping to revive patents their families had been granted and make their fortunes. Some died, some gave up, and a few hunkered down, survived the Revolution, and became important in the District of Maine."

"So the embroidered coat of arms I have could have been owned by a family who came to Maine before the Revolution, believing they owned land here."

"It's possible."

I was silent, thinking.

"It wasn't simple. That's why your school didn't emphasize it when they were teaching classes about the history of Maine. Maine history's not easy."

I nodded. "So, what can I do now?"

"Do you know who owned your embroidery before you bought it?"

I shook my head.

"That's where you should start."

"Thank you. I may be back if I can figure out what I want to know."

"Name's Jonas Beale. You're welcome any time. Wish I could have helped more. If you decide to do any genealogical research, come on in, put on some of our white gloves"—he pointed toward the basket on his desk—"and I'll help you find the documents that might help."

"You did help," I said. "Now I have even more questions than when I came in." I looked at the gloves. "Why the white gloves?"

"So the oils on your hands don't get on the fragile documents in our archives." He laughed. "Welcome to the world of historical research."

I walked outside. Light snow mixed with sleet was falling at a slant, stinging my face. My telephone said it was only a little after eleven. Patrick would just have arrived in Biddeford. What was I going to do for the next couple of hours?

I headed down Congress Street. In summer I would have walked to the Old Port and gone window-shopping, but February wasn't a time for wandering. The Portland Museum of Art was nearby, but I had too much on my mind to appreciate what was on display. Besides, Patrick had mentioned our going together soon. He could explain what I should be looking at there.

Above me, on one of the taller buildings, I saw a sign for Channel 7. Clem worked at Channel 7.

I huddled in the doorway of an insurance building and called her.

"Clem? I'm in Portland and at sixes and sevens. Any chance you could break away for an early lunch? No. He's in Biddeford, at Steve's studio. He dropped me off here. I'm on a quest, but I've come to a dead end. Great! See you there!"

I headed farther up Congress Street, toward her building, striding with a purpose. We'd agreed to meet at a coffee shop near there.

Despite my scarf, snow was blowing down my neck by the time I reached the coffee shop. I pushed through the door and headed for a warm corner booth, far from the door. Hot chocolate and menus came quickly, and the waitress assured me there was no hurry. I could order food when my friend arrived.

Ten minutes later Clem walked in, brushing snow off her hat and shoulders, and recognized by one of the waitresses. "Ms. Walker, I love watching you on the six o'clock news. You're my favorite reporter."

"Thank you," said Clem, giving the waitress a

special smile and sliding into the seat opposite mine. She must have been on camera this morning; she was still wearing heavy makeup, and, despite the sleet and snow and her hat, her hair was immaculate. "Now, Angie, what mysterious quest has brought you to Portland?"

CHAPTER 6

"Youth you must not on numerous years
  depend
For unknown accidents your steps attend
Some sudden illness soon may stop thy
  breath
And prove an inlet to eternal Death."

—Stitched with four alphabets in silk
thread on linen by Charlotte Camp,
aged 13, in an unknown town in Maine.

"Order first?" I suggested, seeing the waitress
hovering and looking toward us.

"Tuna salad, no dressing," Clem ordered without
checking the menu. "And plain black tea."

Despite the hot chocolate, I wanted something
warm. "A bowl of haddock chowder," I told the
waitress. "With extra oyster crackers. And a glass
of water."

"Okay," said Clem. "Now, tell me!"

I made the story as short as possible. "Yesterday
I went with Sarah to an auction in Augusta and
bought an old embroidered coat of arms that
intrigued me. It was in poor condition, but I
hoped maybe one of the Mainely Needlepointers
could restore it."

Clem nodded.

"When I took it out of its frame last night I found a folded paper and a ribbon embroidered with flowers and a heart hidden behind the coat of arms."

"Yes?"

"The paper was a receipt—a billet, they called it when I looked online—from the London Foundling Hospital dated 1757 for a two-week-old boy named Charles."

"Weird!" said Clem, leaning toward me. "Did you bring it with you?"

I nodded, and carefully took the embroidery and the paper out of the portfolio.

She looked at it closely. "Fascinating. You said you looked online?"

"That's how I figured out it was the London Foundling Hospital, from the dates. When an infant was left there, most parents left a token—like the ribbon—which would be attached to the billet, and could be identified by the family if they came back to reclaim their child." I shook my head. "According to what I read, few families did that. But someone must have gone back for Charles, or the billet and ribbon wouldn't be here, right?"

Clem nodded. "And sad how many children ended up at places like that. But how did the coat of arms and its hidden secret get to Maine?"

"That's what I've been trying to figure out," I told her, putting the paper and embroidery back away gently before our food arrived. "I was just at the Maine Historical Society. The historian there told me about a place in England that identifies coats of arms, but their service is expensive. And that still wouldn't explain the Maine connection."

"Did he have any ideas about what the connection might be?"

"He told me land in Maine was given away by the English king way back in the 1600s, and those rights were handed down in some families. By the late 1700s some of those heirs had come to Maine to try to claim the land, but by then, of course, other people had been living on it for generations. During the American Revolution most of those English families left, or laid low, although some stayed here, and a few became prominent in Maine history."

"How cool if we could connect this coat of arms to a notable Maine family!" Clem said. "That would be a real story! Maybe an illegitimate son, or a runaway daughter."

"Could be," I agreed, noting Clem had said "we" might connect the story.

"How would you like to go on television and tell your story?" she asked. "It would be a human interest feature. One of our listeners might recognize the coat of arms, or know something that would explain the story."

"Me? On TV?" I asked. "That's your job, Clem, not mine."

"What if you're just on for a few minutes? We'll show the coat of arms, and the paper, and the ribbon, and you'll say you bought it all at an auction, and you'd love to know the real story; know the family it belonged to back in the eighteenth century."

"I guess," I said, hesitantly. It did sound like fun. And Clem was right. Someone watching television tonight might know the connections I was trying to figure out.

"I'll introduce you as the head of Mainely Needlepoint," Clem tempted. "A little advertisement for your business. Couldn't be bad, right?"

"Right," I agreed, only slightly reluctant.

Our food arrived, and we both started eating. The chowder was thick with haddock and bacon and potatoes. Almost as good as Gram's.

"When would we do this?" I asked.

"How long will you be in Portland?" Clem asked. "Patrick's going to pick you up, right?"

"Right. He's with your friend Steve Jeffries. He said he'd text when he'd be back."

Clem hesitated a moment. "I should tell you: I'm going to break it off with Steve."

"I'm sorry. He seemed like a good guy."

"We're on two different career tracks. I can't see myself living with someone who spends hours each week collecting metal trash at dumps and then bringing it all home. And he wants someone who'd not only have a steady paycheck for when his art didn't sell, but who also promised dinner would be on the table when he got home."

"I'm sorry."

"It doesn't mean Steve and I aren't friends." Clem took out her phone and started texting. A minute later she said, "And I haven't told Steve yet that it's over. Steve and Patrick are going to have lunch together in Biddeford. Patrick won't be back here until at least two o'clock. We have plenty of time. Let's finish our lunches and go back to the studio. It won't take long to tape the segment, and you'll be home in time to see yourself on the evening news."

"I'm not dressed for TV."

Clem looked at me critically. "Your sweater is fine. We'll use headshots. Take off the flannel shirt; the pattern is too bright. I'll have Sophie do your hair and makeup. She's a wizard. You'll look like yourself, only better."

I shook my head. "You win, Clem. Television is your world. But it sounds like fun, if scary. And it might help solve the mystery of the embroidery's history."

"I hope!" said Clem. "It'll be a fun story on a snowy day. I'm tired of covering high school basketball games and snow sculptures. So . . . eat up, and we'll head for the studio." She sent another text. "Sophie is a miracle worker. She'll meet us there in half an hour."

CHAPTER 7

"Jesus Permit thy gracious name to stand
As the first effort of an infant's hand
And while her fingers o'er this canvas
   move
Engage her tender heart to seek thy love."

—Stitched on a linen sampler by Susan
   B. Kinsley (1815–1901) in Grantham,
   New Hampshire. Susan was the second
   of eleven children. In June of 1841
   she married John Harris Bullard.
They had five children, although most did
   not survive past young adulthood.
Susan was eighty-five when she died.

Half an hour later Channel 7's makeup artist was putting mousse in my hair and color on my face. By the time she'd finished I had deeper eyes and sun-touched cheeks. Clem had been right. I looked like me, but a more defined me.

While Sophie had been enhancing me, Clem had the needlepoint, billet, and ribbon photographed.

"You look great, Angie. Told you Sophie was a miracle worker!"

I did look good. But had it taken a miracle?

Clem headed us out into the hall and toward another room. We almost crashed into Dara Richmond, Channel 7's chief anchor on the evening news. She'd been on that desk as far back as I remembered. She looked older in person than she did on television, but I was still impressed. When I was growing up she'd been the voice of Maine news to me.

"Clem! Where are you headed in such a hurry?" she asked.

"I'm working on a feature for tonight's show," Clem answered.

"The schedule's already set for tonight's broadcast," Dara said. She didn't look happy, but no frown lines were visible on her forehead.

"I talked to the producer. He said we could squeeze in a human interest story."

"He didn't talk to me. What does he plan to bump?"

"Something out of local news. Nothing news-worthy came out of the city council meeting."

"That's my segment," Dara said. She didn't look—or sound—happy.

"You'll have to talk with John. He's the one who decided. C'mon, Angie. We have Studio B for only twenty minutes." Clem took my arm and almost pulled me around Dara and down the hall into another room. Presumably, Studio B. Two cameras were set up inside.

"Dara seemed upset," I said.

"Dara can't take competition," said Clem. "Don't worry about her." She handed me the envelope holding the coat of arms and ribbon and Foundling Hospital paper. "We've already photographed this. It's hard to see the needlepoint, it's so faded, but we managed to adjust the light so it shows a little better, and I'll summarize what's on the billet. I'll call it a registration sheet, since people would understand that. All set? You look great, Angie."

She pointed me toward a stool on the side of the room in front of a large blue sheet of paper.

"This is where you'll be taping?" I asked, curiously. It didn't look like the sets I'd seen on news shows.

"We don't need the whole set," she explained. "The audience won't even know you're not live in the studio."

I must have looked confused. I was certainly nervous. The haddock I'd eaten for lunch was swimming circles in my stomach.

"Don't worry. You can do your bit a couple of times if it doesn't feel right, or if it is too long the first time," she assured me.

I was beginning to panic. But Clem knew what she was doing, I told myself. I just had to follow her directions. I sat on the stool, as she told me to, in front of a camera.

"When the red light comes on, talk to me, but look at the light," Clem instructed.

She sat at a desk in the corner of the room and read off a teleprompter. When had she written those words? Had it taken Sophie that long to make me television-presentable? If Clem's future was as a news anchor, I had no doubt she'd be terrific. When Clem set her mind to do something—whether it was losing weight or moving up a corporate ladder—she succeeded.

Sometimes I wished I was as focused as she was. One year ago I'd been the assistant to a private detective in Arizona. Now I was the owner of a business and a home on the coast of Maine. I hadn't planned those changes in my life, but I was happy the way they were working out, at least for now. Would there be more changes? Probably. But I had no idea what they might be, or whether they'd be new goals I set, or just the turning of the tides. The tides had been on my side for the past year. The future? Clem might be sure of hers. Mine was an untrodden path, and I didn't have a GPS or road map.

Clem smiled at the camera aimed at her and said, "Many Mainers love auctions. And one of the delights of bidding is that sometimes you find a hidden treasure. That's what happened yesterday to Angie Curtis, owner of custom needlepoint business Mainely Needlepoint, when she bid on an old piece of embroidery of a coat of arms in Augusta. Tell us what you found, Angie, when you got home and took the embroidery out of its frame."

My red light went on. I was sweating. I tried to imitate Clem's smile. "In back of the embroidery I found a folded paper from the London Foundling Hospital, dated 1757, for the receipt of a two-week-old boy. An embroidered ribbon was attached to the paper, which the parents could describe or match when they went back to claim their son."

My red light went out, and Clem's went on. "The mystery, of course, is who was that little boy? Did he come to Maine two hundred years ago? Whose coat of arms was it? Angie's asking our viewers for help. If anyone watching tonight knows anything about this mystery, please call or e-mail me here at Channel 7, and I'll make sure Angie Curtis gets your message."

All the red lights went out.

"How did that feel, Angie?"

"Good, I guess. But aren't you going to show the embroidery and the paper?"

"We will. We'll show you at first, and then use your words as a voiceover while we show the embroidery and the receipt. You'll see!"

"Why did you ask people to contact you at the station?"

"I should have warned you about that. I didn't want you to get any of the crazy messages people sometimes send. This way we can screen the calls or e-mails. I promise, you'll see anything promising as soon as I do. And you won't be getting weird calls in the middle of the night."

"That makes sense," I agreed. "This will be on tonight's news?"

"I checked with the producer. He shaved Dara's time to get it in the six o'clock time slot. Go and call your grandmother and your friends. You'll be on about seven past six, unless we have late-breaking news, like a fire or a bad accident on the turnpike."

My phone vibrated. I glanced down. "Patrick's on his way back to Portland."

"We timed that right, then! Tell him to pick you up outside the building," said Clem. "Wasn't that fun? Your first time on television."

"It was fun, except for being petrified. Let me know if you get any responses about Charles or the coat of arms," I said, heading for the elevator.

"Promise!" she said. "We'll be in touch."

Fifteen minutes later I was back in Patrick's car, heading home to Haven Harbor.

"So you had lunch with Clem," he said. "The historical society wasn't much help?"

I shook my head. "Not now. They might be able to help if I find out the name of the family involved. They have a lot of genealogical records."

"You look a little different this afternoon," he commented as he glanced over at me. He drove down Congress Street and then turned to get on Route 295 north. "Did you and Clem go to a beauty parlor after lunch? Or did Clem do your hair and makeup?"

"No. Sophie did," I said, excitedly. "I'm going to be on Channel 7 tonight." I told him everything that had happened.

"Call your grandmother and tell her," he suggested. "She won't want to miss your television debut. And Sarah and Dave and Ruth and the whole gang."

I picked up my phone. "I wonder if anyone will recognize the embroidery, or know anything about it?"

"I'm glad Clem suggested people contact the studio, and not you," he said. "Although you said she did use your name."

"She gave a plug for Mainely Needlepoint," I agreed. "Probably no one will remember my name. I'm not in the phone book or even in online directories."

"But the business is, right?"

"Right," I admitted.

"You should let calls from anyone you don't know go to voice mail," Patrick advised.

Patrick's mother was a famous actress. She got calls from crazy people. But Angie Curtis in Haven Harbor? "I don't think there'll be a problem, Patrick. I was only on the air for a few seconds."

"You may be right. Just be careful," he advised. "Now, get on the phone and call all your friends and relations."

I spent the next few minutes telling Gram the

whole story. She was as excited as I'd been. As I still was, I admitted to myself. I could hardly wait to see myself on television.

"Gram said she's going to invite all the needlepointers to her house so we can watch together. Can we stop and get some pizzas on the way home? They can stay warm in the oven until we eat. Gram's going to invite people to come at five o'clock."

"No problem," he said. "It'll be like an Oscars party!"

"Not exactly," I admitted. "But it should be fun. And, after all, it's February, and an excuse to get together with friends." A few miles later I added, "In my excitement I didn't even ask you. How was your meeting and lunch with Steve Jeffries?"

"I offered to show half a dozen of his smaller pieces in May," Patrick said. "He would have preferred a summer show."

"More people," I put in.

"Exactly. But I'd like to see the response to a few of his pieces before I commit to showing more."

"He should understand that," I said.

"I hope so," said Patrick. "But artists have delicate feelings. He implied that either I loved his work or I hated it. It is interesting. But I'm not sure there's a place for it in Haven Harbor. I'm a new gallerist, and I know I'll make mistakes. I just don't want them to be enormous mistakes.

That's why I offered him a smaller show than he would have liked. So . . . we'll see. I left him a contract, and I'll be surprised if he doesn't sign it."

"Are all artists that sensitive?" I teased.

"Of course, my dear. Can't you tell how fragile my ego is?"

"Then I'm glad I'm a patron of the arts," I added. "Or at least of your art. I love the painting you gave me for Christmas."

"Unfortunately, Steve isn't giving us anything," Patrick reminded me. "He has an idea his sculptures are worth more than I suspect customers at my gallery will pay."

"You get fifty percent of the sales prices, right?" I asked.

He nodded. "Standard at galleries. But my predecessor in Haven Harbor showed only a few tabletop sculptures. He stuck to paintings. Steve Jeffries's work is a whole new direction."

I settled back in my seat. "I'm glad you offered him a contract, though, even though Clem said she was going to break it off with him. Clem's being a real friend about my embroidery mystery."

"Clem and Steve are breaking up? He didn't mention that."

I shrugged. "He doesn't know yet. I shouldn't have mentioned it, so don't say anything to him."

"I won't say a word," Patrick shot back. "His

relationship to Clem is none of my business. I visited his gallery because I liked some of his work. He's developing an interesting style. His sculptures have to stand on their own. Clem had nothing to do with it." He glanced at me. "To tell the truth, I'm glad they're not a couple anymore. Maybe Clem won't be calling me as often."

"She's been calling you?"

"Asking me to give Steve a chance."

"I didn't know she'd been doing that. I thought she was just calling me."

"Clem must make a lot of telephone calls," Patrick said, drily.

Most of the ice that had covered branches this morning had melted in the sun, although the snow on the side of the road still glittered. Ice floes crowded the Kennebec River at Bath.

"Decide what kinds of pizza you want," suggested Patrick. "And call ahead to order them so we can pick them up on our way."

I nodded and started figuring guests and slices and toppings. A pizza party for my first television appearance! My first auction was turning out to be more exciting than I'd anticipated. And maybe that television mention would result in some information about the embroidery and baby Charles.

I called my favorite pizzeria and gave them a large order. If people weren't hungry we could take extra slices home for breakfast. Or, better yet, Gram and Reverend Tom (since he was now my step-grandfather, he kept telling me to drop the *reverend,* but I kept forgetting) could take any leftovers to the soup kitchen at the Baptist church. Pizza went with soup, right?

Pizza was good any time of day.

CHAPTER 8

"O may I heavenly treasure find,
And choose the better part
Give me an Humble Pious Mind
A meek and lowly heart."

—Stitched by Eleanor Merrill (1818–
1890) in 1826, when Eleanor was eight
years old, the third of eight children.
In 1843 Eleanor married Ithiel Homer
Silsby. They lived with Ithiel's father
in Newton, Massachusetts.

Gram and Reverend Tom had already preheated
their oven to "warm" when Patrick and I arrived
at the rectory carrying five pizzas (ranging from
cheese to "extra everything"), large bottles of
Pepsi and Moxie, and three six-packs of Sam
Adams.

Maine in February offered a lot more to do than
most summer folks imagined. But, still, it would
be fun to see everyone.

"Bring those pizzas in, out of the cold," Gram
said, ushering Patrick and I inside. "Angie, put the
pizzas in the oven, and, Patrick, there should be
room for the drinks in the refrigerator. I rearranged
a shelf when I heard you were coming."

Tom had already put out heavy paper plates, a stack of napkins, and an ice bucket (full) on the kitchen table, along with an assortment of glasses. He'd also selected two bottles of red wine. I suspected two bottles of white were chilling in the refrigerator.

Gram and Tom enjoyed their wine, even though most people I knew preferred soda or beer with pizza.

"Who's coming?" I asked as soon as all our contributions were stowed.

"All of the Mainely Needlepointers except Dave. He has a home and school meeting tonight," Gram told me. "So we'll have Ruth—Sarah's going to bring her so she doesn't have to cope with that walker and the snow by herself—Captain Ob and Anna, and Katie and Dr. Gus. Ten of us."

"Fun!" I said. I nodded as Reverend Tom pointed at the wine. Red wine before pizza was more than acceptable. Patrick and Gram joined me; we had about an hour before any of the others would arrive. "I hope I didn't make a total fool of myself on camera." I took a sip of wine. "But even if I did, it wasn't for long. Clem said the whole segment would be a minute or less once it was edited."

"I'm sure you did fine, dear," Gram assured me.

"Don't worry," Patrick seconded. "Besides,

you're the first in your family to be on television!"

No one said anything for a moment. Then Gram filled the space with, "On television for something fun, for sure!"

She'd been reluctantly interviewed after Mama's body was found. Being interviewed on television wasn't always for a good reason.

"Come, sit. Did you bring that mysterious embroidery and paper you bought at the auction?" said Tom, herding us toward the living room.

"I did," I said, reaching into the canvas bag I carried as a pocketbook and pulling out the padded envelope.

I carefully put the embroidery, ribbon, and fragile paper on their coffee table.

Gram got a large magnifying glass ("on dark days it helps with small print,") and carefully went over the coat of arms. "It's in very poor shape, Angie," she pronounced. "I'm not sure it can be restored. Where the threads are still visible they could be reinforced. But some parts are missing."

"What about the dirt?" I asked.

"Cleaning might help; it could reveal needle-marks or stains from where threads were originally. But the linen is in poor shape, and very weak. Perhaps if it were backed with new, archival fabric, that might help. But I doubt the piece will ever be anything more than a curiosity.

It would cost more to restore than it's worth."

I shrugged. "I like it anyway. I didn't buy it to display it or resell it. Sarah's the one who does that. But I was fascinated by it."

Tom and Patrick had been looking at the foundling hospital receipt. "This is interesting, for sure," said Tom. "I'd think a receipt like this would be kept at the institution, not given to someone, even if he or she had come back for a child. The British are organized. See the number on the receipt? Anyone checking records—back in the eighteenth century or even today—would question why one of the receipts was missing."

"The hospital is still in London," I said, "although it operates under a different name now. They have a museum and a library with all the old records, I read online. So, you're right. A missing record would stand out."

"But it can't be a copy—they didn't have copy machines or even carbon paper two hundred and fifty years ago," Patrick pointed out.

"Maybe someone at the hospital wrote everything twice?"

"You told me earlier that over sixteen thousand infants were entrusted to the foundling hospital during one twenty-year period. I wouldn't think anyone dealing with that many needy babies would have the time to make a copy of one receipt," Patrick pointed out.

"That many babies?" Gram shook her head.

"How sad, for the children and the parents. I'm amazed the hospital was organized enough to record anything about each child, much less to include a piece of fabric, or an embroidered ribbon, like this one." She hovered her magnifying glass above the ribbon. "This is beautifully embroidered. Someone took a lot of time with it—and used a very small needle."

"The flowers on the ribbon could have been embroidered separately, for a special woman—or one who could pay for the work—and then whoever gave baby Charles to the foundling hospital might have added the heart at the end," I suggested.

Gram looked more closely. "That's possible. The heart is embroidered in a different ply silk than the flowers. But that could mean the embroiderer decided to emphasize the heart more."

"We'll probably never know all the answers," said Patrick. "But it's interesting to guess."

Gram patted my knee. She'd known me when I'd been a child whose father was unknown and whose mother was gone.

I sipped my wine and listened as Reverend Tom tried to convince Patrick (for the nth time) to join the Congregational Church choir. I'd be next on his list.

"I'll get it," I said when the doorbell rang.

Sarah had brought a plate of molasses cookies to add to our evening. She held Ruth Hopkins's arm as Ruth navigated her pink walker into the front hall.

"Good to see you, Angie," Ruth said as I helped her off with her coat. "I can't wait to see you on the television and hear all about this mysterious embroidery."

"Clem said I'd be on shortly after six o'clock," I told her. "The embroidery is in the living room. As soon as everyone gets here, we'll have some pizza and talk!"

"Sounds good," said Ruth. "Sarah was such a dear to come and get me. This time of year I'm nervous about going out, especially after dark, with all the ice and snow."

"Here, Ruth. I've saved the chair with the highest seat for you," said Gram, joining us in the hall.

"You're becoming a real Mainer, Sarah," I said. "Molasses cookies are the best!"

"They're your grandmother's recipe," she called back to me as I took the cookies to the kitchen table and she hung up her coat and scarf and hat and gloves and kicked off her boots in the entryway. "I'm dying of curiosity. I want to see what was behind the embroidery," she said, and I pointed her toward the living room as Captain Ob and Anna arrived. They'd brought a six-pack of 633 beer, brewed in nearby Boothbay Harbor.

Mainers seldom went anywhere for dinner without bringing something.

Katie and her husband, Dr. Gus, weren't an exception. They were the latest to arrive, but they brought a gorgeous amaryllis plant. "It bloomed today," said Katie, "and I know how much your grandmother loves flowers."

"It's spectacular," said Gram. "I'm going to put it in the living room so we can all admire it!"

I glanced at the clock. Almost five-thirty.

"It's time we all got our pizza and drinks," I announced.

"I'm getting Ruth two slices of mushroom and pepperoni and a Moxie. Everyone else is on their own," said Patrick.

Gram and I pulled the boxes of pizza out of the oven and spread them on the kitchen table, while Patrick added the drinks in the refrigerator to the counter and got Ruth her dinner.

It didn't take long. Five-thirty might be early for supper in some places, but we were pretty flexible in Maine, especially in months when it was dark by four in the afternoon.

I moved my auction finds to a table away from the food and drinks, and we all focused on our pizza. I chose one slice of vegetarian and one of plain cheese and added some red pepper.

"Thank you to Patrick for buying the pizza, and to everyone, for what they brought, and, most important, for joining us tonight. I hope no one will be disappointed," I added, as I looked around the room.

A year ago I'd been living in a one-room apartment in Mesa, Arizona, quite possibly eating pizza by myself, or in my boss's car while we were following someone we'd been hired to "follow and photo."

True, February in Arizona was warm and bright, but nothing was warmer than this room full of friends on a snowy night in Haven Harbor.

A year ago I would never have guessed what my life would be like now.

I swallowed hard and sipped from my bottle of Sam Adams.

"Everything okay, Angie?" said Sarah, who'd sat next to me.

"Everything's just fine," I said. I raised my bottle to everyone in the room.

"We're curious to find out about your embroidery," said Ruth.

"It might be from a family with the last name Providence," said Sarah. "The lots at yesterday's auction came from one of two families, and the samplers and mourning art I bought were signed by girls with the last name Providence."

"What did the auctioneer say?" Anna asked.

"He never identified the families," I answered. "Although I'll call him tomorrow and see if he'll tell me off the record."

"If you want me to help with any genealogical research, let me know," Ruth put in. "I'm bored with the book I'm writing now. Plots are hard to come by. I wouldn't mind spending some time on family history sites."

"Thank you," I said as Tom turned the television on.

Suddenly I was nervous. Had I messed up? What would I look like on camera? Maybe we shouldn't have invited all these people to see me make a fool of myself.

I put down my beer and waited.

The early weather report. Dara Richmond reporting on a fire in Portland and a bill not passed in Augusta. An advertisement for the Portland Boat Show. Then, there was Clem. She was sitting at the same desk where I'd seen her that afternoon, but in back of her was a giant enlargement of the embroidery.

Then—there I was! I hardly had time to focus on whether my hair was in place or whether I'd stumbled on my words. Then my face was gone, and the receipt and ribbon were on the screen, and Clem was telling anyone with information to contact Channel 7.

It was over quickly. Tom switched the television off, and Sarah and Patrick applauded. "Not bad for your debut appearance," said Patrick. "You spoke clearly and succinctly and all went well."

"Absolutely," Sarah agreed. "Clem got in a plug for Mainely Needlepoint, too."

"I don't expect we'll be getting in dozens of orders as a result," Katie added. "But that was a nice plus. Now, we have to wait and see if anyone contacts Channel 7 with information."

"A coat of arms," Ruth said, looking over at the embroidery. "And that paper is dated before the American Revolution. I wonder if it all belonged to a Royalist family."

"Didn't most Royalists leave Maine during or just after the Revolution?" Gram asked. "Seems to me a lot of them headed for Nova Scotia or somewhere else in Canada—or went back to England. They weren't welcomed with open arms here."

"But the auctioneer said everything in the sale was from old Maine families," Sarah put in. "If the family had left Maine, that wouldn't be true."

"We'll have to wait and see," said Tom, passing around the plate of molasses cookies Sarah had brought. "We know Angie's good at solving mysteries. If anyone can figure this one out, she can."

"With a little help from my friends," I said, taking a cookie. "Right now I'm not sure what direction to turn."

"You were going to call the auctioneer," Captain Ob reminded me.

"I will. Tomorrow," I agreed. "But I don't know if he'll help."

My cell phone interrupted my thought.

It was Clem.

"It looked great, Clem!" I said. "We just watched it!"

"Angie, this is crazy, but I had to warn you. That segment was only aired a few minutes ago, but someone called the station and left a message threatening to kill you and I and anyone else who tried to find out about that embroidery and the paper."

"What?" I said, incredulously.

"Just be careful. I'll be in touch."

I looked around the room.

"Someone called the station with information?" Anna asked. "That was fast!"

"Someone called the station," I repeated, slowly. "They left a message saying they'd kill Clem and I and anyone else who asked questions about the embroidery."

"What?" said Dr. Gus. "That's crazy!"

"And scary," said Gram. "Maybe you should never have bought that embroidery."

"And maybe you should forget about it now," advised Captain Ob. "You don't want some unhinged person looking for you."

"But who would call in a death threat over a one-minute news story about an old embroidery?" asked Sarah.

"Someone who knows something about it," Patrick answered.

"Because something about it is important, somehow, to someone," I added.

"Or there's some crazy out there who had nothing better to do tonight than annoy the young women he saw on television," Captain Ob said succinctly.

"Or some kid," his wife added. "Trying to stir up trouble. Kids make prank phone calls and send prank e-mails."

"Threatening to kill someone is more than a prank," Sarah put in, frowning.

"What are you going to do about it?" asked Ruth. "I'm still game to help with any research you need. I'm not scared of some anonymous caller."

"Neither am I," I declared. "I'm going to continue investigating. You're right, Anna. That call was probably just a nasty prank."

Patrick nodded. "I hope so, Angie. But if it happens again, I hope Clem, or someone else at the station, calls the police."

CHAPTER 9

"Our days alas our mortal days
Are short and wretched too
Civil and few the patriarch says
And well the patriarch knew."

—Wrought in silk thread on linen by
Jerusia Hill (1819–1889), aged sixteen,
in Wells, Maine, in 1834. Jerusia married
David Hunt, a carpenter, in 1866 (she
was his third wife) and went to live in
Woburn, Massachusetts.

The party broke up shortly after that. Patrick and I each claimed a couple of slices of pizza and took the rest to the Baptist church minister for his soup kitchen.

"Are you okay, Angie?" Patrick asked as we got to my house. "Would you like me to stay tonight?"

We'd been a couple for a while, but we were still happy in separate residences. I lived in the house that had been my family's since 1809, and mine alone for about six months. It was also my Mainely Needlepoint office. I couldn't imagine leaving it.

Patrick had designed a new carriage house,

with living quarters for him and a large studio, after the original carriage house on his mother's estate had burned last June. It was exactly the way he wanted it.

We both respected each other's territories. Maybe we were being cautious; maybe we were smart.

But we always had ready excuses. "I should get home to feed Bette," Patrick added. "If I know I'm going to be away overnight I leave her more food."

"That's what I do with Trixi," I agreed. We'd adopted sister kittens in the same litter last fall, and both of us considered them important family members. "I'll be fine. Some crazy person called Channel 7. That guy didn't call Clem directly, or call me. He doesn't know where either of us live, even if his threat was serious. Which I'm sure it's not. Who wants to kill someone because of an eighteenth-century embroidery?"

Truth was, I was a little nervous. I was almost tempted to turn around, to tell him to go feed Bette and then come back. But I didn't.

I was independent. Strong. I could take care of myself.

I hoped.

Once inside I double-checked the locks on all my windows and doors. That was only smart, right? Not being paranoid. I fed Trixi and assured her nothing was wrong. (She seemed very relaxed about the whole situation.)

Then I took my Glock out of its usual hiding place and carried it upstairs with me.

I jumped when my cell rang.

"Angie? Are you all right?" Gram's voice was, as always, reassuring. "That telephone call to the studio was strange. If you want to sleep here tonight, you know you're welcome."

"I'm fine," I assured her. Who wanted their grandmother to worry? When I'd lived in Arizona I'd done lots of things Gram wouldn't have been happy about. She'd just happened to hear about my current situation. "Trixi and I are all settled in. I'm going to get in bed, turn on some dumb television program, and relax. I'll fall asleep before you do."

"I doubt it. But you're right. You're probably fine. But that call was so weird. And Mainely Needlepoint was mentioned in that story on the news. The business is on the Internet and in the phone directory. With the address."

"Not the street address. I listed a post office box number. But, you're right. We're in the phone book, and someone might be able to figure out where I live. But I'm not worried. I'm fine." The hand holding my cell phone was shaking. But that was silly. I was perfectly safe in my own house.

"Do you have that gun of yours?"

I hesitated. "What gun?"

"The one you hide under the winter gloves and hats in the bureau in the front hall."

"Right. That one." Trust Gram to know every-thing, but not mention it. "Yes, I have it."

"Good. I don't like guns. Never have. But in case of an emergency . . . tonight I'm glad you have one."

"I'm fine. I'll call you tomorrow, okay? Thank you for hosting the television-watching party tonight."

"It was fun. You were great. And I'm as curious as you are about what you got at that auction. Let me know if you find out anything from the auctioneer tomorrow."

"I will. Good night."

"Good night, Angel."

Mama had called me Angel. Now Gram was the only one who did. I touched the gold angel I wore around my neck. Gram worried. She'd lost Mama; she didn't want to lose me. I understood that.

I didn't want to be lost, either.

CHAPTER 10

"Conscious virtue is its own reward."

—Stitched by Jane Virginia Corbin in 1825 at The Reeds, her home in Caroline County, Virginia. She included three alphabets in her sampler.

I slept off and on. At about three in the morning I woke suddenly, certain I'd heard the creaking footsteps of someone in the house. I reached for the gun I'd left on my bedside table.

My guard cat slept on, curled on the rug next to the hot-air vent on the floor of my bedroom.

I listened.

And listened.

After my heart stopped thumping I realized the sound I'd heard was one of the three-foot-long icicles hanging from my roof falling and splintering on the porch roof outside my bedroom window. Not an unusual noise in February.

But tonight my senses were on alert.

I listened a little longer, to be sure, and then fell asleep again, this time muffling any sounds with my pillow.

I managed to sleep another couple of hours before dawn.

Trixi might have been sleeping when the icicle had woken me, but she'd been up and around other times during the night. I almost stepped on one of her catnip mice on the stairs and two of her plastic balls were in the corner of the kitchen.

As far as I knew she hadn't found a mouse in our house . . . yet. A few were probably hunkering down for winter in the cellar or the attic. But she attacked her toys, practicing for the moment when something alive might cross her path.

In the meantime, she sat behind her food dish in the kitchen, staring up at me plaintively.

"There's dry food in the dish, silly," I told her. "You're not starving."

She curled herself around the dish and squeaked plaintively.

She did not consider dry food an adequate breakfast.

I added half a can of cat food to the dry. She purred a thank-you and started gulping. She'd licked her dish clean before my coffee was brewed. If only all relationships were as simple as mine with Trixi.

I scrambled a couple of eggs and put them between two pieces of buttered toast.

She jumped onto the kitchen table and looked at my eggs hopefully.

"You've had your breakfast already," I scolded. "This is mine."

Her tail swished, as she gave up and headed

back to her food dish to make certain it was empty.

I carried my coffee and breakfast sandwich into the living room and turned on my computer. The past couple of days had been so busy I hadn't checked either my personal e-mail or the e-mail for Mainely Needlepoint.

This time of year was quiet. I had a message from L.L. Bean suggesting I buy more flannel shirts and warm silk underwear, a note that I needed to return two books on needlepoint to the Haven Harbor library, and an e-mail from Gram reminding me I'd promised to bring a contribution to the church's coffee hour on Sunday. Cookies? Muffins? I had a few days to figure that out.

I made a note on my calendar about promised food, and checked the Mainely Needlepoint account.

One order from a woman in Georgia for a "Save the Cormorants" pillow cover. No problem. I had two in stock. Although local gift shops sold them complete with the pillow insert, shipping was less online if customers just wanted the cover. I confirmed the woman's credit card and wrote to her, saying I'd received her order and her pillow cover would be in the mail within two days.

One spam message asking if I had any symptoms of diabetes.

Not so far.

And . . . a vile e-mail saying "sharp needlepoint needles could be fatal," with several expletives, and a reminder to "stick to your own business and forget about the past." At the bottom of the note was a clipped photo of a sewing needle.

On another day, under other circumstances, I would have pressed the delete button and forgotten it. Today, I shivered. I checked immediately. A computer expert might be able to figure out who it was from, but I only saw nasty words in the "from" space.

I turned off the computer. Most days I left it on, but this morning I felt that somehow, if the screen were blank, the cruel message would go away. I didn't want it in my house.

The buzz of my phone startled me.

The text was from Clem. **"Studio got more threats overnight. Call me when you're up."**

I was up. "Clem? The same kind of threats?"

"Right. Death to both of us, but no explanation as to why."

"I got a nasty e-mail at the Mainely Needlepoint Web site, too," I shared. "It had a picture of a needle under the message. Luckily, I don't have my home address or telephone number on the Web site." I'd hoped listing a post office box number would prevent salespeople from unexpectedly arriving at my door. It had never occurred to me that someone with a needlepointing business would be stalked.

104

"Just a box number?"

"Right."

"Even with the box number, whoever it is knows you live in Haven Harbor," Clem reminded me. "And he or she knows your name."

"You're right."

"He or she could go to Haven Harbor and ask around. Anyone who'd lived there a while would know you and your family."

My family. That was Gram.

"Angie? The studio is taking this seriously. We always get a few crazy calls. But not like this. Dara Richmond is telling everyone this is why I can't be trusted to come up with my own features."

"That's ridiculous! How could you have guessed an old piece of embroidery would get that kind of response!"

"I agree, but Dara's making a big deal of it. John, our producer, reported the calls to the station security guys and the Portland police. You should let the Haven Harbor police know, too."

"Do you think this guy—or gal—is serious?" I asked. Trixi jumped onto my lap and started purring. I stroked her, absentmindedly.

"I have no idea. But I don't like it," said Clem.

"Did anyone call with any information about the coat of arms, or the paper?" I asked. "Any clues to what might be inspiring the craziness?"

"Nothing," said Clem. She hesitated. "Have

you called the auction house yet about who consigned the lot?"

"No. I'm going to call as soon as they're open this morning."

"Good. How about meeting for lunch? I'll admit I'm a little nervous about this whole situation."

"Portland is a drive for me," I pointed out.

"I have an appointment with my dentist near Haven Harbor this afternoon, so I'd planned to take the afternoon off and then have dinner with my parents. They're always complaining they only see me on the news. Steve's joining us, too. How about meeting at the Harbor Haunts Café at, say, one o'clock this afternoon?"

"I can do that. Maybe I'll have found out something more by then," I agreed. Steve was joining them? Hadn't Clem said they were going to break up? But, of course, that was yesterday's news. Life changed. "Could you bring printouts of the calls Channel 7 has gotten about this?"

"Are you sure you want to see them?"

"No. But maybe there's a pattern to the messages. Some clue as to who is threatening us."

"I'll bring them, then," Clem answered. "Why don't you bring me a copy of the note you got, too? If you can get through to the auctioneer this morning, maybe we'll have names to go on."

I hesitated to turn the computer on again. That was silly. The message might be there, but it was already in my head. What harm would there be to printing it out?

I scooped Trixi up and gave her a fast hug before she wriggled out and jumped to the windowsill to watch the bird feeder. A pair of cardinals and a song sparrow were eating seeds, and a junco and chickadee were breakfasting on the suet. For them, it was a typical morning.

Why had I let Clem mention the business name on the short segment about the embroidery last night? That must be how whomever had written to me had found the e-mail address. It was on our Web site, and easily found in search engines. That was how business was conducted today.

It was only eight-thirty. Still too early to call the auctioneer. I looked through my boxes of completed needlepoint, found the pillow cover the woman in Georgia wanted, sealed it in a heavy plastic bag with an invoice and one of our Mainely Needlepoint brochures, and packaged it in a padded envelope, ready to mail.

I jumped when my phone rang. "Angie? I was worried about you. Were you able to sleep last night?"

Gram always seemed to sense when I needed someone.

"I'm fine, Gram. I slept all right. Not perfectly, to tell the truth. But I'm okay."

"I'm glad. That message was probably a prank or a hoax, but it wasn't funny."

"I agree," I admitted. I didn't tell her about the e-mail I'd gotten, or the new calls to Channel 7. She was already worried. Why upset her more?

"Are you going to call that auctioneer this morning?"

"I was planning to," I said.

"I can't imagine a reason anyone would be upset about that old piece of needlepoint."

"I can't either. Although maybe it's the paper and the ribbon—the connection to the Foundling Hospital—that's the problem," I speculated.

"But who would care about something that happened two hundred and fifty years ago?" Gram said. "I looked up that hospital, too, Angie. You were right. Thousands of babies were left there. The 'Charles' mentioned on the receipt was very lucky if his family reclaimed him. That happened in only a few cases."

"That's what I read too," I agreed. "It was interesting that pieces of fabric or embroidery or ribbons were used to identify the children, though."

"I've done a lot of needlepoint in my lifetime, but never any that had as important a purpose," Gram agreed. "But if someone is truly upset about your investigating it, maybe you and Clem should stop. I'm worried about both of you. And, after all, you're only investigating out of curiosity."

"Clem and I are going to meet for lunch at the

Harbor Haunts." I didn't mention we were going to share our threatening notes.

"I'm worried," Gram repeated. "We like to think Maine is a safe place, not dangerous, like Chicago or New York. But we have our share of troublemakers."

"Troublemakers." One way to categorize people who threatened murder.

"I can't believe whoever called the studio in Portland and made the threat is serious," I assured her. And myself. "It doesn't make sense."

"I wonder if that was the only response you got to that segment on the news. Maybe someone else called in who knew something about the needlepoint."

"Clem promised to let me know if that happened," I said, not mentioning what Clem had told me this morning.

"Give her my best when you see her, and tell her she did a good job last night on the story. I'm guessing putting you and the needlepoint on the news was her idea."

"It was. And it was fun," I admitted. "I hope her doing it doesn't turn into a problem. I'll be sure to tell her you enjoyed the segment."

It was nine o'clock. I pulled my auction receipt out of my desk drawer and dialed the auction house in Augusta.

CHAPTER 11

"She was a blessing here below. An only child of a widow, Subscribed by Sally Parker."

—Stitched by seven-year-old Mary Dealy
in 1806. Sally Parker might have paid
Mary's tuition in an embroidery class
or school, and this sampler might
have been stitched for her in thanks.
Vines are intertwined across the words.

"May I please speak to Mr. Haines?"

"Mr. Haines is busy with an appraisal. Perhaps I can help you? I'm Jessica Winter, his assistant. Do you have items you'd like to consign?"

"No. I wanted to ask him about an item I bought at his auction a couple of days ago."

"All items are sold where is, as is."

"Yes, I know. I don't want to return it. I wanted to ask Mr. Haines if he knew what family it came from. It's a piece of embroidery."

Jessica paused. "A piece of embroidery?"

I glanced at my auction receipt. "Lot number 176."

"Oh, wow. Are you from Channel 7? Clem Walker? Oh, I love seeing you on the nightly

111

news. I've always wanted to be a television reporter. You're my idol!"

"Wait," I interrupted. "I'm sorry, but I'm not Clem, although she is a friend of mine. You saw the story on the news last night?"

"I did. So who are you?"

"I'm Angie Curtis. The one who bought the needlepoint."

"Oh, right. That's what you said before, that you'd bought that embroidery. I would have recognized Clem if she'd been at the auction. Is she as beautiful in person as she is on television?"

"She's very attractive," I said, wishing I could tell this Jessica what Clem had looked like when I'd first known her. High school wasn't everyone's finest hour. "So, you know I'm trying to find out more about the embroidery."

I heard papers shuffling. "I agree. Clem Walker is *so* gorgeous. And smart, too! And you're friends?"

"We went to high school together in Haven Harbor." Where we hadn't exactly been close friends, but, yes, we'd known each other. Two teenagers who hadn't fit in.

"How cool! I grew up not far from there, in Waymouth. I love Haven Harbor. Sometimes my boyfriend, Roger, and I eat lunch there, at that little restaurant near the wharves."

"The Harbor Haunts Café. In fact, Clem and I are going to have lunch there today."

"Oh, wow! I wish I didn't have to work so far from the coast. I'd love to meet her! Or even just see her in person."

"About the embroidery?" I tried to steer Jessica back to the reason I'd called.

"You know, Mr. Haines promises anonymity to people who consign items. You said it was lot 176?"

"Right. I don't want you to get in trouble with your boss, of course. But Clem and I would love some help."

"Oh . . ." she said.

I suspected dropping Clem's name a few more times would get me further than asking for myself.

"Most of our auctions have items from dozens of different people. Hundreds, even, sometimes. But that last auction was from only two families."

"I remember reading that," I said. Actually, I remembered Sarah telling me.

"So I can't tell you what family lot 176 came from. That would be against the rules."

"Jessica, I wouldn't want you to break any rules," I lied.

"But, you being on television and all, maybe"—Jessica's voice lowered to a whisper I could hardly hear—"I could tell you who the two families were. Would that help?"

"It would," I agreed. "And Clem would be so pleased to know."

"Okay! And you'll tell her what a fan I am?"

"I promise." Clem would be thrilled, I was sure.

"Well, because it's Clem Walker who wants to know . . ." Jessica's voice almost disappeared.

I turned up the volume on my phone.

"One of them is the Jonathan Holgate family. You know. The Holgates with all the money."

I didn't know, but I figured I could find out.

"And the other consigning family was the Goulds."

"The Goulds?"

"That's all I can say," whispered Jessica. "I shouldn't even have told you that much! My boss would fire me if he knew I'd told you. But tell Clem how much I admire her!"

The phone clicked before I could promise that, indeed, I would.

I looked at the two names I'd written down.

Jonathan Holgate and the Goulds. Sounded like an old-time rock group.

I'd been away from Maine since I'd been in high school, and I'd never paid a lot of attention to either Maine history or current Maine events. Even if I had, would either of those names have meant anything? Although it seemed I'd heard both names before. Gram or Ruth would know. They were experts on the history of Haven Harbor and Maine.

The samplers Sarah had bought were from the

Providence family. Did either the Holgates or the Goulds have any relationship to the Providences? And, if they didn't, why were the Providence samplers in an auction of goods from another family?

Although maybe, as Sarah had suggested, the Providences had "daughtered out."

I wanted to tell Clem what I'd found out, and, of course, let her know what a fan she had at the Augusta Auction House. But I wouldn't bother her now. I'd see her in a couple of hours. Maybe I could find out more by then.

I could Google Jonathan Holgate and Gould. But I suspected that would tell me a lot about families not related to Maine. Even if the families had been here for generations, they'd been in other places, too. I wasn't in the mood to spend hours looking through hundreds of names.

When my phone rang I checked who it was before answering. "Patrick! Good morning!"

"I hope it is. Everything okay?"

I hesitated, and then decided I had to tell someone. "Clem said the studio got several more nasty calls last night. And I got a horrible e-mail this morning addressed to Mainely Needlepoint."

"Angie, you have to tell the police."

"Clem said the studio did that in Portland."

"And you need to do it here. Give Pete Lambert a call. He's a friend. This time of year he probably isn't too busy."

115

It was Patrick's first Maine winter. He didn't understand that life went on, even after summer visitors had returned to New York or Texas or Pennsylvania.

"I'm going to have lunch with Clem here in the harbor. I'll see what she thinks."

"Tell her what *you* think, Angie. You're an independent woman. But don't be foolish. Letting Pete know what's happened is the smart thing to do."

Trixi jumped down from the windowsill onto my lap. She curled into a circle, her tail neatly tucked at one end and her paws at the other.

"I'm glad you'll see Clem today. I was going to suggest we have lunch together, but I just heard from Sam Gould. He wants me to drive to Camden and see his newest design for Mom's boat."

"Sam Gould!" One of the family names connected to the auction. I knew I'd heard it somewhere. "I met Sam Gould last summer, right? The man who had a crush on your mom's friend Jasmine back in the early seventies?"

"Right. Remember? I told you she'd called him when she was here for Christmas. She's commissioned his company to build her a boat."

"A yacht?" I did remember Sam Gould. Gould's Shipbuilders and Marine Services. His office was in a large brick building next to the shipyard where his company built yachts.

"Not a yacht, Angie. More of a big boat."

"A boat you can sleep on?"

"Only eight."

I smiled to myself. Patrick and his mom had very different ideas about some things than I did. Granted, a ship that slept eight wouldn't be the biggest on the Maine coast, especially in summer. But the biggest boats I'd been on smelled of bait and lobsters and didn't sleep anyone unless you'd had too much beer or were homeless or brought a sleeping bag with you.

But Sam was a Gould.

"Would you ask him if he auctioned off a lot of family pieces in the past week? Or if anyone in his family did?"

"Angie, that's none of our business."

"I talked to someone at the auction house this morning. She said one of the consigning families was the Goulds. The needlepoint could have belonged to them."

Patrick sighed. "I'll see if I can work a question into our meeting. 'How are you, Sam? How many heads will there be on Mom's boat? And, by the way, have you auctioned off any embroideries lately?' "

"Something like that," I agreed, even though Patrick was being facetious.

"Give my best to Clem, despite her being a pain during the holidays," said Patrick. "And for goodness sakes, don't tell her about Mom's boat.

Mom doesn't need publicity every time she buys something. She thought it would be fun to motor around next summer. For us, too, Angie."

"Sounds great," I agreed. I was still getting used to the way Patrick and Skye spent money. I counted pennies; they counted houses. And, now, boats.

"I'll call you tonight," he promised. "Hope whoever that idiot is who's been bothering you disappears by then. Have a good lunch with Clem."

"And you with Sam Gould. I do think it would be great if you and Skye had a boat." I hadn't asked how many feet it would be. He'd said "motor" so I assumed it wasn't a sailboat. I hoped it wasn't so big it would require a captain. I liked the idea of a boat Patrick and I could spend afternoons on. And maybe nights . . .

Plus, it was fun to think of something other than death threats.

Trixi was still curled up on my lap. "Trixi, I want to find out about that embroidery and the London Foundling Hospital billet. But I have work to do, too. Shall we pay some bills? And then maybe I'll stop to see Ruth on the way back from the post office. Ruth volunteered to help if I needed some genealogy research. I think that time is now."

CHAPTER 12

"Endeavour to employ yourself in something useful. Take great pains to learn. Too great a thirst for play is unfavourable to learning."

—Sampler stitched by
Sara Elizabeth Dukes, age nine, in 1815.
It included a rose border, a leopard
between two trees, and dishes of fruit.

"And I need to buy a book of stamps, too," I said to Haven Harbor's postmaster, handing him the envelopes I'd already stamped and the padded envelope holding the needlepoint cushion cover filling this morning's online order. "I never seem to have enough stamps."

"Most folks nowadays pay bills online," said Pax. "Glad you're doing it the old-fashioned way. Helps keep the Haven Harbor post office open, and me employed. That, and your sending out Mainely Needlepoint packages, too." He handed me the stamps I needed.

"I'd pay online if I had a regular income," I told him. "But owning a small business isn't the same as getting a regular paycheck. I rarely send in a payment late, but I never know exactly when I'll have enough money to pay a bill."

"Right," he agreed. "My wife house-sits some-times, and walks dogs. If we had to depend on what she brings in, and when, we'd be in big trouble. That's why I've worked for Uncle Sam all these years." He stroked his bushy red beard, which I remembered being fascinated by when I was a kid. Now it was streaked with gray. "Post office work's not a bad job. Get to work with a lot of good people here in town. In the summer, especially, people act like I'm a chamber of com-merce information center. Thinking of which, did that fellow looking for you this morning find you?"

I stopped. "What fellow?"

"Tall. A little balding, but not too old. One of those men whose hairlines start disappearing in their late twenties or thirties. Navy fleece pullover, sweatshirt, jeans, navy watch cap. Came in here asking about the lady who ran Mainely Needlepoint."

I shivered. A strange man I didn't know? On an ordinary day I wouldn't have thought much about that. But today wasn't an ordinary day. "What did you tell him?"

"Nothing special. Just that you had a box here, but you lived on the green in town. Wondered if I should give him your address, but didn't. Hope that didn't mean you lost a sale, or maybe a date? Did he find you?"

"No. And, please, don't give anyone my address," I said.

Pax leaned over the counter. "You got some problem, Angie? Saw you on the TV the other night. You and Clem looked wicked good. I figured that guy might have information for you about the old embroidery."

"If he did, he should call it into Channel 7," I said, firmly. "That's what Clem said on-air. Did you notice where he headed?"

"Sorry. I didn't pay attention. I was putting today's mail in the boxes about then."

"I'm glad you didn't give him my address." Thank goodness! "You know I live alone since Gram married Reverend Tom and moved to the rectory. I don't want any unexpected visitors."

"I never give out street addresses. That's a post office rule, you know. But him being a young man, and you being a young lady . . . I thought maybe you knew him. I mean, you and Patrick West are pretty good friends"—he winked—"but you're an attractive woman. You might have other friends."

"No. I don't know him," I said. "And if I have any friends, I'll give them my address myself."

"I get asked addresses all the time, you know. Patrick's mom, that actress, Skye West? I must get three or four people a day asking where she lives. That's in the summer, of course. In February, I don't get so many questions about anything."

"What time was that man here?" I asked.

"Oh, can't say I remember exactly. About nine-thirty, maybe. The morning mail had come in from Portland, and I'd just started to sort it. Yup. Maybe closer to ten."

"Thank you, Pax. And . . . don't tell anyone where I live, please."

"No problem, Angie. So what do you have planned for this bright day?"

"Errands. And lunch with Clem at the Harbor Haunts."

"Good to see her coming back to town to see people. Her mom and dad are good people. They miss her since she moved to Portland."

"Portland's only about eighty minutes away."

"True enough," he agreed. "But not exactly down the street. I haven't seen Clem in person in years now. Of course, we all tune in to see her on Channel 7. Local girl makes good!"

I smiled and shook my head slightly. Everyone had an opinion. And Clem was doing well. The magic of television seemed to impress people more than I'd imagined.

I glanced around as I left the post office. I'd slipped my Glock into the canvas bag I used for a pocketbook, just in case. But I didn't see anyone but Arwin Fraser, who waved as he drove his truck by. He'd outfitted it with a snowplow. Not all fishermen lobstered in winter. I waved back, got in my car, and headed for Ruth's house. I'd have time to talk with her before I met Clem.

Who'd been looking for me at the post office? Pax's description could have applied to half the male population of Maine. Maybe it was nothing.

But with the phone calls and messages Clem and I had gotten in the past day, it was hard not to imagine something sinister.

"This is Haven Harbor," I told myself. "Not Phoenix or Mesa. And I managed to take care of myself just fine during my ten years there."

Ruth Hopkins was seventy-nine. She'd lived in the shade of the Congregational Church steeple for as long as I remembered. I remembered her husband, Ben, living there when I was a child. He'd lost his leg in Vietnam and never really found his way after that. She and Ben hadn't lived on his VA disability payments all those years. They'd lived on the money she made from writing erotica. Officially, no one in town knew Ruth was also "S. M. Bond" and "Chastity Falls," but I suspected more people knew than she suspected.

She lived alone now, with her Mainely Needle-point and church friends and her characters to keep her company. Because of her arthritis she wasn't the most productive member of our needlepointing group, but she helped whenever she could. She wrote, watched her Red Sox in the summer and fall, and loved horse races when they were covered by a local cable channel. I stopped in whenever I could, to bring groceries, or just to chat.

I'd sent her a message that morning about needing some help with genealogy, and she'd invited me to come over about eleven.

I rang her doorbell exactly on the hour, and waited. It took Ruth a little time to get to the door with her walker. In summer she left her door open if she was expecting company, but an open door in February would only invite dustings of snow and chill winds.

"Angie, come on in. It's freezing out there."

"It is," I said, stepping into her front hallway and removing my snowy boots. "Spring's only a month away, remember!"

"By the calendar. Not by Maine weather," she pronounced. "In 1986 we had ten inches of snow on the fourth of April."

I followed her into her living room.

"So, you found out what families were involved with that needlepoint?" she said, sitting in her favorite chair, the one covered with red and green-flowered upholstery.

"I talked with someone at the auction gallery this morning. She told me the items at the auction were consigned by Jonathan Holgate and the Gould family."

"Holgate and Gould," Ruth repeated. "Both old-time Maine names. Probably dozens in the state. Senator Holgate, for one."

"*Senator* Holgate?"

"Don't pay much attention to Maine politics, Angie?"

"Not really," I admitted. "I've had other things on my mind since I got back to Haven Harbor."

"You have, indeed. And she's not up for reelection for another couple of years. But her name is identified with Maine."

"Is she married?"

Ruth paused. "Pretty sure she is. Can't recall her husband's first name, but he's the Holgate by birth. I can look all that up for you. I suspect there are a lot of Holgates around. And Goulds?" She shook her head. "Can't begin to think how many Goulds have popped up in Maine history, not to count those who haven't gotten their names into history books."

"I talked to Patrick this morning. He's having lunch with a Sam Gould over to Camden today."

"Shipbuilder?"

"That's the one."

"Goulds have built ships up to Camden for generations. But other Goulds are in Maine, too."

"I'm interested in whatever family might have been related to the Providences. The name Providence was on several of the samplers, including one genealogical sampler that Sarah bought. She guessed they'd daughtered out."

"Not unlikely," Ruth agreed. "Can't say I know anything about a family of that name. But I can check into it. Used to be you had to go to local churches and graveyards and town records and archives to research family histories. But a lot is online today—either here in Maine databases or on national sites. Let me see what I can find out for you."

"Are you sure you want to take the time to do this?"

"I'd love to. Who knows? Maybe by researching family histories I'll come up with some new plot lines."

"Thank you so much," I said. I knew Ruth had been borrowing gossip (and truths) from Haven Harbor families to use as fodder in her erotica, and that had hurt a few people. Maybe looking outside Haven Harbor would help both of us.

"Has Clem gotten any tips to work on? Her story the other night suggested calling Channel 7. I know they got that one nasty call. But I hoped others might be helpful."

I hesitated for a moment, but, after all, someone who wrote erotica had heard a lot. And Ruth hadn't hesitated when she'd heard about some of the murders I'd somehow become involved with in the past months.

"Clem's gotten several calls through the station," I admitted. "And I got one e-mail to Mainely Needlepoint. The business was mentioned on the broadcast, you remember. But none of the messages we've gotten so far were helpful."

Ruth nodded. "No leads, then?"

I shook my head. "Death threats."

"All of them? About a piece of needlepoint done over two hundred years ago?"

"Doesn't make much sense, does it?" I asked. "I'll admit it makes me nervous. Clem and I are going to have lunch together today to talk about what, if anything, we'll do about it. Her producer at Channel 7 reported the messages to the Portland police, but you can't arrest someone for threatening—and, even then, you'd have to figure out who he or she is. So far the messages we've gotten have been anonymous. We can't get a restraining order against e-mails."

"Of course not. But how awful for the two of you. I suspect it isn't unusual for a television station to get crazy messages. Death threats are a whole other kettle of fish."

"Clem said they get crank calls all the time," I agreed. "But, you're right. Death threats go further than the usual craziness."

"Probably nothing will come of it," Ruth said. "I sometimes get nasty letters from readers, thinking I'm writing about them, or saying God will never forgive me for the filth I'm writing. On the other hand, I also get letters inviting me to visit one of my readers and reenact my plots." Ruth smiled. "My publisher forwards them to me. I wonder what some of the men making those salacious proposals I've received would think if they knew Chastity Falls was seventy-nine years old."

We both laughed.

"Not that I'm not up for some fun once in a while," said Ruth, her blue eyes twinkling. "But not quite the fun I write about. Maybe when I was much younger. But writing about it is plenty these days."

I shook my head. "I hope whoever's been writing and calling Clem and me is just pranking us." I hesitated. "One of the messages included everyone who was asking questions about the needlepoint, so that would include you, too, if you help us with the genealogical search."

"Don't you worry, Angie," said Ruth. "I can take care of myself. And don't you have a gun, too?"

I wasn't sure I'd heard her right. "You have a gun, Ruth?"

"I'm a woman alone. Ben got me one years ago. I don't have much ammunition, but I have enough."

I swallowed. "I have a Glock. But I don't advertise it." Not exactly. Although most of my friends knew I had one. I'd learned to shoot in Arizona, ironically. Mainers usually learned to shoot closer to home.

"Good for you. Did you bring it with you today?" Ruth asked, as casually as if she'd asked if I had a kitten, or a credit card.

"Yes," I admitted. Under the circumstances . . .

"Good for you. Maybe you should be carrying more regularly," she suggested. "If whoever sent those messages intends anything wicked, you want to be prepared."

"You may be right," I said, thinking of the "tall man" Pax had told me about at the post office. "For now, anyway."

"Exactly," she agreed. "Now, before you go and meet Clem, tell me about the other things that went on sale at the auction. I haven't been to one in years, and that one sounded interesting."

"It was my first," I said, relieved to be on another topic. "It was amazing to see the variety of things people were bidding on. And the bidders themselves. Auctions are another world, Ruth."

Telling her about the auction and the other bidders ate up time. It was after twelve-thirty before I glanced at the clock over her mantelpiece.

"I need to get going. Clem is always on time, and she's meeting me before an appointment, so I don't want her to have to wait for me."

"You tell her I watch her on the television almost every night," said Ruth. "We're real proud of her in Haven Harbor."

"I'll tell her," I agreed as I pulled on my boots. "And give me a call if you're able to figure out anything about those families."

"I promise," she agreed. "I'll get right to it.

Sounds more interesting than the chapter I was going to write this afternoon."

I waved, and headed my car toward the Harbor Haunts, the only year-round restaurant in Haven Harbor. In summer or fall I would have walked, but this time of year walking took longer, and parking spaces were easy to find. I parked a block from Sarah's store, thinking I might stop in to see her after lunch, and headed for the restaurant.

The dining room was warm. A fire crackled in the fireplace, and I smelled haddock cooking, most likely in chowder, and coffee.

Sergeant Pete Lambert was at the counter, and waved. "Angie! Haven't seen you in a while."

"Winter keeps people inside. Quiet days for you?"

"Mostly vehicle accidents and drunks," he acknowledged. "Always something going on. Join me for lunch?"

"Some other day, Pete. I'm meeting Clem Walker."

"Our local celebrity, eh? Haven't seen her in years, except on the tube."

I glanced around the small restaurant. "I expected her to be here by now. She's usually early."

"Maybe got delayed on the road," he suggested. "Sit and have a beer with me until she gets here."

"Not a beer," I said, sliding onto the stool next to him. "Too cold. Tea?" Pete wasn't drinking beer, either. He was eating a cheeseburger and fries for lunch, but drinking soda. It was a work-day for him.

I ordered, and we talked about the weather, and people we knew. He'd missed my television appearance the other night, so I filled him in. Patrick had been right. I should tell the police, and Pete had the right credentials, as well as being a friend.

"Death threats?" he frowned. "Glad you told me about those. Get me copies, will you? I don't know that I can do much, but at least I can get them on record."

"You can't do anything unless someone follows through and does something about a threat, right?"

"True enough. But I can drive by your house when I'm making my rounds, and keep my eyes open."

"Thanks, Pete. They're probably nothing."

"Hope so. But death threats aren't anything to fool around with."

"I'll get them to you," I agreed. "Clem's going to bring me copies of the ones the station received. I'll make you copies of those, too." I hesitated, and then I told him about the man Pax Henry had said asked for me at the post office.

Pete frowned. "Could be a coincidence. But I'll stop and have a word with Pax. He told this fellow you lived on the green?"

I nodded.

"Anyone who lives here could have given out your address, then. And your name was on that show, too. Not good. If you hear anything else out of the ordinary, you let me know, all right?"

"I will, Pete." I could feel the warmth from my hot tea all the way to my toes. Or maybe I felt safer sitting next to one of Haven Harbor's three-man police force. "Clem said the television station gets lots of prank calls."

I glanced at my phone. Clem was twenty minutes late. That wasn't at all like her.

"How's your friend, Sarah?" Pete asked. "I've seen the lights on in her place, and you and she went to the auction together, so I'm guessing she hasn't left town for the winter."

"Right," I agreed. "She's fine. Her shop isn't open all the time this time of year, but she's buying and sorting through inventory and starting taxes."

Pete stirred his soda with his straw, looking as though his glass held secrets. "Not to be too curious, but Sarah's a good-lookin' woman. And smart. Any special man in her life now?"

"No; she's single," I said, grinning at Pete. "Speaking of which, I heard your separation was official."

"Yup. Wife—soon to be ex—is living down to Bangor. She's got a new friend there."

"How're you doing?"

"Middling. It's been a rough winter," Pete admitted.

132

"Want me to put a word in for you when I see Sarah?" Pete was a good guy, in his thirties, and not bad looking. Had a steady job. Who knows? I hadn't thought about matching him with Sarah, but they were both good people who knew what they wanted in life. They each should have someone to share it with. I had no idea what Sarah thought of him, but I could find out. "You know—I could pass her a note in study hall or something." I elbowed him gently.

Pete's face got as red as the Formica counter we were sitting at. "No need, Angie. Curious, that's all. Sure you don't want to order some food? Looks like your friend Clem's been delayed."

I texted her. **Where are u?**

"I'll give her a little more time," I said. "I'm sure she has a good excuse." But, still. Clem was never late. Never.

Pete finished the apple brown Betty he'd had for dessert and paid his tab. "Sorry to leave you, but I'm back on the clock. You have my number. Don't forget to get me that information about the crazy caller."

"I won't," I promised.

As soon as he left I started seriously worrying. Clem hadn't returned my text. Maybe she was driving? Maybe her car had hit a patch of black ice and gone off the road?

Something was wrong. I was sure of it.

I texted her again.

CHAPTER 13

"Fortuné Gauffreau agé de 12 ans fait a St. Barth'my le 24 Juillet 1816."

—St. Barthélemy is a West Indies island belonging to France, now known as St-Barth or St. Barts. This sampler, stitched by a twelve-year-old boy, includes a house, birds, dogs, cows, vases of flowers, and clover.

Clem had said she'd meet me at the Harbor Haunts at one o'clock for lunch.

Maybe she'd been delayed at work. Or stuck in traffic. Or had to cancel.

But why hadn't she called, or texted, to tell me?

The Clem I knew would have contacted me if she were going to be late. Clem organized her life the way other women organized their closets or their checkbooks. (She organized those, too, of course.)

In the past year she'd moved from behind-the-scenes to being an on-camera reporter. Her next step, either in Portland or in a larger city, would be to become an anchor. Ultimately, a network anchor.

She knew how to manage people and politics as

well as she'd learned to manage herself. It might take longer than she hoped. But she'd get where she wanted to go.

The more I thought about Clem, the more I worried.

"Another cup of tea?" the young woman behind the counter asked. "Or something stronger? Something to eat?"

Suddenly I wasn't hungry. "No, thank you." I fished out my wallet and left her a good tip. I'd been taking up counter space for over half an hour.

I'd parked near Sarah's shop and apartment. This time of day she'd be sorting and pricing items for her shop, or studying recent prices for antiques. I decided to stop and see her.

I was two stores away from her door when my phone rang. I pulled it out quickly. Clem?

But it wasn't Clem. It was Pete.

"Angie, are you still downtown? You were waiting for your friend Clem Walker twenty minutes ago."

"I just left the Harbor Haunts," I answered. "Why?"

His voice was steady. "Sorry to have to break it to you this way, but Clem won't be meeting you for lunch."

I stopped walking. I didn't feel cold or hot, despite the wind whirling fallen snow around me. "What's happened?"

"We had a call from someone else who had lunch at the Harbor Haunts. He'd parked next to Clem at the town wharf." He paused. "She never got out of her car."

"What?"

"She's dead, Angie."

I stood in the snow. My mind went blank. "No!" Not Clem. I'd coped with death before. Even murders. But none of the victims had been my friends. "When? How?"

"Shot. But you know that's officially up to the medical examiner to determine. I've called Ethan. He'll want to talk to you."

Ethan Trask. My high school crush who was now a Maine state trooper in the homicide division; the one Pete called in whenever there was a murder, or suspected murder, in Haven Harbor. I'd seen him all too often in the ten months since I'd been home.

"Can't you tell me . . . ?"

"I can't say anything more. If we hadn't happened to meet earlier, I wouldn't have known you were even connected with this. But under the circumstances, you need to be careful. I'm thinking you shouldn't even go home, in case whoever killed Clem is also looking for you."

"Someone killed Clem . . . because she did a television feature on a piece of old embroidery?" I was still trying to make sense of what I was hearing.

"I don't know, Angie. I don't know anything more than I've told you. The crime scene crew is on their way, and I can't leave here."

"You're in the wharf parking lot?"

Pete paused. "Yes. But don't come here. You know the drill. We're closing off the scene." He hesitated. "Besides, you don't want to see her. Where are you now?"

"On Main Street. I was going to stop to see Sarah."

"Good. Get off the street, and stay at Sarah's. Don't leave."

I was numb.

"Angie? Are you still there?"

"I am."

"Walk to Sarah's now. Tell me when you get there."

I walked, quickly, ignoring the snow on my eyelashes and my cold feet. I couldn't focus on the street, or the cars passing me, or other people walking on the sidewalks. I kept my feet moving. Sarah's store wasn't far. I had to get to Sarah's store.

"Pete? I'm at her place now. The store isn't lit, so I'm going to her apartment," I reported.

"Good. Go."

The steps to Sarah's second-floor apartment over her store were icy. I held onto the phone with one hand and her railing with my other. At the top of the iron steps I knocked on her door.

A minute later she opened it. "Angie! What are you doing out there? You look pale as the snow."

"Pete, I'm going into Sarah's apartment now."

"Good. Take it easy. Try to relax. And don't leave there. I have to notify Clem's parents. And her station may send a crew. You don't want to be connected with any of that, hear me?"

"I hear you," I said as I walked into Sarah's kitchen.

She closed the door and raised her eyebrows questioningly.

"I'm hanging up, Pete. I have to tell Sarah what's happening."

I put my phone on her counter. She took my parka and hung it on one of the hooks inside her door.

"Was that Pete Lambert on the phone?"

The gallery-style light over Sarah's grand-father's painting of the harbor was lit. Its glow brightened the kitchen and the small living room filled with cozy furniture and a stack of books next to the couch she must have been using when I knocked.

Two of her living room windows overlooked the harbor. Below us, the waters were a wintery gray-blue. Edges of the mainland shore and the rocks surrounding the Three Sisters, islands across the harbor, were lined with snow and ice. The afternoon tide was full, and only two lobster boats were at the town wharf. Lobsters wintered farther out to sea. Most lobstermen spent their winters repairing nets and traps, repainting, and doing other chores and jobs like snowplowing or carving decoys for summer buyers or improving their own homes.

Looking out Sarah's windows you wouldn't know a young woman had been murdered three blocks away.

"Angie? Talk to me? What's wrong?"

I turned back to Sarah's living room, where everything was peaceful and warm. And safe.

"Clem's dead," I managed to say. "Killed. Shot, in the parking lot at the town wharf. Pete's worried whoever did it is looking for me next."

"No!" Sarah sank into one of the cozy armchairs she'd bought at an auction a couple of years ago. She didn't say anything for a few minutes. Then she added, "About the embroidery?"

I shook my head and sat on her couch. "I don't know. But Clem and I were both getting threats, and now she's dead." I looked at the wall where Sarah had hung the needlepointed map of Australia her grandmother had given her. "Clem was going to meet me for lunch. I talked to Pete while I was waiting for her, and told him about the threats. I didn't take them seriously." Maybe not, but I'd brought my gun with me.

"But why?" Sarah shook her head. "It makes no sense."

"I found out who the families were who

consigned everything at the auction," I told her. "Jonathan Holgate, and the Gould family."

Sarah shrugged. "Neither name means anything to me. You think someone from one of those families killed Clem?"

"I don't know. I don't know anything, Sarah. And I can't guess. Whoever shot her didn't leave a calling card. But . . . he might have been looking for me earlier this morning."

"You? How do you know?"

"The Mainely Needlepoint site had a nasty death threat on it this morning, written in on that spot where it says 'contact.' And Pax Henry said a tall man was asking about me at the post office this morning. The man wanted to know where I lived."

"Did Pax give him your address?" Sarah frowned.

"No. But he told the guy I lived on the green."

"How many homes are on the green?"

"The church and the rectory and Ruth's house are at the far end, and then, let me see, six houses on each side. And another five on the east end, near Main Street."

"Not that many," Sarah concluded.

"No. And several of those homes are owned by people who're in Florida or North Carolina for the winter. Their drives are plowed, so at first glance the houses don't look empty, but anyone paying attention could figure out pretty fast that no one was there."

"What are you going to do?"

"I don't know. Pete said to stay here right now. He's calling Ethan and the crime scene folks."

"You're welcome to stay here, of course. My couch folds out," Sarah said. "But what about Trixi?"

"She'll be all right today," I said. "I left her plenty of food. She won't be happy, but she won't starve."

Sarah nodded. "Ruggles doesn't forgive me right away if I leave him overnight. But he's my best friend again after I open a fresh can of cat food."

I looked around. "Where is Ruggles?"

"Probably under the bed. He's shy when I have guests. He'll join us later." She went back to our original subject. "Clem's parents are here in town, right?"

"She was going to the dentist this afternoon, and then going to have dinner with them and Steve." I shuddered. "Pete said he'd call them and tell them what happened." Should I tell Sarah Pete had asked about her? Maybe. But this wasn't the right moment.

"What an awful thing to have to tell parents. To tell anyone," said Sarah. "I can't believe we saw her on television last night—you saw her in person—and now she's dead."

"And . . . why? It doesn't make sense why finding a piece of old embroidery—I'm sorry,

Sarah, antique embroidery—would cause some-one's death. Much less Clem's."

"So, it would make more sense if you were the one to be killed?"

I started pacing. "Yes, in a weird way. If there's some secret in the embroidery, I'm the one who bought it and am investigating. Clem just used it as a filler on the news." I hesitated. "So, yes, I feel guilty."

"I sympathize. But the whole thing is crazy. And from what you've told me, Pete's right. You could be in danger. So, take it easy. Did you ever eat lunch?"

"I had some tea, but I was waiting for Clem before I ordered food."

"Then what about a bowl of bean soup? I made it yesterday; it's hearty and tastes good, too."

"The old-fashioned kind? Starting with dried beans?"

"Yes, ma'am. I believe your grandmother gave me the recipe."

"I'd love some. Thank you."

Sarah headed for the kitchen to heat the soup, and I followed. "How do you think whoever killed Clem even knew she was in town? She lives and works in Portland, right?"

"I don't know," I said. "At the moment I don't know anything."

"Relax. Take deep breaths. You're safe here." Sarah glanced at her door. "Both doors downstairs are locked, and this one will be, too." She slid the bolt shut.

I tried to keep my voice even and calm. "Ruth is checking online for genealogical records about the Holgates and Goulds. I didn't recognize the names either. Although Patrick told me he was going to Camden today to meet with Sam Gould, the shipbuilder, and I remembered I'd talked with him last summer. He'd known Skye and her friend Jasmine back when he was in college in New York City."

"A shipbuilder? Doesn't sound like someone who'd kill Clem over your buying an embroidery."

"Agreed. Besides, Sam Gould would have been in Camden with Patrick when Clem died. But, still, he's the only Gould I've heard of. Although I'm sure there are a lot more people in Maine that have that name now, and were more in the past."

"Isn't there a Senator Holgate?"

"Ruth said that, too. She's going to try to find any genealogical connections between the Providence family, since their names are on your needle-pointed samplers, and the Holgates or Goulds."

"If anyone can do that, it's Ruth."

"That's what I thought."

Sarah put a steaming bowl of soup in front of me with a package of crackers and some cheddar. She sat across from me and cut herself a piece of cheese as I started eating.

144

"Up to your standards?" she asked.

"Definitely. A little hot, but I can cope with that." Gram's bean soup had been a staple of winter lunches when I'd been a child. Delicious, filling, nutritious, and, thinking back, inexpensive. Filling my spoon again I was comforted in a way I must have been when I was little, and cold weather was my only enemy.

I focused on the soup and tried to forget why I was at Sarah's.

Gram's call interrupted my focus on food. "Angie! Are you all right? Mrs. Walker, Clem's mother, just called Tom. Have you heard?"

"Pete told me," I said, swallowing the last of my bean soup and giving Sarah a thumbs-up. "I'm at Sarah's." Of course, Gram would be one of the first to hear. The Walkers were members of her husband's congregation.

"Good. Then you're not alone. I knew you and Clem were going to have lunch together. I still can't believe what happened. Tom's gone over to be with the Walkers. I don't think they're coping well."

How could they? Their daughter had been killed. "I'm still trying to understand how this could have happened. Clem was late for our lunch date, so I was a little worried, but I never dreamed she'd been killed."

"Does Pete know about the threats you were both getting?"

"Yes; I told him. He suggested I stay at Sarah's,

at least for today, in case this crazy person is looking for me, too." Saying it out loud made it sound even scarier than it was.

"How are you, Angie? Really?"

"Nervous. Still finding it hard to believe Clem's gone."

"Is Sarah okay with your staying at her place?" As always, Gram was worried about bothering other people.

"For now, yes. I don't think I'll be here long."

"You'll be here for the night, at least," Sarah put in, loudly, so Gram would be sure to hear her.

I could almost see Gram smiling. "You thank Sarah for me."

"She just heated me a bowl of bean soup she'd made, following your recipe. I feel like I'm at home."

"Good. And you're keeping in touch with the police?"

"Pete Lambert's going to check on me. I'm all right, Gram."

"You let me know if you need any help from Tom or me, hear? You're welcome to stay with us, too. Any time. Do you need me to get Trixi?"

I hesitated. But I hadn't told Gram one of the threats also included my family. I didn't want her near my house. "Trixi will be fine for now. I'll let you know if I need anything."

"I'm so sorry about Clem, Angie," she said. "Sometimes life isn't fair."

She was right about that.

Sarah'd already washed my soup bowl. "What's next?" she asked, heading us both into her living room. "Who else should know what's happening?"

I looked out her front window. I couldn't see the wharf, but cars were parked in areas near the waterfront that had been empty earlier. The crime scene van? More police, including Ethan? Had anyone called Channel 7 to tell them they'd lost a reporter . . . and maybe their next anchor?

Sarah came and stood next to me. " 'By my Window have I for Scenery / Just a Sea.' "

She, and Emily, were right.

And Clem was dead. I still couldn't believe it.

CHAPTER 14

"Liberty Peace and Prosperity Ever Prevail in America."

—Stitched within a border of hearts and flowers by Hannah Jones in 1801.

"Why don't you call Patrick? He'll be worried about you if he hears what happened to Clem," Sarah suggested.

"You're right. I should call him. But he was going to Camden. He may still be having lunch with Sam Gould. I'll call Ruth first. She may have found some genealogical information that would help us."

Sarah nodded as I settled myself on her couch.

"Ruth? I didn't want you to hear it on the news. Clem was shot this afternoon."

"No! Are you all right?"

"I'm fine. I'm at Sarah's," I assured her. "The police know about the threats."

"And how is Clem?"

I hadn't been clear about that. "Clem's dead," I told her. "Her body was found in her car, at the town wharf parking lot."

Ruth didn't say anything. Then, "She was so young! Bad enough if something like that happened to an old bird like me. But she had so much of her life ahead of her. Angie, I'm so sorry. I knew Clem, but not well. Selfishly, I'm glad you're all right."

"I am," I assured her. At least for now. I was trying hard not to worry about whether whoever had killed Clem would now be looking for me. "Have you found out anything about those names connected with the embroideries Sarah and I bought?"

"Not much so far," Ruth answered, her voice still shaking a little. "But all the families—Providences, Goulds, and Holgates—were originally from England, and I'm pretty sure some members of each family were in the District of Maine before the American Revolution."

"That sounds as though you've gone back a lot of years in a few hours," I said. Ruth's research skills were amazing.

"I didn't start with now and go back. I checked Maine data for early families. All three were listed. The Holgates were one of the families to whom the English king awarded Maine land grants back in the sixteen hundreds."

That fit what Jonas Beale at the Maine Historical Society had suggested.

"Most of those that got land grants never came to the States—or, colonies, as they were then. And the farmers and fishermen and lumbermen who settled on the land didn't pay attention to what

150

was happening in England. There were no maps or borders or guards to say, 'Don't settle here.' "

"That was when they marked the pines, right?" I remembered some things from my Maine history classes at Haven Harbor Elementary.

"Exactly. The tallest and straightest white pines in the Maine woods were claimed by the English king for his navy. They were marked with large *X*s; only agents of the crown were supposed to cut them."

"But some people did."

"Representatives of the English crown weren't exactly guarding them. Some of those trees were included in the land grants."

"What about the Goulds?"

"I still have to check some sources. The first mention I found of a Gould here in Maine was in 1774."

Almost twenty years after that London Foundling Hospital billet dated 1757. "Englishmen were still immigrating to the wilderness of Maine then?"

"Either that, or they'd been here for a while, but their presence wasn't recorded before that," Ruth explained. "Records were scarce then."

"What about the Providence family?"

"The first Holgates were the earliest of the three. The Goulds came next, and the Providences, just after the Revolution. So the three names you're looking for were all here—or had been here—by eighteen hundred."

"What do you mean, 'had been here'?"

"I have a lot more work to do on this, Angie, but the Holgates seem to have disappeared for a while during and after the Revolution. Despite the earlier references, I can't find anything more about the family until eighteen ten, when a Geoffrey Holgate married in Gardiner."

"Gardiner's not far from Hallowell or Augusta," I pointed out. "At least one of those estates was supposed to have come from near Augusta."

"You're right. Gardiner's not far down the Kennebec from there," Ruth agreed. "I'm sorry I haven't found information helpful to you or Sarah. Or, unfortunately, to Clem. Even if the coat of arms embroidery you have is connected to one of those families, I can't imagine why someone today would care about it, or be so angry about your finding out about it that he—or she—would kill anyone."

"Let me know if you find out anything more," I said.

"I'm not giving up," said Ruth. "I'm going to take a break for a little while to rest my hands—carpal tunnel, you know, from all the hours I spend on my computer—and then I'll get back to it. I'll let you know. And, Angie, I'm so sorry about Clem. Take care of yourself, now."

"I will," I promised, although I wasn't sure how I was going to do that. I wasn't going to hide in Sarah's apartment for the rest of my life.

CHAPTER 15

"Diligence and Perseverance are the Keys to improvement and Subdue all difficulties."

—Stitched by Mary Ann Lewis, eight years old, at Miss Pierce's School in New Haven, Connecticut. It also includes three alphabets and a row of cross-stitched flowers and strawberries.

"What did Ruth find out?" Sarah asked, coming back into the living room after washing my lunch dishes. She stopped for a minute and glanced into my canvas bag, but then kept going.

"The Holgates and Goulds were in Maine before the Revolution. The Providences arrived after that. None of the families seem to be connected. Or at least Ruth hasn't found any connections yet."

I glanced down as my cell rang. "Yes, Pete?"

"Everything all right where you are?" he asked.

"Quiet as a snowy day," I answered.

"Snowy day wouldn't be quiet for me. Wicked bad accidents happen when stupid people drive on snowy roads," he answered. "You still at Sarah's?"

"I promised I'd stay here. What's happening at the wharf?"

"I'm on guard duty at the moment, freezing my rear off. Crime scene folks are here; medical examiner arrived about ten minutes ago. Ethan's on his way. With his wife back from Afghanistan, he spends as much time at home in Hallowell with her and Emmie as he can. Used to be easier on me when he and Emmie stayed with his parents here in the Harbor."

"I understand that," I agreed.

"I don't know any more than I told you earlier. But under the circumstances, I still think you should stay away from your house right now. Maybe for a few days."

"Pete!"

"Until we know whether whoever killed Clem is looking for you. I know you'd rather be at home. But do you have somewhere else you could stay?"

"Sarah said I can stay here tonight, and I will." Sarah nodded at me.

"But she doesn't have enough space for me to stay long. I could go to Gram's."

"Better not at your grandmother's. The rectory is too close to your house. Someone might see you—or even go to look for you."

I shivered. "What about Gram and Tom?"

"I'll call them and make sure they know to keep a low profile. Aren't you seeing Patrick West? He lives far enough out of town that no one would look for you there."

"Unless they knew I was . . . dating . . . him. I'll ask him," I said. Stay with Patrick? How would he feel about that? How would I feel? That would be crossing our unwritten red line. On the other hand . . . "Gram might stay out of sight. But a minister can't hide. Last I heard Tom was over with Clem's parents."

"I'm glad. The Walkers were wicked upset, of course. They also said they expected a friend of Clem's . . . a Steve Jeffries . . . to be arriving there soon. What do you know about him?"

"He's a sculptor. Lives in Biddeford. He and Clem have"—I corrected myself—"had been seeing each other for a couple of months."

"Any problems there you know of?"

Could Pete be thinking Steve killed Clem?

I didn't understand the relationship Clem and Steve had. When she'd talked about him it had seemed private, personal. But when you're murdered, nothing is private. "Yesterday she told me she and Steve were breaking up. But then this morning she said he'd be here in Haven Harbor to have dinner with her and her parents tonight. So I don't really know how close they were."

"She say why they were breaking up? Was he violent? Ever hit her?"

"She never said anything like that!" I'd only met Steve a couple of times. He hadn't seemed the violent sort, although you couldn't always tell. "Clem was trying to get Patrick to show Steve's sculptures at the gallery here in Haven Harbor. But she said they disagreed on future plans."

"I'll talk to him myself," Pete said. "Seeing as how Clem's future plans are now limited. Ethan'll want to talk with him too, and with the Walkers. They might know if Clem had been having problems with anyone outside of this embroidery situation."

"You think the death threats about the embroidery weren't serious?"

"I have to take them seriously, since they were followed up by someone's being murdered. But I can't see why anyone would kill over an old piece of stitching."

Me either.

"So, talk to Patrick, and see if you can stay out at his place a couple of days. And I know you'll want stuff from your house. Make a list of what you'll need and have him get it for you, or I'll do that. I don't want you at your place even for an hour."

"Yes, Pete." I raised my eyebrows at Sarah. Patrick going through my clothes and toiletries would be bad enough. I didn't want Pete doing it. "Let me know if you hear anything."

"I will. You rest easy, now."

"No news," I told Sarah after the call ended.

"But Pete's determined I shouldn't go home for a few days. He suggested I stay with Patrick because his place isn't near downtown."

Sarah grinned. "Patrick will like that."

"I'll have to talk to him to be sure." I didn't want to make any assumptions. Patrick and I were close, but not living-together close. "And his Bette and Trixi haven't seen each other since we divided that litter. I don't know how they'll get along."

"I'd offer to take Trixi here, but I'm afraid Ruggles wouldn't agree," said Sarah. "You took her to your grandmother's house once, right?"

"When I lost power right before Christmas," I agreed. "Her Juno wasn't thrilled, but it worked out all right."

"Settle in here for now. Call Patrick pretty soon. And if he's hesitant, you can stay here more than one night. For now, let's take advantage of a bad situation and have a girls' night in."

I smiled. Sarah was trying to keep me from thinking about Clem. She and Clem had met a few times, but Clem had been my friend.

She'd been the organized one. The ambitious one.

Who'd killed her, and why? Pete, and soon Ethan, would be working on that. But if I hadn't bought that embroidery, or showed it to Clem, would she still be alive?

I wanted to do something. To talk to people. To think through the history of the needlepoint.

"What about pasta?" Sarah was saying. "And streaming a good movie or two. And wine, of course."

"Wine sounds good for a start," I agreed. "And, yes, a movie." Maybe someone else's story would get my mind off mine. And off the possibility that whoever killed Clem also had my name and picture on his list.

I'd been involved in murder investigations before, but I'd never thought I might be a victim. It wasn't a good feeling.

"Do you need anything for tonight?" asked Sarah. "I have extra blankets and pillows, and you can wear one of my sleep shirts. I'm pretty sure I even have an extra toothbrush. The dentist gave me several when I had my teeth cleaned last week."

Clem had been going to see her dentist this afternoon. That was the reason she'd been in Haven Harbor.

"I'm fine, Sarah. All that sounds good." I glanced over at the canvas bag I'd left near the couch. My Glock was in it, loaded and ready. "I have everything I need." Except answers.

CHAPTER 16

"Imitate the Best."

—Sally Amy Vickery stitched these
words on her sampler with three
alphabets and a border in black cross-
stitch, perhaps because she was in
mourning. She completed it in 1807
in Taunton, Massachusetts,
when she was ten years old.

Two glasses of wine later (after all, I wasn't going to be driving) Sarah began cooking pasta for dinner. I stood at her window, looking into the darkness. A February day in Maine was dark by four-thirty in the afternoon.

Had Pete and Ethan and the police crews removed Clem and her car? Had they found anything that would help them figure out who'd killed her?

And, in the shadows below the window, was anyone looking for me?

Sarah was my best friend, but today her apartment felt like a jail. I hated being confined, even if the confinement was for my own safety.

Patrick should be home from Camden by now. I was about to call him when my cell rang. "Angie? It's Pete. Everything okay there?"

"Fine. Any news?"

"Ethan's here. He'd like to stop in to see you." Pete paused. "I'm coming along, too. We don't think anyone is watching us, but we're going to play it safe and leave the wharf heading in different directions. Tell Sarah to answer the door in the next ten minutes if someone knocks three times. It'll be Ethan or me."

"You sound like you're on a spy mission," I said, shaking my head.

"We don't want to take any chances. We don't want to lead anyone to where you're hiding."

Hiding. That's what I was doing, wasn't it?

"Fine. I'll see you both in a few minutes." I ended the call and told Sarah about the three-knock code.

"Sounds like a movie script," she agreed. "But we're here, and they're welcome. I'll start coffee brewing. If they've been out by the wharf, they'll be freezing."

"Good plan," I agreed, wondering if I should hide my glass of wine. But, then, there was no reason I couldn't have wine. Even two glasses.

The first set of three knocks came about five minutes later. Sarah opened the door carefully, and let in a snow-covered Ethan Trask. He stepped inside and took off his gloves and hat. Snow falling from his boots and jacket left small puddles on the floor. "Sorry, Sarah," he said, looking at the melting snow.

"No problem," she assured him. "It happens in winter. In the dark we didn't even know it was snowing again," she said, taking his jacket and hanging it above a hot-air register in her kitchen.

"Started about half an hour ago," Ethan said. "Coming down wicked hard, now."

"Angie's in the living room," she said, as three more knocks on the door announced Pete's arrival. She opened the door, calling to Ethan, "Coffee's about ready."

"Sounds great," said Pete, grinning as he hung his jacket in the kitchen. He glanced at Sarah a few more times than necessary, but she was busy with the coffee and didn't notice.

"Looks like the gang's all here," I commented as Ethan and Pete joined me in the living room.

Sarah brought in mugs of coffee a few minutes later and went back to the kitchen. Her apartment was small; she couldn't help hearing what we all said. But she was trying to give us some privacy.

"Pete told me about the threats you and Clem got yesterday," said Ethan, getting to the point immediately. "I want to hear about them, make sure we all have the same information."

"Clem interviewed me on Channel 7 yesterday about a piece of embroidery and what looks like a receipt for a child abandoned at the London Foundling Hospital in 1757. The segment aired for about a minute. Maybe less."

"I've called the studio, Ethan," Pete put in. "They're sending us each a link to the clip."

"Good," said Ethan. "And you were both named on the air, Angie?"

"Clem was named, as always, because she's a reporter for Channel 7. She introduced me and said I owned Mainely Needlepoint."

"She didn't say you were in Haven Harbor."

"No. But the town is named on the Mainely Needlepoint web site."

"So, Clem said if anyone had information to help identify the embroidery, to call Channel 7?"

"Right. And only a few minutes after the segment aired Clem called me to say the station had already received a call. Whoever left the message didn't have information about the embroidery. He—or she," (I'd never asked whether the voice was male or female), "threatened both Clem and me with death if we didn't stop investigating."

"I assume you both thought that was strange," Ethan said, raising his eyebrows, as if to say that he sure thought it was strange.

"Of course. It was spooky. We had no idea what to think. I was at Gram's house with Patrick West and the Mainely Needlepointers when I got the call. Some people wondered if it was a joke, or a prank. Others said we should take it seriously."

"And did you?"

I didn't want to admit how scared I'd been. "I

162

made sure all my windows and doors were locked last night." I didn't mention I'd kept my Glock next to my bed, or that my heart had practically stopped when an icicle had fallen off the roof in the middle of the night.

"And then there were more threats?"

"One was on my computer, at the Mainely Needlepoint web site link. It said no one should be asking questions about the embroidery. Then Clem called. She said the station had gotten more calls during the night. I don't know how many. She was going to bring the printouts of the calls with her to show me when we had lunch, and I told her I'd bring the message I'd gotten."

"We found her printouts in her car. Do you have yours with you?"

"I'll get it for you." I dug into my canvas bag and handed the printout to Ethan.

He glanced at it. "Have you gotten any more threats since then?"

"I haven't checked since mid-morning, so there might be messages there." I paused. I didn't add that I hadn't wanted to look. "Have you any idea who killed Clem? Were there footprints, or fingerprints or . . . anything?"

"We'll have to wait to see what the crime scene technicians and the ME come up with," said Ethan, telling me nothing. "Her body's been taken to Augusta."

I shuddered. All the work she'd done, all her

dreams, and she'd ended up on an autopsy table. Maybe that would happen to most of us, some day. But Clem was only twenty-seven or eight. My age. Too soon.

"One thing I shouldn't tell you, but I will," said Ethan. "But you have to promise to keep it to yourself."

I nodded.

"The reason we're taking these threats to you and Clem seriously is not only because she was killed. But because whoever killed her left an embroidery needle sticking out of her throat."

I gasped.

"That's why we're all taking this seriously. Pete told me someone had been looking for you this morning," said Ethan.

"Pax Henry said a man came into the post office asking for my address. I don't think Pax paid too much attention to him, but he did tell the man that I lived on the green."

"Pete, let's make sure we talk to Pax," said Ethan. He turned to me. "Did this man ask anything about Clem?"

"Pax didn't say, if he did," I answered.

"Have you seen that man since? Or anyone else out of the ordinary?"

"I don't know what he looks like." Where had I been today? "I was at home, then mailed a package at the post office, and stopped to visit Ruth Hopkins. After that I went to the Harbor

Haunts, to have lunch with Clem, and talked to you, Pete. I waited for about thirty minutes, and then left, came here, and haven't left. I haven't seen anyone else today." I looked at the two officers. "Except you guys."

"One more question," said Ethan. "Clem doesn't come to Haven Harbor often, from what I've heard. Who knew the two of you would be having lunch together today at the Harbor Haunts?"

"I don't know who she might have told," I said, thinking. "Her parents? Someone at the studio?"

"Who did you tell?"

"Patrick, and Gram. I mentioned it to Ruth Hopkins. I told you, Pete. And—I mentioned it to someone at the Augusta Auction House." I thought back to early this morning. "Jessica Winter."

"Okay," Ethan said. "That's a start. Now I'd like your house keys, so we can pick up your computer. I'm hoping our technicians can figure out who sent that message to you. They'll also see whether any more messages came in this afternoon."

My computer! "How long will you need it? All the Mainely Needlepoint records are on it, and our online shopping web site is, too." I handed Pete my house key. I probably should have saved my business records to the cloud. But I hadn't. "I understand you need to look at it. But I need it back as soon as possible."

"We'll get it back to you as soon as we can," Ethan promised. That didn't give me a warm feeling. But I had no choice.

I touched the gold angel necklace Mama had given me so many years ago. Sometimes, when I felt stressed, I hoped she was an angel now, looking down at me. I wasn't religious, but that idea calmed me.

"Angie, you know Pete and I well enough to trust us. We don't know why Clem was killed, or by whom. It could have been random. But with that needle left at the crime scene, there's a good chance it has something to do with your embroidery. Until we have a better idea of what happened, we want you to stay safe. Pete said you might stay with Patrick West, out at Aurora?"

"I haven't talked with Patrick yet, but I think that will be okay." Did everyone know about Patrick and me? And if they did, could the killer know, too?

"Keep in touch with Pete or me, and let me know if you hear anything more, from anyone, or think of anything that might help us. Or, certainly, if you get any more threats. We suggest you stay out of downtown Haven Harbor for a few days. Aurora's not far, but at least it isn't in the center of town. Even there, stay low. Out of sight. No long walks in the snow or visiting your grandmother in town."

"Got it."

"And, for the record, Clem Walker was your friend, right?"

"We went to high school together and reconnected when I came back to Haven Harbor from Arizona last May."

"Was she happy?"

I looked at Ethan. "Happy? That's a funny question. She was living the life she chose. No one's life is perfect." I glanced at Pete. Since his wife had left him last fall I knew he'd been having a hard time. "She wasn't suicidal."

"I didn't know Clem, other than seeing her on the news. I don't remember her from high school. Knowing more about her might help us find her killer."

"Okay. Clem was focused and dedicated to succeeding. She went through U Maine on a scholarship, and has been working her way up at Channel 7. Her goal was to be an anchor on a national news show. She was hoping to get a promotion soon."

"A promotion?"

"She told me the producer was thinking of replacing an older anchor with a younger one, and she was high on the list of possible replacements."

Ethan frowned. "Replace Dara Richmond? She's been at Channel 7 forever."

"I'm pretty sure that's what Clem meant. She didn't use Dara's name, though."

"And Clem was happy about replacing her?"

"Excited at the possibility," I said.

"We know about Steve Jeffries. What about other friends in her life? Enemies?"

"She lived in Portland. We didn't socialize a lot. We saw each other when she came back to Haven Harbor to see her family. I met Steve because Clem hoped Patrick would give his work a show in the gallery here in town."

I'd only seen Clem when she wanted something from me, I realized. Or, I admitted, when I wanted something from her.

"I don't know anything about her friends. She seemed to spend most of her time at work," I concluded, weakly. I wished I knew more about her that would help Pete and Ethan.

Ethan closed the small notebook he'd been using. "If you think of anything else that might be helpful, let us know. We'll stop by your house, check it, and pick up your computer, before we go to see Mr. and Mrs. Walker."

"My computer's on the desk in the living room."

"Good. Remember to let us know when you leave here, whether it's to go to Patrick's house or somewhere else."

Where else could I go?

"Oh—and is your car near here or at your place?"

"Down the street," I answered.

"Do you have someone who could get it off the street and into your barn? In case anyone knows it's yours and is watching it. Not to speak of plows needing to clear the streets."

I nodded. My car. One more thing to take care of; one more favor to ask.

But speaking of favors . . . "Would you mind doing me a favor?" I asked as Ethan and Pete were putting their coats on. "When you're at my house, would you give my cat some more food and water? Her food and dishes are in the kitchen. She should be all right tonight, and I'll find some way to get her out tomorrow."

"I'll feed her," Pete agreed. "Not a problem. But remember—don't *you* go to your house tomorrow. If you need anything, have someone else get it." He looked over at Sarah, almost shyly. "Thanks for the coffee, and for watching out for Angie. If we can help in any way, call me. The police station is only a couple of blocks away."

"Don't keep my computer longer than you have to," I reminded the two men.

"We won't," said Pete, as he and Ethan went down the now snow-covered steps.

I watched them leave, separately, heading to their cars.

Sarah closed the door, brushing off the snow that had blown onto me as I'd stood in the doorway.

"It's going to be all right," she said. "They'll find whoever killed Clem. It just may take some time."

"But it will never be all right for Clem," I said. I realized I was crying.

CHAPTER 17

"Industry is the law of our nature, the indispensable condition of possessing a sound mind and a sound body."

—Ann Stoddard, an eleven-year-old
from Hingham, Massachusetts,
stitched this in 1801. She included
three alphabets and a trefoil border.

Sarah let me cry for a few minutes. Then she handed me a cup of chamomile tea. "Maybe this will help. Wine's a depressant. Right now you don't need any more of that."

"You sound like Gram," I said, wiping my eyes.

"Of course you're upset. And scared. And confused, because none of this seems to make sense. But it will. I've known you less than a year, Angie Curtis, but I've never seen you give up trying to find the truth when something bad happened. Ethan and Pete are like that, too. Between the three of you, you'll find out what happened to Clem. And you'll be fine." She glanced over at my bag. "I saw what was in your bag. In Australia you wouldn't have that gun of yours. Weapons make me nervous. But I understand why you want to have yours near you now." She smiled at me, half-jokingly. "Just don't take it out of that bag or point it at me."

"It's a deal," I said. "Thank you for the tea. And whatever you're cooking smells terrific." The whole apartment warmed with the scents of tomatoes, garlic, and anchovies.

"Supper's almost ready. While I'm cooking you should try to reach Patrick. You'll feel better once you know what you're going to do tomorrow."

I picked up my phone.

"Hi! I was about to call you. How was your day?" Patrick's cheerful voice was too much. I started crying again. "Hey, Angie. What's wrong?"

"Clem's dead."

"What?" Patrick hadn't heard.

"Remember, I told you we were going to have lunch at the Harbor Haunts? She didn't make it. Someone found her in her car at the town wharf parking lot. She'd been shot."

"That death threat last night," Patrick immediately connected. "Are you all right?"

"I'm fine. The police say I shouldn't go home for a while. I'm at Sarah's."

"Good. You're not alone. What about Trixi?"

"Pete Lambert is going to feed her when he and Ethan stop to get my computer."

"Your computer? Why do they need that?"

"Because I got another threat this morning, through the Mainely Needlepoint Web site. They want to see if they can trace it." And see if any more threats came in this afternoon. "How was your lunch with Sam Gould?"

"Good. Meeting went well. Sam's doing a nice job with Mom's boat. I had a couple of suggestions, but not many. He knows a lot more about boats and yachts of all sizes than I do. I've only been on a few, and I never paid much attention to them."

Of course, Patrick would have been on yachts. His uncle had sailed one into Haven Harbor a few months ago. My experience with boats was limited to small sailboats, skiffs, and lobster boats. I'd never paid much attention to yachts either.

"Will the boat be finished by next summer?"

"That's the plan. Mom's hoping to be in Maine then. There's talk of making a movie nearby."

"I thought she was against that."

"She was. She is. But two producers are enthusiastic about it. But that's not important now; you're important. Did you say Pete and Ethan don't want you to go home?"

"Maybe not for several days. They're afraid whoever hurt Clem might be looking for me."

"Then you'll come stay with me," he said firmly. "We can roast marshmallows in the fire-place and drink champagne."

My tears had stopped at the yachts.

"You wouldn't mind?"

"Mind? No way. I'd mind if you didn't come."

The line was silent for a few seconds. I suspected we were both thinking that my staying with him was a new step. One, maybe for different reasons, we'd both been avoiding.

"Not sure about the marshmallows and champagne combination. But, yes, tomorrow? I'm going to stay at Sarah's tonight. Maybe tomorrow you could go to my house and get Trixi and some of my clothes."

"That should be interesting. Trixi and Bette together again. A reunion of sisters." Patrick's voice dropped. "Seriously, Angie, are you all right? Are you sure you don't want me to come and get you now?"

"I'm fine. Really. And Sarah's good company."

Sarah walked by and gave me a high five.

"We're going to have a girls' night. Talking boys and makeup and murder. The usual stuff."

"I'm glad you're smiling. But . . . Clem. Does Steve know?"

"I assume so. Pete called Clem's parents. Before all this happened Steve was planning to join Clem at her family's house for dinner."

"I'll call him, make sure he's okay," said Patrick. "He may need someone to talk to. And if he wants to stay in the area, maybe he'd feel more comfortable staying at my place tonight than with Clem's family."

"That's a good idea," I agreed. "Offer, even if he turns you down."

"Call me if you need anything tonight, or if anything else happens. I'll talk to you first thing in the morning, and you can tell me what you need from your house besides Trixi." He paused, and I could hear the smile in his voice. "Does this mean I get to go through your unmentionable drawers?"

"Very funny," I said, smiling back. "I'll make a list. Have a good evening. See you tomorrow." I'd be staying with Patrick tomorrow night. My first night at the carriage house. I should be excited. Under these circumstances romance wasn't a priority. And yet . . .

"Sounds like you have tomorrow organized," said Sarah. "I made pasta puttanesca and a salad. Dinner is served!"

Thank goodness for Sarah. "Smells delicious," I said. Then I added, hesitantly, "Would you mind if we turned on the Channel 7 news? I'd like to know if they are covering Clem's death."

Sarah didn't hesitate. "The pasta can wait." She turned on the television.

Tonight's snowstorm would only result in four to six inches. (My friends in Arizona would have been freaked out by that much, but in Maine it was only borderline "plowable snow.") Nothing to worry about. Besides, Sarah and I were inside, Patrick was home. And Clem . . .

Dara Richmond was at the anchor desk after the weather. "Tonight we have sad news. A member

175

of our Channel 7 family left us today." A smiling picture of Clem filled the screen. "Features reporter Clem Walker died in her hometown of Haven Harbor this afternoon. As we have more details, we'll bring them to you. For now, we send sympathies to her family and many friends."

A commercial was next, advertising a sale on used cars.

I turned off the set. "No details. She didn't even say Clem was killed."

"Maybe the police asked the station to keep that quiet for now," Sarah suggested.

"Maybe," I said, almost to myself. "I wonder how her 'Channel 7 family' is reacting off-air. Clem only worked there a short time, and she once told me some of her coworkers resented the amount of airtime she was getting."

"They can't resent that now," Sarah pointed out.

"With Clem gone, I wonder who's keeping track of telephone calls about the embroidery," I added. "If any more calls came in." The helpful kind or the unhelpful kind. Would Clem's killer call to brag about what he did? "I don't even know who to call to find out. If messages are still coming in, I could still be in danger."

"Pete and Ethan seemed to think so," Sarah agreed as she set her kitchen table with ceramic pasta bowls and salad plates. "They're in touch with the studio. The studio knew she was dead."

"But Pete and Ethan didn't tell me they'd heard of any new messages or threats."

"If they had, would they? They probably wouldn't want you to worry."

"I'm all grown up. And it's my life. If Clem died because of the embroidery I bought . . ." I sat and unfolded my bright cotton napkin. "I know I'm supposed to stay away from my house and downtown Haven Harbor. But no one said I couldn't go to Portland."

"What are you thinking of doing?" Sarah added oil and vinegar dressing to her salad and handed the cruets to me.

"Going to the studio myself. I could talk to Dara Richmond. She and Clem might not have been best of friends, but she might know what was happening about any messages."

I took a bite of the pasta. "Delicious, Sarah. I don't think I've ever had this. Cooking the garlic and anchovies and red pepper together melded them."

"Pasta puttanesca is easy. It's a meal I make for myself when I want something comforting, but with a little spice. I'll give you my recipe," Sarah promised, pouring us each a half glass of red wine. "If you get weepy again, we'll go back to tea. But red wine with pasta is required."

I didn't disagree.

"You're right. Dara Richmond might know what was happening there. She might even have ideas about anyone who didn't get along with Clem. Ethan asked you questions about that. But would Ethan want you going to Portland?"

"He didn't say I had to stay at Patrick's twenty-four/seven," I pointed out. "Clem had a strong personality. She could be abrasive sometimes. She and Dara might have competed at the station. That could have resulted in conflict that had nothing to do with embroidery."

" 'Success is counted sweetest / By those who ne'er succeed,' " Sarah said quietly.

Another Emily Dickinson quote, I was sure. I liked that one.

"You're right. Her ambition might have had something to do with her murder," Sarah continued. "Although we've all been assuming she was murdered because of what you said on television yesterday." She took a sip of wine. "To be honest, Angie, I'm hoping Clem was killed for some reason totally unrelated to the coat of arms you bought. After all, I'm the one who took you to that auction. But I couldn't help overhearing what Ethan said about that embroidery needle. That does sound like a reference to embroidery. If your going with me to that auction resulted in Clem's death, I'd feel responsible." She looked at me. "But I'm selfish. If anyone kills you, I'll be devastated."

My telephone rang. I didn't feel like talking to anyone but Sarah. But cell phone calls followed you everywhere, unless you turned the phone off, and I didn't want to miss any calls from Gram or Patrick. Or Pete or Ethan.

At first I didn't recognize the name that appeared. J. Winter. Then I connected. "Hello?"

"I'm sorry to bother you, but this is Jessica. At the Augusta Auction House? We talked this morning?"

"Yes, I remember, Jessica."

"Is it true? What was just on the news? Is Clem Walker dead?"

"I'm afraid so. She died early this afternoon."

"Oh, no! What happened? She looked fine on the news last night, and you said you were going to have lunch with her today. I'm so upset. After I talked to you I thought, maybe someday I could meet her. And now . . . I had to call you. You were her friend. Her real, in-person friend. And, oh, you must be so devastated."

"Jessica, how did you get my number?"

"This morning you told me the number of the lot you'd bought, and of course I could cross-reference it to the information you gave us when you registered for a bidding number."

Of course. "It wasn't on the news. Not yet. But Clem was murdered." I knew Pete said we shouldn't give out any details, but Jessica had helped me this morning, and she was a big fan of Clem's. I couldn't lie to her.

"No! But, why? She was so young, and smart, and beautiful."

179

"The police are investigating, of course. They don't know much right now."

Jessica sounded as though she was crying. "Who would kill someone like Clem Walker? I can't believe it."

"I'm sorry, Jessica. But it's true. Thank you again for giving me the information on the consigners this morning. That will be a help."

"Not help in finding Clem Walker's killer!"

I didn't disagree. But she might be wrong about that.

"I'm sure there'll be more details about Clem as they develop. I'm afraid I can't talk right now."

"It's all so awful."

Yes. It was.

"Who was that?" Sarah asked.

"The young woman I talked with this morning who works at the auction house in Augusta. She was a major fan of Clem's, and gave me information she wasn't supposed to because I knew Clem. She heard on the news tonight that Clem was dead."

Sarah shook her head. "I know Patrick's mom has fans, some of whom are a bit over the moon, but it never occurred to me that local television reporters would have fans, too."

"The world is full of strange people and events," I agreed.

CHAPTER 18

"Not always must we think while here to
  share
Pleasures unmingled with corroding care,
The rose its thorn, the sweet its bitter
  yield,
And blended good and ill, spread o'er
  life's field."

—Stitched by Esther Warrington at
the Westtown Boarding School,
a Quaker school in West Chester,
Pennsylvania, in 1808.

Sarah and I vowed not to think about murders anymore that evening. Instead, we watched *You've Got Mail* and *The American President* and *Notting Hill*. Romantic comedies that were light and funny. If life worked out as well for real people as it did for those fictional characters, the world would be a different place.

I couldn't forget what had happened to Clem, or that I could be in danger, too, but I tried to focus on the movies, not on what had happened today . . . or what might happen tomorrow.

We said good night after midnight. I collapsed on Sarah's fold-out couch and slept better than

I'd expected. Ruggles joined me at some point and slept on the pillow next to me. Did he sense my anxiety and want to comfort me?

By morning the snow had stopped and been replaced by sea smoke . . . winter fog that lingered over the ocean and nearby land. Beams of sunlight only occasionally shone through the billows of white, low-hanging clouds close to the dark blue harbor water.

My home was only a few blocks inland, but far enough from the harbor that I rarely saw sea smoke from my windows. Seeing the swirling mists outside Sarah's windows was a treat. When I was a child I'd loved fog in the summertime and sea smoke in the winter. Both seemed like nature's magic, covering the world, and making parts of it appear and then disappear.

Sea smoke was still hypnotic. Only the tantalizing smell of coffee pulled me away from the window.

Sarah brewed coffee dark, the way I liked it. We ate cinnamon toast and didn't say much. Last night's wine was slowing us down.

After breakfast and putting Sarah's couch back together I made a list of what Trixi and I would need if we stayed with Patrick for a couple of days. I hoped it wouldn't be more than that. Patrick might try to make my visit amusing or romantic, but the reason I needed to stay with him wasn't fun. And, although Pete and Ethan wanted me out of Haven Harbor, if anyone in town was asked about me, they'd say Patrick and I were together. Most people in town knew me, and since Patrick was Skye West's son, and now owner of the gallery in town, people knew him, too. Secrets were hard to keep in small towns.

Sarah peeked over my shoulder. "How long a list are you giving him?"

I hadn't been focusing on the list. "Do you think Trixi and Bette would use the same litter pan? Or should he bring Trixi's with him?"

"I vote you let the cats work that out. If it doesn't seem to be working, he can always go back another day for your litter box. Does Patrick have a key to your house?"

"He does. Like you do. Last fall I got nervous about living alone."

Sarah looked at me oddly.

"I know, I know. You live alone. Patrick lives alone. Dave and Ruth live alone. Pete lives alone, since his wife left him." I glanced over at Sarah to see if she'd reacted to that. She hadn't.

"And I lived alone in my apartment in Arizona. But I have a big house, and there are funny noises. Anyway, I gave you a key, and Patrick one, and Gram already had one. I figured, if I were ever in trouble, someone could get in to help me."

"Not a bad idea, actually," Sarah agreed. "You

183

have a key to my place, but no one else does anymore. I should think about that."

I suspected Ted Lawrence had had a key to Sarah's apartment. Or maybe someone else I didn't know. Sarah had her secrets, too.

I went back to my list.

A few basic toiletries, and, yes (sigh), underwear. Flannel shirts, a fresh pair of jeans, a nightgown. I hesitated about that, but then added, specifically, "flannel nightgown." That would be more comfortable than sleeping in my underwear. And I didn't want to take the sleep shirt Sarah had loaned me for last night. I didn't need much. Toothbrush, comb, hand lotion, lip moisturizer. What I wanted most was my computer, but Ethan and Pete had already taken that.

When Patrick called, my list was set.

"I'll pick you up about noon. What about your car? Is it near Sarah's?"

Oops. I'd forgotten my car. "Yes. But Pete and Ethan said I couldn't go near it, in case someone knows it's mine and is watching it. I'll ask Gram or Tom to move it."

"Do they have your car keys?"

"Gram has an extra set, in case I lock myself out of the car. I'll call her."

Patrick's voice lowered. "Steve's here with me. He spent the night. That's why I won't be by for a little."

"How's he doing?"

"All right, considering the circumstances. I can't say much now."

Of course. Patrick's carriage house, where he lived on his mother's estate, Aurora, was relatively small. If Steve was there, he could hear Patrick's end of our conversation.

"Everything okay with you?" Patrick asked.

"Fine. I'll see you when you get here." I turned to Sarah. "Steve spent the night at Patrick's place. Patrick won't be here to get me until noon."

"No problem here," said Sarah. "But I'm going to open the store today. I have some new inventory items to put out, and some accounting to do, and that's easier to do downstairs. I might as well put the 'open' sign on the door since I'll be there. You can come along or hang out here."

"I want to call Gram and ask her or Tom to move my car," I said. "I'll call Ruth, too. And I should let Dave know what's happening, since just about everyone else knows."

"Fine," Sarah agreed. "If you find out anything interesting, let me know." She pointed at the inside steps to her shop. "You might leave a message for Patrick to pick you up at the shop. Avoids the slippery outside steps, and he'd look like a customer, since the store will be open."

"Good thought," I agreed.

The apartment was quiet without her. Ruggles came over and rubbed against my legs. I guess his

185

sleeping next to me meant we were now friends. What would Trixi think when she smelled him on my jeans?

First call was to Gram. "Good morning, Angel! I've been thinking about you. How are you?"

"I'm okay. Sarah and I watched movies and relaxed as much as we could last night."

"You're still at her apartment?"

"Right. But I'm moving to Patrick's at about noon. He's going to get Trixi and some of my things and then get me."

Gram was silent for a second or two. "Sure you don't want to come here, Angie? I know you're all grown up, but being with family is important."

I suspected she was also questioning my staying with Patrick. But she was Gram. She had a right. "I first thought of staying with you and Tom. But Pete and Ethan felt I shouldn't be anywhere near my house. And, Gram, he said for you and Tom to be careful, too. At least one of the threats included my family."

"Your family?"

"And that's what you are. How are you and Tom doing?"

"Tom spent a lot of time with Clem's mother and father last night. That fellow she's been dating was there, too, for a while, but he didn't stay long. Her parents were, of course, very upset. And the police came to question them."

"Pete and Ethan told me they were headed

there. Steve, Clem's friend, spent the night with Patrick at the carriage house."

"Then he wasn't alone either. That's good. If you can't come here, can I do anything else to help?"

"Actually, yes. I left my car near Sarah's apartment yesterday. It's parked between her store and the Harbor Haunts. The police don't want me near it in case anyone recognizes it, but it needs to be out of the street and in my barn. Would you or Tom mind moving it?"

"Of course not. Tom's over at the church office right now, but, when he takes a break or comes home for lunch, we'll drive down there and take care of it. Are you sure you want Patrick to get Trixi?"

"Sure. She's probably lonely."

"Hope she gets along with her sister," warned Gram.

"I hope so, too. But she got along with Juno when we stayed with you and Tom at the rectory before Christmas."

"Because Juno stayed out of sight most of the time," Gram reminded me. "So it should be interesting. It all depends on how territorial Bette is, and how indignant Trixi is about being taken out of her comfort zone. So Pete and Ethan paid you a visit yesterday?"

"Right. They asked a lot of questions. I told them what I could, but, unfortunately, I didn't

187

have a lot of answers. I knew someone was upset about the embroidery I bought, but I didn't know much about Clem's personal or work life. Ruth is trying to trace the genealogy of families who might be connected to the needlepoint."

"Captain Ob called last night to see how you were. I told him you were coping as well as anyone could."

"Thanks, Gram. I'll let him know when I get to Patrick's. I'll be right across the street, so he should know that. Where I'll be is supposed to be a secret, of course."

"Of course. But not to your friends and family."

"I meant not to mention it to a lot of people. I have no idea who sent those messages, or who killed Clem, or even if those things are connected. I don't know for sure that anyone's stalking me. But Ethan and Pete seemed to think I need to keep a low profile for a day or two." I took a sip of my now-cold second cup of coffee. "I hope they figure out who killed Clem, and soon. I'll go crazy if I have to stay in hiding very long."

"I'm sure they will, dear. And if you and Patrick need anything, you let me know. I could bring some food over."

"Thank you, but, no, please don't do that. I'm beginning to feel paranoid myself. I'm afraid if someone is looking for me, he or she will check your house—which is why you and Tom have to be careful!—and they might follow you. Pretend I'm on a vacation somewhere far away. I'll check in and let you know how I am. I promise."

"If you're sure, Angel," said Gram. "I feel so helpless."

Me too. "We'll all be fine," I assured her. "Let's hope this is only for a day or two."

I hated telling Gram she couldn't see me, or help, except for moving my car. But I'd never forgive myself if anything happened to her because of me.

I was imprisoned. I couldn't leave, and I was a possibly lethal package being handed from Sarah to Patrick. I was already restless. I wanted to smell fresh sea air and get snow on my boots. Most important, I wanted to find Clem's killer.

CHAPTER 19

"Friendship's a name to few confirmed
The offspring of a noble mind
A generous warmth which fills the breast
And better felt than e'er exprest."

—Part of elaborate sampler worked
in 1824 by Anna Braddock, who was
fourteen. She included many birds,
branches of trees, animals, a horse, sheep,
two children holding hands, and her
school building in Pennsylvania.

Next call was to Ruth.

"Angie, I'm so glad you called. I could hardly sleep last night I was so worried about you. And Clem, dead, so young. Life is full of unfairness, isn't it?"

"Sometimes it is," I agreed. "I'm all right, but restless. Sarah doesn't have much space here, and the police want me out of downtown Haven Harbor, so I'm going to move to Patrick's house later today."

"The big house?"

"No. Patrick's place. The carriage house."

"I'm sure that will be as nice. Maybe nicer."

"When Skye isn't in town they turn down the heat and turn off the water at Aurora."

"Of course. That makes sense," said Ruth.

"So, did you find out anything about the families involved with the needlepoint?"

"A few things. But I'm not sure how much help they'll be. First, I found the Providence family connection."

"Great! Sarah will appreciate that. The embroideries she bought were done by Providences."

"In 1788 Jonathan Holgate's daughter Verity married Joshua Providence in Saco. I couldn't find more details last night, but that could be the connection."

"That sounds right. I'm pretty sure Joshua and Verity are listed on the genealogical sampler Sarah has."

"If the list of people on the sampler is correct, and the Providences daughtered out, there are two possibilities. One is, of course, that the family continued, but hidden, under the married name of one of the daughters. Or, two, that the family dead-ended, and perhaps the possessions— including the embroideries—were taken by a Holgate relative, a cousin, perhaps. Many Maine families stayed in the same geographic areas, often in the same towns. I know of one couple in Damariscotta in the late nineteenth century who had seventeen children. All but one of them married someone else from Damariscotta. The lone holdout married someone from Boothbay. That's only a few miles down the peninsula, but he rarely saw the family after his marriage. In their eyes, and perhaps in his, he had left them."

"Incredible," I said. "And you found something else?"

"It's not definite yet, but do you remember I said the Goulds seemed to disappear about the time of the American Revolution, and then reappeared later?"

"I remember. Strange."

"Maybe not so strange. Several Goulds popped up in Nova Scotia about then, and then disappeared."

"What?"

"My guess is the Goulds were Royalists who got out of Maine during the colonies' rebellion, and went to Nova Scotia. They must have been wealthy—many Royalists were. The Goulds had enough money to get to Canada, and then after the Revolution they came back to try to reclaim their lands. Men who were Royalist-sympathizers going to Nova Scotia wasn't unusual during the Revolution. Who would want to stay here and be tarred and feathered? But not many families came back. The Goulds might have been an exception."

"Interesting," I said.

"Of course, none of that explains who auctioned off their estates this week, or why anyone would be angry enough about that to threaten you and Clem."

Or kill Clem, I added to myself. "Maybe some other information will pop up," I told Ruth. "Patrick had lunch with Sam Gould from Camden yesterday. I asked him to find out if Sam knew anything about the auction, but I don't know yet if he did. I'm going to see Patrick around noon."

"We'll keep in touch," Ruth promised. "And . . . take care of yourself, Angie. You're more important than any embroidery."

She was right, of course. "I'll check the dates you found with Sarah's embroidery," I promised.

"Good," said Ruth. "I'm going back to my own writing today for a while; I just got a manuscript in for proofing. But later today I'll be able to take more time for genealogy. It's a lot more interesting than reading my own book for the twentieth time. And, who knows? Maybe I'll set one of my next books during the American Revolution."

"Is erotica set then?"

Ruth laughed at the other end of the line. "Angie, dear, there's been erotica since the Greeks, and probably before. I can set a book in any time period I choose."

I'd been planning to call Dave, but, of course, he'd be at school. This time of year high school teachers were busy. Instead, I called Captain Ob.

His wife, Anna, answered. "Angie! I was

194

wondering how you were. I heard about Clem. Sad. So very sad."

"It is," I agreed. "Gram said you and Ob had asked about me. I wanted to let you know that I'd be staying with Patrick starting this afternoon."

She hesitated. "Temporarily? Or longer?"

"Only for a day or two," I assured her. "Since the threats were about me as well as Clem, the police want me to be safe, and away from my house."

"We'll be neighbors then, for a few days."

"We will," I agreed.

"Maybe you and Patrick could come over for dinner," she said.

"Thanks for asking, but for the moment I'm supposed to stay put. Police orders," I explained. "But after the police are sure they know what happened to Clem, and that I'm safe, Patrick and I would love to stop in."

"You do exactly what the police tell you to, dear. I don't want to hear about any more deaths."

I understood. She wasn't just talking about Clem. There'd been a death in Anna's family not long ago.

"I will, Anna. I promise," I told her. "I'm being good." At least for now.

Of course, I hadn't asked Ethan whether I could go to Portland to talk to Clem's coworkers at Channel 7. And I was talking to Ruth, who was checking family history information for me. Several of the threatening messages had said not to talk to anyone about the embroidery, or ask questions.

I went downstairs to Sarah's store. "Ruth thinks she found the Holgate-Providence connection," I explained. "Could I see the genealogical sampler you bought?"

"I hung it on the wall," said Sarah, pointing.

"Ruth's right," I said, looking at the names. "The two names at the top of the sampler are Joshua and Verity—the two names she mentioned. It doesn't say Verity was a Holgate before she married Joshua, but that's what Ruth found. She said they were married in 1788. Verity would have been fifteen and Joshua sixteen then."

"Young," said Sarah, coming over to look.

"From what Ruth saw, the Holgates were wealthy. Maybe Verity's father was helping them out—buying them land or having Joshua work in a Holgate business."

"What was their business?" Sarah asked.

"I don't know. I don't know what the Goulds did, either," I admitted. "Maybe Ruth can find out. Or someone at the Maine Historical Society would know. Ruth does think both families were from England."

"Where the Foundling Hospital was," Sarah pointed out.

"Exactly," I agreed. "But what relation was that foundling to either family? And how can we find out?"

"Maybe we need to start with this end of the search first," Sarah suggested. "What Ruth's discovering is fascinating. I'll write up what she finds out about the Providences and attach that to the back of the samplers. But no one in 1788 killed Clem or threatened you. Someone in a current generation did that."

My next thought was interrupted by an ear-shattering explosion, followed immediately by a series of a dozen smaller booms, one right after the other. It didn't sound like gunshots; it sounded as though all of Haven Harbor was exploding. Sarah's building shook. Her display of teacups rattled in their saucers, and a large gold-framed mirror fell off the back wall, breaking the frame and shattering the mirror. Seven years bad luck. As we looked at each other, fearing what would be next, a long crack spread diagonally across one of Sarah's store-front windows, dividing it into a spider web of lines and spaces.

"What?" Sarah said. "Is the town blowing up?"

We both headed for the front door of her shop.

"Stay inside," she said, waving me back from the door. "Between the sea smoke and real smoke I can't see what's happening anyway. No one's

197

supposed to know you're here. Let me go and check. And stay away from the window. Someone could see you from the street."

Real smoke? As soon as Sarah said that, I could smell it. Smoke mixed with gasoline. Not a good combination.

I stepped back, clenching my fists in frustration. I wanted to run out into the snowy street. I wanted to know what had happened.

Despite Sarah's admonition, I moved back a little, but peeked through the cracked front window, hoping I'd see something to explain what was happening. As I watched, as though in slow motion, the glass in the wide window wavered, split, and collapsed. Splinters of glass covered everything in Sarah's display and the floor near it. Sharp fragments of glass covered my sweater and jeans. Without thinking, I started to brush them off, and splinters cut into my skin.

Trying to keep the blood on my fingers from dripping onto the floor or the antiques or my clothes, I ran back to Sarah's counter and reached for the box of cloths she used to wrap fragile ornaments.

Outside in the street the commotion continued. The explosions had stopped, but the smoke was thicker, darker now. Was it from a fire? Sea smoke? A mixture of both? I couldn't tell.

Sirens from the Haven Harbor fire engine and

ambulance added to the cacophony. Both vehicles passed Sarah's store and headed down the smoky street toward the harbor. People somewhere were shouting. Several men ran by Sarah's open shop door.

I sopped up my blood and brushed the fragments off my clothes. I could feel pieces of glass in my fingers.

Snow started blowing through the broken window into the shop. Melted snow would destroy many of Sarah's antiques already covered with glass shards.

Despite Sarah's warning that I should stay away from the window, I had to do something. I covered my hands as best I could so no blood would get on the antique dolls and toys in Sarah's display and stretched my arm through the broken window glass. I managed to retrieve two nineteenth-century wax dolls and started to lift out a Victorian wicker doll's carriage.

Before I'd gotten the carriage out of the window Sarah was back. She looked in horror at her store, and at me, dripping blood.

She helped me with the carriage and then said, "Sit down, Angie."

I moved back from the window, but I didn't sit. "What happened?"

"Where did you park your car?" she asked, so calmly that I knew something was seriously wrong.

"About a block from here. Two blocks from the Harbor Haunts."

"It's hard to see in the smoke and confusion. I may be wrong. But I think it's your car that's on fire."

CHAPTER 20

"Mrs. E. Folwell, intending to resume her former school of embroidery, takes this method of informing her friends and the public in general she will commence as soon as she has a certain number of Young Ladies engaged. Mr. Folwell, being a Master of Drawing, the Ladies under her tuition will have a double advantage in shading, which is all the merit of the picture."

—Advertisement in *Poulson's American Daily Advertiser,* a Philadelphia newspaper. Ann Elizabeth Folwell (1770–1824) ran a well-known embroidery school for girls in Pennsylvania.

"My car?" I asked. "But . . ." Then it hit me. "Gram and Tom were going to move my car about now. Were they in the street? Were they all right?" I ran toward the shop door.

Sarah was faster than I was. She tried to block me. "No! You can't go out. What if whoever is looking for you is there? Maybe he started the fire to get your attention. It's just a car."

"But it's *my* car," I said, in frustration. My little

red Honda. I hesitated a fraction of a second. Then I pushed her aside. "I don't care about the car. Gram or Tom may be there; they may be hurt. Besides, no one can see anything in all this smoke."

As I left Sarah's shop a Haven Harbor Hospital ambulance, siren blaring, passed me, heading for the hospital. Someone had been hurt.

The fire engine was stopped close to where I'd parked my car less than twenty-four hours before. Yesterday, when Clem was still alive, and I was looking forward to lunch with a friend.

Sarah followed me, both of us slipping and sliding on the ice under the snow on the street. Neither of us had stopped to put on boots.

Several dozen people had gathered on the sidewalk. Smoke filled the air. I didn't see any flames. Had the fire already been put out? Flames in this narrow street could set buildings on fire. No wonder the fire department had responded so quickly.

I pushed my way through other people who'd gathered to see what was happening. Where was Gram? Where was Tom? I didn't see their car. Maybe they hadn't gotten here yet. Would my car have burst into flames by itself? Without help?

No way.

Sarah'd been right. The smoke was from my car, and it merged with the sea smoke, obscuring everything. When it parted I could see my little

Honda being hosed down. Water from the fire engine's hoses was already turning to ice, covering the car and freezing it to the street. Smoke from the car's engine was mingling with the water the car was being doused with.

I got as close as I could.

Were Gram and Tom here, too?

I hadn't seen this many people in downtown Haven Harbor since the Christmas Cheer Festival.

Today no one in the street was celebrating.

"Hey, Angie! Get back! Get away!" Pete Lambert's voice was close to my ear. He grabbed my arm and pulled me through the crowd into an alleyway between two stores. "What are you doing out here? You should be with Sarah, in hiding." He glanced at my hands, still covered in a bloody cloth. "Are you hurt?"

"That's my car," I said, pointing. "Gram and Tom were going to move it for me. I was trying to find them." My fingers had almost stopped bleeding. They seemed unimportant. "I'm fine, Pete," I said. "Just a few glass cuts. A window in Sarah's store shattered."

Pete put his hand on my shoulder. "I wasn't here when the fire started, but Gus Gleason at The Book Nook was rearranging his front window and saw it all." Pete hesitated. "Gus saw Reverend Tom opening the door of your Honda right before the explosion. He said it was like fireworks—colors and all."

Tears now covered my cheeks. "He and Gram have only been married about six months."

Sarah had caught up with us. She put her arm around me, but I felt like stone.

"I don't know how badly hurt the reverend was. The fire department ambulance took him to the hospital," said Pete.

"Where's Gram?"

"Maybe with him? Either in the ambulance or following it in her own car."

I hadn't seen her car in the street. That must be what had happened. "I need to get to the hospital," I said. "Now."

Pete nodded. "I'd take you, but I have to stick around and make sure nothing else happens here." He looked at Sarah.

"I'll drive her," she said. "Angie, come back to the store with me and get your coat on. You're freezing out here."

"I need to get to the hospital," I said again. All I could think was that Tom was dead, or seriously hurt. Gram loved him so much. She deserved to be happy. And it was my fault. I shouldn't have asked them to move my car. "And your storefront window is broken. You need to cover it, or the snow will ruin everything."

Sarah hesitated.

"I'll get someone to cover your window, Sarah," said Pete. "Don't worry. You take care of Angie."

"Thank you, Pete," she said gratefully, and started to move away when Pete touched her arm. "Are you okay with this. Sarah? We don't know who—or what—caused the explosion or fire. Or if whoever set it up is still around. He or she could be watching Angie. If so, he'd expect her to head for the hospital to check on Reverend Tom."

"The hospital isn't far," Sarah assured Pete. "I'll take Angie to the emergency room door and then come back and help fix the window."

"I'll alert the security guys at the hospital that you'll be coming," said Pete, pulling out his phone. "Get going. I need to get back to the street." He headed back to the crowds on the sidewalk, leaving us in an alleyway that ended in a small tenants' parking lot in back of the stores.

"Let's go the back way," Sarah said, heading me in that direction. "No one in the street will see us."

"You were outside before I was. Did you see anyone who might have done this?" I asked her. "Anyone you didn't know?"

"I wasn't looking at the people on the street," said Sarah. "I was trying to see what had exploded. At first no one seemed to know what had happened. But then it became clear."

"Gus Gleason saw Tom open the car door. He might have noticed someone tampering with my car before that."

"I'm sure Pete will talk with Gus," Sarah assured me.

My teeth were chattering, and my feet were numb. My mind hadn't paid attention to the cold, but my body had.

Sarah kept me walking toward the back door of her store.

"You go upstairs, take off your shoes, and put on your boots. I'll pull anything that might be hurt by the snow out of the window and then close the store and meet you in a couple of minutes." She opened the back door to her shop.

Two people were inside.

I ignored them and headed up the inside stairs to get my bag and boots and coat. Sarah could deal with unexpected customers.

Who would drop into an antiques store when all the excitement in Haven Harbor was happening a block away?

My mind pictured Reverend Tom, bleeding. Or burned. Patrick had been burned last spring. How was Gram coping?

Why hadn't Sarah gotten rid of those customers by now? I needed to get to the hospital.

CHAPTER 21

"Jesus Permit Thy Gracious Name to stand
As the first efforts of an infant's hand
And while her fingers o'er this canvas
  Move
Engage her tender heart to seek thy love
With thy dear children let her share a Part
And write thy name thyself upon her
  heart."

—Twenty-inch square sampler, including alphabets of upper and lowercase letters, sewn on linen in silk thread. A house, two trees, an urn of flowers, and a fence are below the words. Sampler stitched (as a child) by American poet Emily Dickinson (1830–1886) and now in the Dickinson Room at Harvard University. Although Emily chose an elaborate pattern for her sampler, her stitching is not as even and measured as that on many other girls' samplers, and she did not sign or date it.

When I'd left home yesterday morning I hadn't intended to be away for the night, so I didn't have much with me. A padded envelope, a pair of boots and a coat, my canvas bag, and my Glock.

I quickly texted Patrick not to come for me until he heard from me again. I didn't take the time to explain why.

Sarah was still talking to those customers.

Three minutes later I couldn't stand waiting any longer. I grabbed Sarah's coat (she needed one, too) and headed downstairs. Those customers had better be spending thousands of dollars for her not to have come upstairs.

I was halfway down to the store when I heard the words "samplers" and "auction." I stopped abruptly. What was going on in Sarah's shop?

"These are the ones. Interesting. Do you have any other samplers?" A woman's voice.

"No, not right now," Sarah answered. "But I do try to keep several in stock. If these don't interest you, would you like to register on my customer list? I could call you if I find any others."

"No; that's all right. These were the samplers sold at the auction in Augusta a few days ago, right?"

"Three of them, yes," said Sarah. Her voice got a little louder. Maybe she wanted me to hear what was happening. "How did you happen to know that?"

"Oh, I know the auctioneer. He mentioned them to me. But I wasn't able to get to the auction that day."

"She had a previous appointment," put in a male voice.

That didn't make sense. Even I knew you could leave a bid at an auction if you couldn't get there in person.

"But how did you know I'd bought them?" Sarah asked.

Silence. Then "We saw on Channel 7 the other night that someone from Haven Harbor had bought them. We were driving by and saw your sign. We thought it must be you, since there didn't seem to be any other antique shops in town."

"I didn't buy the embroidery mentioned on the news. I didn't buy every embroidery at the auction. The Saco Museum bought the best one . . . a beautiful sampler. They'll probably add it to their collection, and you can see it there." Sarah sounded a little dismissive. I hoped she was getting rid of the couple. It didn't sound as though they were going to buy anything.

"But what about the embroidery on the news? A coat of arms, the newscaster said." That was the male voice.

"It sounded unusual," added the woman.

"I didn't buy it. It was in poor condition," said Sarah. "And, I'm sorry, but I need to finish covering my antiques near the broken window, and then I have an appointment. I do love needlework of all kinds. And did you see my antique needleworking tools on the table in the corner?"

"We're just interested in the embroideries themselves," said the man.

"Are you sure you don't want to leave your names in case I get any other pieces in?" Sarah asked.

"No; no, thank you," said the man. "But if you should hear anything about that coat of arms"—I heard him ripping a piece of paper—"here's my e-mail address. We'd love to see it."

"Thank you," said Sarah.

I heard the front door of the shop close.

"Sarah!" I said, from the stairs. "What was that all about?"

"I don't know exactly, but I didn't like it," she said. "Something was weird about those two."

My last steps took me behind her counter.

Sarah was trying to move the rest of her antiques out of the window without cutting herself. She shook an iron fire engine to remove the glass splinters. After the second toy she gave up and shook her head. "I hope whoever Pete finds to fix that window gets here quickly. The children's books I had in the window are already ruined. I'm not going to try to bring them inside now. Snow will ruin so many of these things."

"Can I help you move anything else?" I asked. I wanted us to leave, but Sarah's store was important, too.

"No! You stay away from the front of the store. Someone in the street could see you through the window. Hand me my coat, and we'll get you to the hospital," Sarah said. "I'll drop you off and then come back and see what I can do here."

I followed her out the back door to where her van was parked. It only took a few minutes for the two of us to brush off the snow that had fallen since yesterday. The street had been plowed, but her van was heavy enough to bump over the piles of snow left at the entrance to the small back parking lot.

"Who do you think those people were?" I asked once we were out in the street heading for the hospital. "The couple in your store."

"I don't know. The e-mail address he gave me was a generic Gmail account; no name, just the word *sampler* and a number."

"I didn't see them, but they sounded strange," I said. "Right now I'm nervous when someone seems to know about old needlework. Especially if they know about the coat of arms." I was talking to Sarah, but my mind was on Tom, and Gram. Were they both at the hospital? How was Tom?

"I agree. It was strange they happened to show up—driving by, he said—right after the fire in your car. And a day after Clem was killed."

"Thanks for not giving out my name, or saying you knew anything about the coat of arms," I said. "What did they look like?"

"The woman was late middle-aged. Short and post-menopausally plump. Brown hair beginning to gray, but sculpted well. No makeup; wore slacks and a heavy ski sweater."

"More Talbots than L.L. Bean then?"

"Exactly. Wouldn't stand out in a crowd around here, but I had the impression she could buy any sampler she wanted. The man with her was younger—maybe early thirties? I figured he was her assistant. Or even her son. Tall, slim—almost skinny. Pale face and hair. Big ears."

"Not ringing any bells with me."

"Sorry. Neither of them had any distinguishing characteristics. Not much to remember. But if Pete comes to help with the broken window I'm going to tell him about them. They were looking for you, not me. They were interested in the coat of arms. And they didn't say anything that made me think they were really interested in samplers or embroideries. Neither of them looked closely at anything I had, or asked any questions about them. Serious collectors of needlework do." Sarah turned her van into the circular driveway that led to Haven Harbor Hospital's emergency room entrance. "If you need a ride back, or to Patrick's house, call me. And let me know how Reverend Tom and Charlotte are."

"I will," I said, nodding as I opened the van door.

"I wish I could stay, but I could lose hundreds—thousands—of dollars' worth of merchandise unless that window gets covered and everything dried off. Not to mention that right now someone could walk into the store through the window and take anything there."

"No problem," I said, waving my hand to dismiss her concern. "I'll let you know how they are. And thank you for last night. And for keeping cool and not telling that couple anything about the coat of arms. They might be harmless, but today I don't trust anyone interested in antique embroidery."

Sarah smiled, grimly. "And you'd be absolutely right."

I headed for the emergency room door.

What would I find inside? My fingers were crossed inside my mittens.

CHAPTER 22

"As one contemplates the millions of stitches worked by these young girls, one wonders what their thoughts were as they sewed them. Children are conventional and conservative beings, and so perhaps the universality of the employment kept most from boredom. But there must always have been a residuum of the discouraged and of the rebels 'who hated every stitch,' and so made their samplers badly or left them unfinished if they could possibly shirk their task."

—From *American Samplers* by Ethel Stanwood Bolton and Eva Johnston Coe. The Massachusetts Society of the Colonial Dames of America, 1921.

Haven Harbor Hospital wasn't a large medical center. If you needed specialists you went to Portland, or even to Boston, as Patrick had last spring.

Boston had a burn unit. Would Tom need intensive care?

In Phoenix I'd once taken a neighbor to an emergency room and, despite the blood dripping (slowly, but steadily) from her forehead after a fall, we were told she was number fourteen to see a doctor. Here the chairs in the emergency room waiting area were rarely filled.

Serious bleeding, strokes, broken bones, and heart attacks received immediate care—even though that care might mean pulling an extra doctor or nurse in from a nearby office. A sign inside the entrance read, "Maternity patients seen at any point in pregnancy." Good to know. But not relevant today.

Usually patients and their families walked through the outside doors and straight to the emergency admissions desk.

This afternoon a large woman in a uniform was standing inside the doors.

"Miss Curtis?" she asked, blocking my way.

"That's right," I said, prepared to push past her.

"Welcome to Haven Harbor Hospital. I'm with hospital security. Sergeant Lambert asked that we watch this entrance. He said someone might be following you. Did you notice anyone on your way here?"

"I didn't look, actually," I said. I'd been so focused on what injuries I might find here at the hospital, and on what the pseudo-customers at Sarah's store were interested in, that I hadn't looked around. I glanced over my shoulder, out the plate-glass doors. "I don't think so."

Pete had said he was going to call security here. I'd forgotten, but he hadn't.

"If you have any problems while you're here at the hospital, tell whomever you're with to call Shaundra in security," she said protectively. "I'll know what to do."

I looked at her, and thought of the gun in my bag. Shaundra was big. And muscular. I was glad she was on my side.

"Thank you, Shaundra."

"I was an MP in the Army. I'll know what to do," she continued. "No one should be hassling you when you're at a hospital."

"I agree. Thank you." I moved past her and on to the registration desk. "Is Reverend Tom McCully a patient here? Or his wife, Charlotte?"

The young man behind the window didn't hesitate. "Reverend Tom is with Doctor Mercer now. Are you a relative?"

"I'm his granddaughter," I said, not hesitating to fudge. "Step-granddaughter" didn't sound as connected.

"I'll buzz you in," the young man said, pressing a button. "Reverend Tom's in room eight."

I'd been in this emergency room before—too many times. I knew room eight wasn't for the most critically ill patients; they were in rooms ten and higher.

I waved to Shaundra, went through the double

doors, and walked down the corridor of small patient rooms.

A toddler in room three was crying in her mother's lap.

An elderly man was lying quietly on the bed in room five, an IV in his arm.

Rooms six and seven were empty.

It was a quiet day in the emergency room.

I paused at the door to room eight.

"Angie! I'm so glad to see you!" Gram jumped up from the chair next to Tom's bed. "Are you all right?"

"Me? I'm fine." If you didn't count being on someone's hit list. "What about Tom?"

"I'm all right," he said. "Just a few scratches." His words were mumbled.

"Pain meds," Gram said softly. Then she added, in her normal voice, "And a shattered leg and a couple of broken ribs, they think. The doctors have ordered another set of X-rays and a CT scan. Do you know what happened? Does anyone? I dropped him off by your car and started to drive home, and there was an awful explosion. It all happened so fast."

"I don't know any details about what happened. Broken bones . . ." I winced. "But at least he's not burned." I'd been remembering the burns Patrick had endured last spring, and how they were still changing his life. And always would.

"Whatever caused that explosion blew him

218

right onto the curb, thank goodness. That's why he isn't burned," explained Gram, shaking her head.

"Threw me out of the way," Tom managed to say.

"He hit the curb, which is how his ribs were broken," Gram explained. "And landed on his leg. After the fire started he was hit by pieces of shattering glass."

"He'll be all right?" I asked. Those injuries weren't minor. And how badly was his leg broken? It was covered by a sheet.

"I hope so. It could have been a lot worse," said Gram. "I'll feel better after we get the results of the scan. You're not a young man anymore," she scolded Tom.

Gram was sixty-five. Not a young woman anymore. Although I'd never tell her that.

"Thirteen years younger than you are, my love," he answered. "I'm grateful we'd decided it would be me who'd drive Angie's car home, and not you." Those words were clear.

"I'm so sorry this all happened," I said. "If it wasn't for me, we wouldn't be standing in this room wondering how badly Tom's been injured."

"Life in Haven Harbor hasn't been boring since you came home," Gram agreed. "Baked-bean suppers were never this exciting. But everything will be all right. Except . . . I think you're going to have to buy another car."

"I suspect so," I agreed, looking from one of them to the other. Gram was holding Tom's hand, and, despite the pain he was in, they seemed to be doing fine. Would I ever have a relationship like theirs? "Pete Lambert was on the street. He'll be investigating. Although it might fit into what Ethan Trask is doing about Clem's murder."

"You mean the two events could be related?" said Gram.

"It was my car, and I've received death threats." Saying that out loud made this crazy situation sound almost logical.

"I'm glad it wasn't you opening that car door, Angie," Tom's face showed pain, but he kept talking. "I'm a tough old bird. If I add a scar or two, it'll just make me more distinguished. If anything had happened to you, I don't think I'd ever have forgiven myself."

Gram had married the right man. I wished she'd found him years ago.

A nurse arrived to wheel Tom, bed and all, to X-ray. He waved as he left.

"Gram, is he really going to be all right?"

"I hope so, Angel. All signs look positive so far. We've done a little praying, and I think the good Lord's come through for us. An orthopedic surgeon's going to have to fix his shattered leg, but, as long as they don't find bleeding in his chest, he'll be frustrated and not able to hike for a while, but he'll be all right."

I hugged her, tight.

"I hope so. I'd like to stay here with you both, but I need to let Patrick know what's happening and where to pick me up. Sarah dropped me off here. Her shop window was broken in the blast. She'll want to know how you both are."

Plus, despite Shaundra's presence outside the emergency room, I didn't think it was smart for me to stay near Gram and Tom. If anyone was looking for me—and it was hard to believe that explosion hadn't been meant for me—they'd look for me where my grandmother and Tom were. Gram and Tom would be safer if I were somewhere else. Anywhere else.

"You call whoever you need to, Angel, and get to Patrick's, or wherever the police think you'll be safe. Tom and I'll be fine here. I'll let you know the official diagnosis once we hear it. Don't you worry about us. I don't know what that crazy person is thinking, but you don't want to be anywhere near where he is."

"You're right. We need to end this as soon as possible. We need to know who killed Clem, and who hurt Tom."

Gram held my hand, tight. "Just don't let it be you next time, Angel. Keep safe."

"I'll do my best, Gram," I assured her. I was assuring myself, too.

CHAPTER 23

"To move me For to Watch and Pray
To Strive to be Sincere
To take My Cross Up Day By Day
And Serve the Lord in Fear."

—Stitched, with alphabets and numbers,
by Mary Chamberlin, age ten, in
Rhode Island, sometime during
the mid-nineteenth century.

I asked Shaundra to keep an eye on anyone looking for me or Gram or Tom.

She waved when Patrick picked me up outside the emergency room twenty minutes later. Trixi was meowing pitifully in her carrier in the backseat of his BMW.

"I would have been here earlier," he said, "but Trixi was not enthused about getting into her carrier." He pushed up the sleeve of his jacket to show me a nasty scratch still oozing blood.

I decided not to show him my matching fingers. At least not until we were out of the car and in a place with good light and tweezers. I hoped I didn't still have shards of glass in my hands.

"So—talk. What were you doing at the hospital?" He headed his car for home. His home.

"I suspect you hadn't just stopped in to say hello to the doctors." Patrick's lips were tight. He was upset. "What happened to you? Are you all right?"

"I'm fine. Tom's the one who's hurt," I explained quickly. "I asked Gram and Tom to move my car from downtown to my barn. When Tom opened the car door, something exploded. Tom shattered his leg and broke some ribs. Gram's with him. He's having more tests to make sure there's no internal bleeding, and, assuming there isn't, he'll have surgery to set the bones in his leg."

Patrick glanced over at me, as though to make sure I was really all right. "Angie, that could have been you in that hospital. You could have been killed!"

"I know. We're lucky Tom wasn't hurt more."

"A shattered leg isn't good," Patrick said. "But, selfishly, I'm glad you're all right. I should hire bodyguards to keep an eye on you, and on the house." He was serious.

"I don't think that's necessary," I said. "Did you bring my extra bullets?"

"I got everything on your list. I thought I'd be collecting Trixi, and some of your makeup or underwear, and instead I was rummaging in the back of drawers for bullets." He wasn't smiling. "I assume your car's totaled?"

"It burned. The fire department doused the

flames, but the foam they used and then the water from the hoses all froze. My car is now black instead of red, and looks like a giant ice cube." I tried to make a joke of it, but the reality was sinking in.

Clem was dead. Tom needed serious surgery on his leg. I'd have to buy a new car.

And whoever was causing all this was still out in the world somewhere. Most likely, somewhere nearby. Or at least he or she had been there recently. How long would it take for him to figure out where I was? Pete was right; staying at my home wasn't smart. But staying with Patrick would, for anyone who knew me, be an obvious alternative.

I didn't want anyone else hurt. I might not have a car, but I had a telephone. I could talk with people.

Patrick was looking grim. I suspected he wouldn't loan me his car. But maybe I could convince him to drive me to Portland tomorrow so I could talk to Clem's colleagues. Pete and Ethan were covering what was happening in Haven Harbor, but I couldn't believe this problem had started in my hometown. Somehow it had started at an auction house in Augusta.

I should call that gallery assistant again.

Ideas swirled through my mind, like the sea smoke that had invaded the town earlier.

"What are you thinking about?" asked Patrick as we neared his home. "You look serious."

"Just tired," I assured him.

"We use the same cat food, so I didn't bring yours. I have plenty. But I did bring Trixi's food and water dishes." He glanced at me. "I think I found the right hand lotion and toothpaste. And I'll admit your clothes weren't as interesting to go through as I'd hoped. A flannel nightgown? Really, Angie?"

"I have a whole drawer of them."

"As I now know," said Patrick.

"It's winter in Maine!" I said.

"Which I am also well aware of," he agreed. "But, still . . ."

"Trixi thinks my nightgowns are fine. Cozy and warm. If I leave one out on my bed, she sleeps on it."

Patrick shook his head, his eyes sparkling. "I suspect no additional comments from me would be appropriate just now. I'm happy for you and Trixi."

I almost laughed. It felt good. I hadn't laughed in a while.

"I stopped at the grocery, too. If we need to hunker down and hide you for a week, we won't starve."

"Thank you," I said, although I hoped I wouldn't be imposing on him for a week.

"Only thing I'm concerned about is whether Bette and Trixi will recognize each other, as sisters, and get along."

"We've always joked we should get them together. You're right. It'll be interesting."

"Since Bette is used to my house and Trixi isn't, why don't I put Bette in my bedroom and close the door while we get the food and your stuff out of the car. That way our cats don't need to confront each other immediately, and Trixi can explore a little."

"Good plan," I agreed.

The gates to Aurora's driveway were closed. Usually Patrick left them open when his mother was out of town. He stopped, pushed a button on his keychain, and they opened for us. "A precaution," he said, glancing at me. "All my windows and doors are locked, and the back entrance to the estate is closed."

As the gates closed in back of us, I felt as though I were entering a prison.

But at least I had a handsome guard.

CHAPTER 24

"Sacred to the Memory of the Illustrious Washington."

—Samuel Folwell (1764–1813), who worked at the school run by his wife, Ann Elizabeth Folwell (1770–1824), in Philadelphia, designed this needlework memorial stitched in 1800. It depicts a Revolutionary War soldier with an inverted musket, next to Liberty, who is mourning at a grave under a willow tree.

We carted everything into the house: Trixi in her carrier, groceries, and the garbage bag Patrick had used for what I'd needed from my house. I'd forgotten to tell him my duffel bag was in the closet in the room that had been Mama's. In my mind it would always be her room. But I didn't think she'd have minded my using her empty closet for storage.

Patrick captured his Bette, who'd immediately come to check out her guest, and locked her in his bedroom while I started putting away the groceries he'd bought.

He'd bought enough food for a week, maybe two. I shook my head at the several bottles of champagne and the case of wine. Clearly he had plans that didn't include crime solving.

And I could probably be talked into eating part of the thick steak he'd bought that I assumed would go with the baking potatoes. Three-dozen eggs and two pounds of bacon would be more than enough for two people. He'd also bought a lot of cheeses and crackers and Italian sausage and bread, and enough pasta, vegetables, and fruit for several dinner parties.

I filled one of his salad bowls with oranges. Had I eaten lunch? I didn't think so.

"I put your stuff in the bedroom," Patrick said as he joined me in the kitchen.

I'd just peeled the orange and put two slices in my mouth. The citric acid stung the cuts on my hand.

"What happened to your hands?" he asked, looking at my fingers.

"The explosion broke the front window in Sarah's shop. I was trying to rescue some of her antiques from blowing snow, and the shards of glass cut my fingers."

He put his arms around me, and for a few moments I felt safe. Was that being anti-feminist? I hoped not. After all, I was the one in this relationship with a gun.

Trixi meowed loudly from inside her carrier.

"We should soak those hands of yours. But cats come first. Children are so demanding." Patrick ruffled my hair as we headed back to the living room. I opened the carrier. Trixi hesitated a moment, and then galloped (can a cat gallop?) out and raced across the room. After a frenetic few minutes she slowed down and started inspecting (and sniffing) every bit of furniture.

I filled her food dish with her favorite canned cat food, put fresh water in her water dish, and put them both in a corner of the living room, far from Bette's dishes in the kitchen. Trixi sniffed, nibbled, and then went back to exploring.

"We should show her the litter pan, right?" I asked.

"Good idea," said Patrick.

I carried her into the small hallway between Patrick's living room and studio where the litter pan was. Trixi looked unimpressed, other than sniffing a lot. She probably smelled Bette. Then she headed into the studio.

"Have you got any open paints or jars of water in there?" I asked Patrick. "I don't want her to mess up anything of yours."

"Everything's sealed, and, if not, it's behind doors in the cabinet," Patrick assured me. "I already have a cat, remember?"

Several of his oils, partially finished, stood on easels in his studio. Two were Maine scenes, like the one he'd given me for Christmas. Another was spirals of blue and green and white. "Supposed to be the inside of a wave," he explained. "A work in progress."

A larger abstract, this one in oranges, reds, and yellows, was on the inside wall of the studio. "I like that one," I said. "It's a little like the one hanging over your couch in the living room."

"I'm trying to decide whether it's finished or not," he said. "My hands are still giving me problems, and sometimes paint ends up in places I didn't intend. If I'm lucky, that works. If not, I start again."

"I'm glad you're painting," I said. Patrick's hands had been badly burned when the original carriage house at Aurora had burned early last summer. He hadn't started painting again until December.

"Me too," he said, squeezing my shoulder.

"How do you manage to paint, with Bette here?" I asked as Trixi sniffed her way around the studio. She liked the floor-to-ceiling windows that gave the room the feeling of being outside, even if the bottom of the windows was now blocked by snowdrifts.

"If I'm going to have open paint that she could get in trouble with, I close the studio door for a while," he said. "She's pretty good about it all; seems to know paint isn't food, and that water used to soak paint brushes doesn't taste good."

"We'll have to watch Trixi, to make sure she understands, too."

Trixi went back to the living room and settled in to have some lunch. That reminded me I still hadn't eaten.

"Mind if I make a sandwich? Peanut butter would be fine," I said. (Patrick's kitchen supplies included a two-pound jar of peanut butter. It would have lasted me months.) "With the explosion and Tom's being hurt and all, I haven't had much to eat today."

"No wonder you were eating an orange in the kitchen! Tell you what. I'll heat water for you to soak your hands in, and you check with your grandmother about Tom. I'll make you a sandwich. You sit and relax. Your job is to keep an eye on Trixi."

I curled up on Patrick's couch and watched as Trixi followed him into the kitchen. I couldn't see her when she was in there, but Patrick could. A few minutes later he brought me a bowl of hot water on a pile of towels and put everything on the glass-topped coffee table in front of me.

"Hands in," he instructed. "After you're sure those cuts are clean, we'll see if you need bandages. Why don't you call your grandmother on the speaker while you're soaking?"

I obeyed instructions.

"Angel? I've been thinking about you. How are you, and where are you?"

"Trixi and I came straight to Patrick's. We're fine," I assured her. "What did Tom's CT scan show?"

"His leg is broken in several places, which isn't good, but the orthopedist assures us it will mend, with a little help from surgery and a cast. And time. Turns out two of his ribs are cracked, but not broken, so they should heal, too. The scan didn't show any internal injuries."

"Thank goodness."

"They're preparing him for surgery now. He's pretty much out of it with the pain meds they've given him. Just as well. He'll have to stay here a night or two. After the swelling goes down, they'll send him home with a cast and a walker."

"I assume he's not supposed to do much walking at first."

"I'm glad our bedroom and bath are on the first floor. I've already called a friend of his over to Brunswick who's a retired minister. He's agreed to take over the service Sunday."

"Does Tom know?"

"Not yet. But he'll need some time off. After this Sunday we'll see how he feels and what his doctors say."

"Gram, I'm so sorry you both have to go through this."

"Life is full of bumps. There are worse ones. Like those Clem's family is dealing with. Which reminds me that I should talk to them about her funeral. I'm not sure what they have in mind, or when. Tom usually takes care of church business. But his secretary knows the drill. She and I'll manage until he's feeling better."

"Gram, he's lucky to have you."

"And I'm lucky to have him. And you. But let's not get mushy about it all. Angel, I have to go now. They've come to take Tom to the operating room, and I'm going to walk along with him as far as I can."

"Call me when he's out of surgery."

"Will do."

Patrick came in, carrying a plate of peanut butter sandwiches, all neatly cut in triangles. "How're your hands doing?"

"They feel much better," I said. "Really." He handed me one of the towels he'd brought in earlier, and I dried them gingerly.

"Need bandages?" he asked.

"I don't think so. Nothing is bleeding right now, and the cuts are clean."

"Good," he said, sitting next to me, handing me the plate of sandwiches, and taking one for himself. "I haven't had lunch either, although I did make breakfast for Steve this morning."

I picked up one of the triangles and started eating.

"How was Steve?"

"Considering that the woman in his life had just been murdered, I'd say he was coping well."

"When did he get to Haven Harbor?"

"I didn't cross-examine the man, Angie. When he got to the Walkers' house they'd already heard about Clem. He stayed there until Ethan and Pete had questioned him. I called him right after I talked to you. He was relieved to have somewhere to go, to leave the Walkers to grieve, but not have to drive far."

"Did he say anything about breaking up with Clem?"

"Breaking up? No. Not at all." Patrick shook his head. "He said the dinner with the Walkers last night was supposed to be the unofficial 'meet the parents' night. He was nervous, and had dressed up. Buttoned shirt, slacks, sweater."

Patrick wore clothes like that all the time. It was fun to hear him noticing that not many men in Maine did, unless they were doctors or lawyers, and, even then, not always. Painters and sculptors? Most didn't even own suits.

"He'd thought last night might be the beginning of a future for him and Clem. Instead, it was the end."

"Did he say anything about Clem's having enemies? Problems at work?"

"Steve drank a stiff scotch, and then we shared a bottle of wine. I cooked steak and potatoes for dinner. I didn't cross-examine him. He and I both assumed Clem had been killed by whomever left those threatening messages. Do you know anything else?"

"No. I keep hoping that there might be a reason someone would kill Clem, other than the embroidery. If that were true, then I wouldn't be in danger."

"Angie." Patrick took the now-empty plate and put it on the table. I curled up with my head on his chest. "I know someone killing over an embroidery sounds crazy. But crazy people do kill sometimes. And a crazy person blew up your car today. I don't like to think about these things either, but someone out in that world is very troubled."

I nodded, and, cuddle over, sat up. "And that person was in Haven Harbor yesterday and today. He or she knew I was here, and somehow he or she knew Clem would be here, too. Did Steve know Clem and I were going to have lunch in town?"

"Sure."

"So he could have told someone else. Or her parents could have. Or someone she mentioned it to at Channel 7 might have told someone else," I said.

"Or it could be someone in town that you mentioned it to," Patrick added. "More people than you might have imagined could have heard about your going to the Harbor Haunts. Neither you nor Clem considered it a secret."

"Maybe we should have," I said, cuddling against Patrick again. "If we hadn't mentioned it to anyone, Clem could still be alive. And I'd still have a car."

We sat there for a while.

"One more question?" I said. "Did you ask

Sam Gould if anyone in his family had consigned anything to an auction?"

"I did," said Patrick. "I told him what you'd found. He knew nothing about any needlepoint, and said no one he knew in his family had auctioned anything off."

"Thanks for asking, anyway. There must be a lot of Goulds in Maine."

"Probably are."

I couldn't just hide out at Patrick's and pretend nothing had happened.

Or maybe I could, for right now.

CHAPTER 25

"Next unto God dear Parents I Addrefs
My self to You in Humble Thankfulnefs
For all Your Care and Charge on me
    Bestowed
The means of Learning unto me Allow'd
Go on I Pray and Let me still Pursue
Those golden Arts the Vulgar never
    knew."

—Cross-stitched sampler with alphabet,
numbers, and triangular floral designs
in each corner, worked in 1768 by
seventeen-year-old Eliza Dearn
in Norfolk, England. (Now in
Strangers' Hall museum in Norfolk.)

Sarah called a few minutes later. "Angie? How are you? And Tom and Charlotte?"

"Sorry I didn't call earlier," I apologized. "I'm fine. Trixi and I are at Patrick's, and all's quiet here. Last I heard Tom was having surgery for a broken leg. He also has broken ribs, but nothing anyone seems worried about. Just a pain for a while. Gram's coping terrifically, as always. What about you? And your antiques?"

"Pete was incredible. By the time I got back

from dropping you off he'd found someone to put a plastic sheet over the space, to keep the snow out. And about an hour later someone else he knew came and replaced the glass. All I have to do is sweep up and make sure no pieces of glass are on any of the merchandise."

"Pete's a good guy."

"He is," she agreed. "And he made those calls about my store when he was in the middle of clearing the street and calming people down. Your car's been towed, by the way. I'm not sure where, but he said they'd be looking at it to figure out what started the explosion that caused the fire. And, you won't believe . . ."

"I won't believe what?"

"I'm having dinner with Pete tonight at the Harbor Haunts. He said we might have gone somewhere fancier, but he has to stay close to town because of the investigations."

"That's great, Sarah!"

"He's separated from his wife, right?"

"And it sounds pretty permanent. She couldn't take being married to a cop and went home to Bangor in . . . November, I think it was. Several months ago. Pete told me she's already with another guy."

"Just checking. I don't have dinner with married men unless their wives are present."

"Nothing to fear. He's eligible. I hope you have a great time."

"I feel a little guilty about it. Clem dead, and you in hiding, and I have a dinner date."

"I'm cuddling up with Patrick. All safe and sound. You go ahead and have a fun evening. I'm so glad your store is all right."

"Me too. I panicked when everything happened at once. I did lose a few things—but not as many as I thought at first. Other than needing a little more cleaning, all is back in order. I'm going to take a shower and relax for the rest of the afternoon."

"And put on something fetching, of course."

" 'Fetching'? Maybe one auction was enough for you, Angie. I don't think anyone's used the word 'fetching' since the nineteenth century."

I smiled. "Thanks again for taking me in last night, Sarah. And one more question before you head for the shower. That couple who were in your store earlier today?"

"The ones asking about the embroideries? Strange people."

"That's what I was thinking. I was hiding on your staircase when they were there, so I heard them, but never saw them. The man gave you an e-mail address, right? Do you remember what it was?"

"I wasn't focusing on much besides my broken window and getting you to the hospital right then. But I did stick that address somewhere." I heard papers shuffling. "Here it is. No name. Sampler1757@gmail.com. Angie, I have to go.

Ruggles just got into the shop, and I don't want him to step on any little pieces of glass. I swept the store, but haven't vacuumed."

A few minutes later Patrick released Bette from his bedroom, and we were sitting in front of the fire in his fireplace, watching the two reunited sisters establish who was the boss of this house. So far they'd batted each other a little, Trixi had hidden under a chair for a few minutes (her tail revealing her whereabouts), and Bette had growled once. I'd never heard a cat growl before.

"Don't take it personally," Patrick said. "She growls at gulls and crows, too. And at me, if she wants some of my dinner and I say 'no.' "

"Trixi's not that aggressive," I said. "She peeps at birds on my feeders, or at me, when she thinks it's time for food. Which is anytime."

"They have their own personalities," Patrick agreed as Bette swatted at a catnip-filled felt mouse and then pounced on it. Trixi watched from behind the couch. "At least they're not killing each other. Given cat behavior, they'll both be sound asleep in fifteen minutes." He rearranged a log on the fire. "Your grandmother called. Everything all right with Tom?"

"He's in surgery. If all goes well he should be released tomorrow."

"And how's Sarah? Did I overhear you saying our Australian friend is going to dine with our valiant local defender of law and order?"

"So she said. I'm glad. They're both good people. I hope it works out. Pete was wonderful today. He got someone to replace her broken window much more quickly than she'd thought possible. She did tell me one thing that was strange when I talked with her earlier."

"About Pete?"

"No. About two people who came to her shop after the explosion and asked about the coat of arms embroidery."

"Interesting timing." Patrick frowned.

"Exactly. Of course, she didn't tell them I had the coat of arms. They said they collected samplers and knew about the auction, and they'd seen someone from Haven Harbor on television."

"That's plausible," he admitted.

"I guess so. I'm sensitive to coincidences right now. They didn't give Sarah their names, but they did give her an e-mail, in case she heard anything about the coat of arms embroidery. I asked her for it, in case I decide to contact them for any reason."

"So?"

"It was a strange address. Sampler1757@ gmail.com"

"What's strange about that? E-mail addresses often include numbers. And Sarah once said lots of people are interested in samplers."

"1757 was the year baby Charles was left at the London Foundling Hospital."

"It's a coincidence, Angie. But the world is full of weird things that don't mean anything. What more could it be?"

"I don't know. But I don't like it."

"You, my lady, need to relax. Forget all about needlepoint and embroideries and coats of arms. Forget that it's February outside. Here, it's June. And you're on vacation."

"What?" That stopped me. I might be at Patrick's carriage house, but—vacation? June? Last time I checked in with myself, I was hiding out from a murderer, and it was snowing outside.

"And while you're on vacation," Patrick continued, "you and your handsome escort decide to have a private picnic."

"A picnic?"

He went over to a pine chest in the corner of the room, pulled out a navy and green plaid blanket, and arranged it on the floor in front of the fireplace. Then he reached for my hand, to pull me up from the couch, and we sat on the blanket. "This is not February. There is no snow on the ground. We're sitting on a beach, with a fire of driftwood, looking out toward the ocean."

"There's a sailboat out there," I said, pointing at the flames.

"A small one, with a red sail. Very far out," conceded Patrick. "Other than that, we're alone."

Trixi leapt from her hiding place behind the couch and curled in my lap.

"Except for a few friendly animals," I agreed.

"For dinner, we'll cook hot dogs over the fire," Patrick said. "And toast rolls in front of it."

"And—let me guess—make s'mores for dessert," I put in.

"Absolutely correct, my dear." Patrick stood. In a few minutes he was back, with hot dogs, bamboo skewers, hot dog rolls, and the makings of s'mores.

I laughed in delight.

"Mustard for the lady?"

"Of course," I agreed, and he next appeared with a jar of Raye's Mustard. (Mustard from Maine. Finest kind of mustard.)

"And to drink, my dear . . ." This time Patrick reappeared with an ice bucket, a bottle of champagne, and two flutes.

It was the best picnic ever.

Before it was over both cats were curled together on the cushion of one upholstered chair, and Patrick and I were sticky with marshmallows and silly with champagne.

Outside, a "wintery mix" was covering the ground and buildings and trees with a lethal combination of sleet and ice. We didn't care.

And I wasn't thinking about murders, or exploding cars, or antique needlework.

Like Scarlett, I'd think about those things tomorrow.

CHAPTER 26

"Adore no other Gods but only me.
Worship no God by anything you see.
Revere Jehovah's name; Swear not in
   Vain.
Let Sabbath be a rest for beasts and men.
Honour thy Parents to prolong thy Days.
Thou shalt not kill nor Murd'ring Quarrels
   Raise.
Adultery shun, in Chastity Delight.
Thou salt not Steal nor take Another's
   Right.
In bearing Witness never tell a Lye.
Covet not what may others damnify."
"Finished October 5, 1776, by Elizabeth
   Houghton, Wells."

—Elizabeth was seven years old,
lived in Wells, England, and included
an alphabet, a bird, flowers, and
a geometric border on her sampler.

The next morning dawned, revealing a sparkling, ice-covered world.

"We're lucky. We don't have to go out today. We don't have to cope with the roads, or with other drivers. We can stay in and enjoy the beauty of the

247

world." Patrick put his arm around me and kissed the top of my head as we stood in his studio, looking out at the back field, glittering with ice.

Beyond the snow-covered field, far in the distance, was the blue of the ocean.

"I'd hoped to go to Portland today," I said. "To talk to some of Clem's coworkers. And stop at the Maine Historical Society again."

"I thought you were supposed to stay here. Undercover. Or—under covers, as I might prefer," Patrick said.

"I can't just sit here and wait for something to happen." I started to pace. "Too many questions need answers."

"I understand. I've seen your sleuth persona on other occasions. But since your car has, sadly, been murdered, and I have the only keys to mine, and the roads are awful, why not investigate from here? At least for today."

"How?" I asked.

He held up his hands in surrender. "I was thinking of that newfangled device, the telephone."

"The police have my computer," I complained. "Could I use yours?"

He grimaced. "Sorry. Mine's in for servicing. It had a nasty virus. Could Sarah or Ruth help?"

I turned to him and hugged him. "You're right, of course. I can call Ruth, and maybe the historical society." People had solved crimes without computers for generations. I could search on my phone, but it wasn't a high-end model, and searches were slow and hard to read.

But I had no choice. If I was going to solve Clem's murder I had to do it with a telephone and a little help from my friends.

And I wasn't alone. I had Patrick. He shook his head. "Why don't you figure out who you need to talk with? Make a list or something, while I put together bacon-and-onion omelets for breakfast?"

Trixi raced past me, in hot pursuit of Bette. They seemed to be coping well with each other.

"Omelets sound delicious," I agreed. "And coffee?"

"As many mugs full as you'd like," he agreed, tossing me a pad of paper and a pencil. "Here's paper so you can organize your sleuthing."

I curled up on one of the chairs in his living room and had started writing when my phone rang.

"Good morning, Pete. Any news?"

"Just checking in to make sure you're all right, and still at Patrick's."

"I am. I heard a rumor you had a dinner date last night."

I could hear the smile in his reply. "No secrets in Haven Harbor. But gentlemen don't tell."

"You're right," I agreed. I'd find out how the dinner had gone later, from Sarah. "Did anyone figure out what happened to my car? Was it a bomb?"

"Hard to believe, but it was a box of fireworks, hidden under a blanket on the passenger's seat."

"Fireworks!"

"They're legal in Maine now, and we've had some accidents with them, not surprisingly. But this is the first time I've heard of them setting a car on fire." He hesitated. "What looked like an embroidery needle was pinned to what was left of the blanket. Any chance you've been embroidering in your car?"

"No," I said, almost whispering. "Like the needle found in . . . Clem?"

"That's what the crime lab guys said," he answered grimly.

"Which definitely links the murder and the explosion."

"Yes."

I struggled to focus on the explosion. "So wouldn't whoever put the fireworks in my car have to have been close by when they blew up?"

"The ATF guys think the fireworks were set off by an electronic triggering unit under your car that was activated by a cell phone. Whoever did it could have been anywhere. Could have been in New Hampshire." Pete paused.

"But Tom said the explosions—the fireworks—went off when he opened the car door. Wouldn't that mean someone activated the fireworks when they saw him at the car? Otherwise, what would have been the chance they'd go off just when someone was getting in?"

"You're right, Angie. So the guy—or gal—wasn't in New Hampshire when the fireworks exploded."

"In fact, he or she must have been in Haven Harbor, and close to the car. With the sea smoke, no one could see far yesterday morning."

"True."

"No fingerprints on the car? Or cameras on the street?"

"No fingerprints. Your car was burned badly. And, come on, Angie. This is Haven Harbor. No cameras."

"Some stores have them."

"In summer months. Focused on merchandise and cash drawers. No cameras record what happens in the street."

"My car was in front of The Book Nook. Gus saw Tom opening the door and the car seeming to explode. Did Gus see anyone else opening the car and putting a box in it? Or a blanket? My only blanket in the car was in the trunk, along with my flares and jumper cables. Nothing was on the front seat when I parked it two days ago."

Two days ago. When Clem was still alive, Tom wasn't injured, and I was excited about a mysterious embroidery and paper from 1757. It seemed weeks ago.

"Gus says he didn't see anything. We asked

around, and no one else saw anything either. Of course, Clem was killed two days ago. The guy who set up your car could have done it late afternoon that day, or even at night. Darkness comes early this time of year."

"True enough," I agreed. "But to have the fireworks explode at exactly the time Tom was opening the door couldn't have been a coincidence."

"You're right. Whoever set off the fireworks was in Haven Harbor. And might still be here. You're going to spend a quiet day, inside, at Aurora, right, Angie?"

"At the carriage house here. Yes. But I assume I'm allowed to make phone calls?"

Pete sighed. "You're allowed to make phone calls. Just don't tell everyone in the State of Maine where you are."

"I promise, Pete."

"Hi, Pete!" Patrick said loudly, next to me. "Angie needs to eat breakfast now."

"Have a good breakfast," said Pete. "I'll check with you later if there are any developments."

"So," Patrick said as he headed me toward the kitchen, where our omelets were waiting. "Did he and Sarah have a nice evening?"

"I think so," I said. "He wouldn't say. I'll talk to Sarah later. Maybe she'll tell me more. First, I have breakfast to eat." I sniffed. "Love the smells of bacon and onion."

Patrick was a good cook.

"While you're making a list of people to call, you should make a condolence call to Clem's family, if you haven't already," he reminded me as we sat to savor our omelets.

He was right. I'd been focusing on what was happening in my life, and on who would have had a reason to kill Clem.

My first call of the morning was to her parents.

"Mrs. Walker, this is Angie Curtis. I called to tell you how sorry I am about what happened to Clem."

"You have some nerve, calling here to say that, when Clem's death was all your fault. It was that piece of embroidery that started all this. If Clem hadn't done that segment on the news, she'd still be alive."

"I'm so sorry, Mrs. Walker." Had she put the telephone down? "Mrs. Walker?"

"This is Mr. Walker. My wife is too upset to talk with you. We know you were Clem's friend, but we blame you for her death. Although, I'll admit we weren't surprised she ended this way. We did what we could for her from the beginning. But maybe it was fated."

"Fated?"

"Biologically. Nature stronger than nurture. That's what they say. We did everything we could to raise that girl right, but it was a struggle all the way. After she graduated college and went

253

to Portland, we hardly ever saw her. She didn't appreciate what we'd sacrificed for her over the years."

"She was your daughter, Mr. Walker. I'm sure she loved you. She was focused on her career. She told me she wanted to see you more often." Well, she'd told me something like that.

"When we decided to adopt, people said we'd never know what we'd be getting. If she'd stayed at home, like we wanted her to, none of this would have happened. But, no. She had to go and change herself, looking like someone who'd never lived here. She didn't care for anyone but herself, and we knew it. She should have stayed to home and helped her mother, like any decent girl would have done."

"I didn't know Clem was adopted, Mr. Walker. She always spoke of you and your wife with love, and respect."

"Respect? And then she tells us she's bringing home a man for us to meet, and the guy shows up, and he's a sculptor. Not even a serious sculptor. Someone who collects junk and welds it together! That's the man she chose to be in her life? No wonder she seemed focused on her career. She was probably supporting the guy."

This was getting more horrible by the moment. "Mr. Walker, I called to let you and your wife know how sorry I was. And I am."

"After what you've done, I hope you don't

come to her funeral. It would be too upsetting for Clem's friends and family to see the woman responsible for her death."

I dropped my phone. The call was over.

"Hard call?" asked Patrick, who'd been putting dishes in the dishwasher while I'd been on the phone. "Condolence calls always are."

"Her mother wouldn't talk to me, and her father yelled at me. They both said I was responsible for Clem's death. Her father told me not even to come to her funeral." I put my head down on the table. I wanted to forget everything her father had said to me. "He was angry at me, and he sounded angry at Clem, too. Said, if she'd stayed home like she should have, she'd still be alive."

"Whew. Wicked harsh. Did you know her parents felt like that?"

"She never talked about them. I assumed everything was all right. But her father sounded a little crazy. He said something about 'nature versus nurture.'" I looked over at Patrick. "I didn't know Clem was adopted, but that shouldn't have made any difference."

"Of course not. Some people need to find someone or something to blame when there's an unexplained tragedy."

"They found someone to blame all right. Me."

I'd felt guilty about Clem's death before, but that conversation with her parents was beyond anything I could have imagined.

"Clem's death wasn't your fault. You know that. You could have put something in motion . . . or not. Until Ethan and Pete figure it all out, we don't even know that. Life isn't easy. It isn't always fair."

"Sometimes it's easier to deal with horrible things if there's someone to blame." For years I'd blamed myself for my mother's disappearance. I'd thought she didn't want to be with me anymore. That I'd cramped her social life. For ten years I'd lived with that guilt, until I'd found out what really happened.

"You were curious about an old sampler—a coat of arms. That's all. It's crazy that Clem's dead, and you're in hiding. But neither of you did anything wrong."

"I'm going to call Gram," I said.

"Okay. But try to relax, Angie. You have all day to make telephone calls. I'm going to leave you to your calls and go into my studio. If you need me, call, or come and get me."

"Thanks."

Patrick was right. But my mind was spinning right now. Maybe Gram would help me slow it down. Besides, I should check in and see how Tom was doing.

"Good morning, Gram. Are you at home or at the hospital?"

"Good to hear your voice, Angie. I'm home. I had trouble sleeping last night, between what happened to Clem, and then to Tom, and worrying about you. And the roads are bad this morning. I talked to Tom. He didn't have a good night, either. Of course, his leg hurts, despite the pain medications. The doctor told him they'd like to keep him one more night, which he's not at all pleased about. I'm not going to visit him for a few hours. I'll let him sleep a little more, and make sure the roads are clear first. How are you? Still at Patrick's?"

"I am. Planning to stay in today; that's what Pete and Ethan want me to do, and I can talk to people on the phone."

"Sounds reasonable. Tom won't be expecting you to visit him. He knows you're keeping away until they find whoever it was who killed Clem."

"I called Clem's parents this morning."

"You didn't! Oh, I should have warned you about that, Angie. It was kind of you to call them, but . . . how did they react?"

"They're blaming me for Clem's murder—not claiming I killed her, but saying my embroidery put her in danger. Plus, Mr. Walker sounded angry at Clem. He said she shouldn't have left home and moved to Portland. She should have stayed home and helped her mother."

Gram sighed. "The Walkers and Clem have had their issues over the years. When Tom went over there the night Clem was killed, they were full of blame and anger, and, even then, just after they'd heard about her death, they were angry with you, too, Angel. I'm sorry I didn't tell you. You did the right thing by calling. But I'm sure they didn't respond the way they should have."

"Mr. Walker said Clem was adopted. I didn't know that."

"No reason you should have. I didn't know the family until you and Clem were in fourth grade together. I saw her mother at school meetings and such, and one day she blurted it all out. They'd lived in South Portland when they were first married, and about a year or two later they had a little boy. I don't remember what was wrong with him, but he wasn't well. Something genetic. He died before his first birthday."

"Sad."

"They took it hard, from what Jeannine said. They decided not to have other children because of the genetic problem. But a few years later Oliver felt Jeannine needed a child to keep her company while he was traveling for work. So they adopted Clem. Shortly after that they moved somewhere in the Boston area. I'm not sure what they expected, but Jeannine said Clem was never an easy baby or child. I suspect by then Jeannine had an idealized fantasy of a child that no real daughter could have lived up to."

"That must have been hard—for Clem and for her mother."

"It was," Gram confirmed. "By the time they'd moved back to Maine, here to Haven Harbor, things were a little better, Jeannine said. But she always referred to Clem as her 'adopted daughter.' Never just her daughter. That struck me as strange, and unfortunate."

"Clem wasn't happy in high school," I said. "But I didn't know she had problems at home."

"She had all the basics—a mother and a father, a house, a peaceful community, and so forth—but she wasn't the child they'd dreamed of."

"Their son who'd died. Or other biological children."

"Exactly. That wasn't fair to Clem, of course. And then Clem went off to U Maine and then moved to Portland. Steps many families would have been proud of. But Jeannine and Oliver somehow expected Clem to stay home and take care of her mother."

"That's practically Victorian!"

Gram laughed. "Not quite that long ago, but, yes. Clem and her parents had different expectations of parent-child relations. I hoped they were resolving them. I know her parents watched her on television, and I've heard her father tell people how well she was doing there. But her death must have brought back all the pains of their past."

"When Clem died they lost a second child."

"Exactly. That can't be easy, no matter what a family's relationships are."

"I wonder why Clem never mentioned she was adopted."

"Maybe she was embarrassed. Certainly her parents treated adoption as a problem, not the blessing it is for so many families."

"Thank you for telling me all that. It helps me understand why the Walkers were so upset this morning, and so angry with me."

"The past doesn't excuse their behavior, Angie. But I suspect they're mourning not only the death of their daughter, but the death of their dreams of having a family. Don't take it personally. You have your own situation to deal with today. Any word on progress from Pete or Ethan?"

"I talked with Pete earlier this morning. He said the explosions in my car were caused by remotely activated fireworks."

"Fireworks?"

"So he said. I don't know exactly how it worked, but it totaled my car and hurt Tom. I'm glad more people weren't hurt. The fire engine and ambulance got there quickly."

"I'll tell Tom. It was bothering him that he didn't know exactly what had happened."

"I hope we will know more than that, soon," I said. "I hope we'll know who rigged the fireworks to begin with."

CHAPTER 27

"To the education of her daughters Lady Bertram paid not the smallest attention. She had not time for such cares. She was a woman who spent her days in sitting, nicely dressed, on a sofa, doing some long piece of needlework, of little use and no beauty."

—From Chapter 2 of *Mansfield Park* by Jane Austen (1775–1817), published in 1814.

After talking to Gram I felt better about my call to Clem's family, but sad about what I'd learned about Clem's life. I'd been lucky. Mama might have had her problems, as most people in Haven Harbor knew, but I'd never doubted that she'd loved me, and Gram's love and care had made up for anything I'd missed. I wished Clem had had the same love and acceptance.

If I were ever a mother (not something I was planning in the near future), I hoped I could be as good a parent as Gram had been.

I sat on Patrick's couch, thinking about families. Trixi and Bette raced around the room in some mysterious kitten race. They seemed to be getting along, although once in a while Bette nipped Trixi. Bette was definitely the dominant kitten. I hoped the two wouldn't miss each other once Trixi and I returned home.

I'd decided to call Ruth, when Sarah called me.

"So, how was the dinner?" I asked.

"Very nice," Sarah said. "Pete and I agree that mustard on haddock is gross—we saw someone near us combining the two—that Shipyard is the best Maine beer, and that Haven Harbor is a wonderful place to live, but there have been too many murders here recently."

I couldn't disagree with any of that. "So . . . are you going to see him again? Socially?"

"I think so," she said. "We were both a little nervous last night. Pete said I was the first woman he'd asked out since his wife left him. I'm afraid he still misses her, which could be a problem. But I was nervous, too."

"Why were you nervous?"

"Pete's your friend, Angie. I kept thinking that if he and I went out for a while and didn't get along, then it might get in the way of our friendship. Or of your relationship with him."

"Sarah, you're thinking too much. Pete's a good guy, and we've been involved in some police situations together in the past months. But Pete's not my best buddy. You are! I want you to be happy. If you and Pete are happy together, that's great. If not . . . that's too bad, but not a problem for me."

"Okay. You're right. Maybe I was nervous because I hadn't dated anyone recently. Both Pete and I were out of practice."

"You're going to see him again?"

"Maybe after he and Ethan figure out who killed Clem, and whether anyone is stalking you."

"Good. And other than my car burning . . ."

"Which was not by chance," Sarah put in.

"Other than that, nothing seems to be happening. I'm at Patrick's, and he's confining me to the house today, which is what Pete wanted."

"It started out a beautiful day, but now it's dank. Cloudy, and the top layer of snow and ice turned to slush. You're better off staying inside. I'm going to finish cleaning the shop, and then relax and make cookies. I need a calm day after the last two."

"Cookies! Yum. That sounds like a good idea."

"You can do that, too, if Patrick has the right ingredients. Snickerdoodles aren't complicated." Sarah reeled off the ingredients.

"I'll keep them in mind." Patrick would probably like me to bake something. He'd done all the cooking so far.

"How are *you* doing, staying at the carriage house? With two cats?"

"The cats are getting along remarkably well."

"And you and Patrick?"

"Not bad. He's working in his studio now." I

lowered my voice, in case he could hear me. "Last night we cooked hot dogs in his fireplace, and made s'mores, and drank champagne."

Sarah laughed. "Sounds wonderful. Romantic and practical at the same time."

"Definitely romantic," I whispered. Then I raised my voice. "I'm going to call Ruth and see if she's found out anything more about the families we've been researching. Maybe call the Maine Historical Society, too. The guy I talked to there said they could help with family research if we had more information. Ruth may have found what they need."

"So you're still working on the coat of arms."

"I can't just sit here, Sarah. Not when someone may be stalking me."

"But you could make cookies," she pointed out. "You shouldn't sit around stewing and trying to solve Clem's murder. Ethan and Pete will do that."

"I could do both," I said. "I can't forget what's happened in the last couple of days."

After Sarah hung up I poured myself another mug of coffee. Did Patrick have ingredients for cookies? I wasn't Sarah; I didn't often make cookies. I was pretty sure Patrick didn't either.

He had sugar. And butter. But no cinnamon. No flour. The snickerdoodles had sounded good, but they needed cinnamon. And even sugar cookies required flour. I was pretty sure I'd need vanilla, too, and I didn't see any. If I was going to stay here a few more days, I should give him a shopping list.

I shuddered. A few more days? A shopping list? I wasn't moving in. I was trying to solve my friend's murder.

Back in the living room I sipped coffee and called Ruth.

"Good morning, Angie! I heard about your car. How's Tom doing?"

Nothing in Haven Harbor stayed a secret for long. I'd known that since I was old enough to eavesdrop on grown-up conversations. "Tom's leg was broken. He had surgery yesterday, but should be getting home tomorrow."

"Poor man. And I'll bet he's more worried about the state of his congregation than he is about his body."

"That's possible," I agreed. "Gram's on the case. Between her and the church secretary, they'll have everything in place. She's already lined up a guest minister for Sunday."

"Good for her! And how about you, Angie? You're carless. Where are you? At Patricks', as you'd planned?"

When Pete told me not to tell anyone where I'd be staying he couldn't have meant Ruth. "I am," I told her. "Just for a day or two. Until Ethan and Pete find whoever killed Clem and blew up my car."

"Good for you. Try to enjoy your time together. And you do have the gates locked, right?"

"We do," I assured her. Patrick and his mother had the only gated home in Haven Harbor. I hoped Pete or Ethan was driving by periodically to check it anyway. "I was wondering if you'd found out anything more about the Gould or Holgate families."

"I may have found your Charles."

"Baby Charles? The one left at the Foundling Hospital?"

"That very one. Now, I'm not positive it's him. Charles wasn't an unusual name in the eighteenth century. But remember Jonathan Holgate? His daughter Verity married Joshua Providence in 1788."

"Right." I needed a chart to remember all these relationships. Ruth probably had made one.

"Jonathan was married, of course—we know he had a daughter, Verity. But he also had a sister, named Letitia."

"Pretty name," I put in.

"It is, and not common nowadays. Letitia had a son named Charles. I don't know when he was born—I know you were hoping for 1757—but he did marry in 1782, so he could be your Charles. He'd be about the right age."

"Was Letitia married?"

"Interestingly, I can't find a reference to a husband. It's hard to trace a woman's family, because after she married she became, for example, Mrs. Gilcrest, and even her first, given, name disappeared. Jonathan had a wife, for example, but I don't know her name. But Letitia isn't listed as anyone's wife. In fact, I'm assuming she's a sister, since she and Jonathan have the same last name. I suppose she could have been a cousin or some other relation who came with Jonathan and his wife to the wilderness of Maine."

"Do you know when they got here?"

"The first reference I've found to them is in 1765. They could have arrived then, or perhaps they'd been here for a while, but their presence wasn't recorded anywhere I've looked so far."

"So," I said, "Maybe Letitia had Charles out of wedlock in England in 1757 and went back to reclaim him a few months later, and sometime, not much later, they came to Maine with her brother to start over."

"That's possible. If they waited several years to sail, I wonder where she lived in England. She wouldn't have brought a bastard child home with her to whatever grand house they lived in. Remember, the Holgates were one of the families with land grants. More to your purpose, they might also have been a family with a crest, and even a coat of arms."

"That's exciting! I wonder if Jonathan or Letitia brought that embroidered coat of arms with them from England."

"I can't imagine why anyone would have stitched it here, from a practical point of view. Flaunting ties to nobility wasn't popular on this side of the pond in the late eighteenth century. But, on the other hand, that embroidery isn't fine stitching. Someone who wasn't an expert embroiderer might have based it on a sketch, or even a verbal description. By most standards, even when it was new it wasn't well enough done to be framed."

"But it was framed," I said. "I took it out of a frame."

"And the papers for baby Charles were behind it, right? Maybe Letitia embroidered it herself. She or her brother would have been the one who reclaimed the baby, and somehow managed to get that receipt—that billet, you said they called it—at the same time. Could the embroidery of the coat of arms be a message of some sort?"

"A sign that Charles was from a grand family?" I frowned. "And yet he was a bastard, or we're assuming he was. Here in Maine no one would have asked questions about his heritage. Letitia could have said her husband had died. She wouldn't have been the first woman with a child to say that."

"True enough. And we may never know," agreed Ruth. "The real question is why someone today cares about it."

"The Holgate family consigned a lot of household furnishings, most of them old, to the auction house in Augusta. Those furnishings could have included the embroidery. Whoever consigned it couldn't have been impressed by the coat of arms. It was in bad condition, as you saw. The embroidery hadn't been out of the frame in years. The nails holding it in the frame were short, with square heads. The kind a blacksmith would have made. It looked like something that had been under the eaves in someone's attic for years."

"So the family today might not have known about the concealed paper," said Ruth. "That must be what they didn't want you to investigate. Maybe they first heard about the paper when they heard you on the news."

"It makes sense," I agreed. "Although since Charles was born and left at the Foundling Hospital more than two hundred and fifty years ago, I can't imagine what difference it would make to someone today."

"Some families are sensitive about illegitimacy," said Ruth.

"I suppose so," I said. "But two hundred and fifty years ago?"

"I'll take a look at more recent descendants of the Holgates," Ruth promised. "We already know Senator Holgate's husband is one. I'll start with him. After all, he's a Jonathan Holgate, too, like the eighteenth-century Holgate I found. It could be a coincidence, or it could be he was named after his ancestor."

"Thank you, Ruth! I appreciate all the work you're doing on this. And, before you hang up, one more question. I was thinking of making cookies for Patrick this afternoon. He doesn't have any flour or vanilla. Is there anything else I could use?"

Ruth laughed. "I can't think of any substitute for flour. Maybe Anna, across the street, could give you some. Lemon flavoring would work. Or even almond, depending on the variety of cookie. Some people use rum or sherry, but I wouldn't do that to sweet cookies. Maple syrup? Does he have shortening and baking soda?"

"I don't know," I said, feeling a little discouraged. Patrick was a guy. Steak, he had. Eggs, he had. Baking supplies? Not so much. "Thanks for your help, Ruth. I'll check in with you later."

I looked through the cabinets in his kitchen again. I'd been right the first time I'd looked. No baking supplies.

"What're you looking for?" asked the man in question, joining me in the kitchen. He glanced at my mug. "I needed more coffee, too. Last night was fun, but . . ."

"A little too much champagne," I agreed. "I was thinking of making cookies. But you don't have all the ingredients I'd need."

"Cookies! That would be great. But you're right

about ingredients. I don't bake." He looked at me and then glanced out the window. "The roads are better now. I could do a little shopping."

I joined him at the window. True. The sun was gone, but cars were moving along the road at usual speeds.

"Make a list of what you need. I'll go to the supermarket and get everything. I'll pick up something for our lunch, too. It's almost noon."

I was still full from breakfast, and yesterday he'd bought enough food to feed half of Haven Harbor. Maybe his work wasn't going well and he was looking for an excuse to go out. "Did you do much work this morning?" I asked.

Patrick shrugged, and then smiled. "A little. Touch-ups. It's hard to concentrate on painting when my lovely lady is in the next room."

I was flattered, but, at the moment, jealous. He was going out into the world. I'd promised I'd stay in hiding for at least today.

He washed the paint off his hands and gulped a little coffee as I made out a short list. Snickerdoodles, like Sarah was making, would be the easiest, and I could call her if I had any questions. "Thanks for doing this. I'm not a great cook, but cookies will keep me amused for a while."

"I want my lady to be amused, of course," he said. He pulled on his heavy jacket and boots and headed for the door.

"Wait! I forgot to check. Do you have a cookie sheet?"

He stopped. "A flat pan, like for pizza?"

"Round or square. Either."

"Glad you asked. I'll get one. Or two. Be back soon."

He kissed me soundly and left.

I turned on the television, looking for an amusing old movie. I'd started switching channels when Patrick came back in.

"Call your friend Pete," he said. "We need to talk to him. Now."

CHAPTER 28

"Short is our longest day of life.
And soon its prospect ends,
Yet on that day, uncertain date,
Eternity depends."

—Orphaned Mary Pennell Corbit was raised by her uncle, William Corbit, in Appoquinimink, now Odessa, Delaware. When she was eleven Mary finished this sampler, which included the initials of her relatives, and flowers, on linen with beige, brown, and blue embroidery. On May 14, 1823, her uncle noted in his account book that he had purchased "a gilt frame for sampler." Mary's sampler is now at the Winterthur Museum.

I looked at Patrick's face. He was serious. Too serious. I called Pete.

"Pete? Angie. No, I'm fine. Patrick wants to talk to you." I handed the phone to Patrick, switching it to speaker so I could hear their conversation too.

"Pete? Angie and I've been here in the carriage house since yesterday afternoon. I just went outside, and there are fresh footprints around the house."

"Are your gates closed and locked, Patrick?" Pete's voice was alert and concerned.

"Both gates. Sure. Since we got here yesterday. And the doors and windows are locked."

"Don't touch anything. I'll be right over. Don't open the gate until I get there. And stay away from the windows, just in case someone is still out there."

Patrick handed the phone back to me and pulled off his jacket.

"Did you walk all around the house?" I asked.

"No. But the footprints seemed to be circling it. You heard Pete. He's coming over to see for himself."

I was shaking a little. "Whoever it was could have been looking in the windows. You don't have shades or blinds."

"We're out of town, far from anyone else, with fields and woods as neighbors. The road's on the other side of the stone wall. No one can see in."

Not unless they were right outside. "How could someone get into the estate? Past the gates?" I'd felt safe here. Maybe nowhere was safe.

Patrick had started pacing. "Someone could have climbed the wall. It's only three feet tall. This place wasn't built as a fortress. Or someone could have walked through the woods on the far side. With all the snow pack, that wouldn't have been easy. But their steps would be visible. Pete can check that."

My mind shifted from mysterious footsteps outside, and what someone might have seen through the windows, to why all this was happening. Did all these threats and Clem's murder come down to someone's being embarrassed by illegitimacy? I was illegitimate. Clem was adopted. There was a decent chance she'd been illegitimate. Something we'd had in common that I hadn't known.

Not knowing who my father was had never bothered me.

Clem probably didn't know either of her biological parents. Had that bothered her? Jeannine and Oliver Walker hadn't been easy parents to live with. But who knew what her biological parents had been like? At least the Walkers had wanted her.

Mama and Gram had both wanted me, too. That made the difference, no matter what your birth. Today many women had children without being married. At least in the United States, most people accepted that, even if they believed children were better off with two parents.

This was the twenty-first century. Why would knowing a child born in 1757 was illegitimate be important to anyone? And Charles hadn't even been totally deserted at the Foundling Hospital. He'd been boarded there for a while, until someone, most likely his mother or uncle, went back to get him.

If he had been born into a family that hadn't wanted to accept him, whoever reclaimed him deserved a lot of credit. It must not have been easy.

I stretched and took my coffee mug to the kitchen.

Patrick was still pacing, looking out his front windows, getting ready to remotely unlock and open the estate's gate when Pete arrived.

This wasn't a time to think about cookies, but I could have used some sweetness. Preferably chocolate. I had a feeling I wouldn't be making cookies today.

"He's here," said Patrick, using the front gate remote. I joined him at the door, as Pete drove through the gate and parked in front of the carriage house. By closing the gates yesterday, Patrick had not only kept out any intruders (he assumed), but he'd also kept out the guy who plowed his driveway. Luckily, the wintery mix we'd had last night had only turned into three or four inches of new snow and ice.

Pete joined us at the door. "Thanks for calling me. Where are these footprints?"

"I'll show you," said Patrick, putting his jacket back on.

I started to follow the two men.

"You stay inside, Angie. Just in case."

I didn't want to be inside. I didn't want to be protected. But I obeyed. Right now Pete needed to concentrate on figuring out who had been on the estate and when. Until we knew that, I wasn't stupid. I knew I should stay out of sight.

Although if someone had been looking in the windows, he or she would have been able to see me clearly. Patrick and I hadn't felt self-conscious about being next to windows.

Ruth was checking genealogy. Sarah was cleaning her store and making cookies. By now Gram was at the hospital with Tom.

What was I doing? Hiding. Being a target for some crazy.

I wandered through the house, peeking out windows when I could, trying to see where Patrick and Pete had gone. They weren't near the house; they were probably checking one of the gates, or following the footprints into the woods on the far side of the estate. No one could hide footsteps in fresh snow.

I ended up back in the kitchen. Patrick didn't have any lemon or rum flavorings. But he did have maple syrup. Could I make something with that? It wasn't chocolate, but it was sweet.

Next month Maine would celebrate Maine Maple Sunday, an annual event at the end of March when sugarhouses all over Maine opened to the public. Farms attracted families by offering rides on oxen-pulled wagons, visits to baby animals, and fresh maple syrup served on snow or ice cream. Gram had taken me every year when I was little. Maine Maple Sunday was a sign of spring. I should take Patrick next month.

In the meantime, maple syrup was nice in tea.

But I was too restless even to heat water.

I wandered through the house. I could make more phone calls, but I wanted to wait until Pete and Patrick returned. In any case, I was tired of talking to people about depressing subjects, like murders. Hospitals. Illegitimacy. Sad families.

My mind spun from one subject to another.

Would Sarah and Pete have a future together?

Patrick and I were coping with each other. Very well, in fact. I smiled, remembering the night before. And Bette and Trixi were curled up together as though they'd been together all of their lives.

The sun had even emerged again. Plows and sanders had been driving by for several hours.

Where were Pete and Patrick?

I looked out the living room windows, past where Pete had parked his car, down the long drive to where Aurora, Skye's Victorian mansion, stood, isolated, waiting for her to return. I didn't see the guys. Maybe they'd gone around to the other side of the carriage house, toward the seldom-used back entrance to the estate.

As I looked, my telephone rang.

I almost didn't answer. But it was Ruth.

"Yes, Ruth?"

"Angie. I've found something interesting. I

don't know whether it will help, but it's a parallel situation to baby Charles's being born in 1757."

"Yes?" I listened to Ruth, but walked into Patrick's studio, where the floor-to-ceiling glass walls overlooked the field in back of the estate. Where were the men?

"We decided I should start with the present Holgate family and work backward."

"Right," I agreed.

"We knew one current Holgate—Jonathan—was married to Senator Julianna Holgate. She's been in Washington for several terms now. Jonathan usually stays here in Maine. He's a philanthropist who's endowed college scholarships at many high schools here, is one of the major donors at several Maine museums, and a few years ago he donated a cancer wing for one of our hospitals."

"Okay. Sounds like he's doing good things with his money."

"He is. He and his wife don't have any children, so they don't have to think about leaving inheritances. In fact, the Holgate family is pretty small now. Jonathan is the last Holgate on his side of the family."

"He was an only child?"

"He has a sister named Barbara. But according to articles I found when I was researching their family, Barbara was disinherited by their father when she was a teenager."

"Disinherited? Do people still do that?"

"The Holgates do. Or did. In any case, Barbara had a son whose father was deemed inappropriate for the Holgate family. If she married, I can't find any mention of it."

"Interesting," I commented, walking back into the living room to check the windows. There were the men! Pete was carrying a camera, and he and Patrick were heading back for the house. "Ruth, can I call you back? Pete's here."

"Of course, dear," said Ruth.

I opened the door and they tramped in, knocking snow and slush and ice off their boots. They didn't look happy. "So? What did you find?"

"Patrick was right," Pete said. "Someone was walking around this place, probably late last night, based on the depth of the boot prints in the snow."

"How did he get in?"

"The prints led back to the woods on the other side of Aurora. We followed them out to the road—must be at least a quarter mile. The stone wall doesn't go that far," Pete explained. "There were tire prints at the side of the road there, too. Someone parked his car and then waded through the deep snow in the woods until he ended up in back of Aurora, and then walked up the drive and around the carriage house."

Patrick nodded. "We turned the lights off pretty

early last night, so chances are whoever it was didn't see either of us in the house, even though the footprints were close enough to the windows that it appeared he—the boot prints were pretty big—tried to see in."

"Patrick told me he parked in his garage. So we don't even know if whoever was here knew anyone was in the house. There didn't appear to be any attempts to break in."

"Thank goodness," I said softly.

"I've taken pictures of the tire tracks and boot prints, but with this weather—sleet and snow has obliterated the prints in some places—I'm not sure the crime scene folks will be able to tell much except that a large man was wandering about."

"Trespassing," said Patrick. "Whoever it was should be arrested on a charge of trespassing if nothing else. We have 'no hunting or trespassing' signs posted all over the place—beginning in the section of woods where he entered our land."

"Looked as though he'd slipped and fallen at least once," said Pete. "But I don't think he was hurt. The fall didn't seem to slow him, although, of course, we couldn't tell exactly when the tracks were made."

"He must have had a flashlight or lantern," I said. "February nights are dark, the snow covers a lot of brush, and that woods is full of downed branches and trees. No clear paths lead through it."

"I was going to get some tree guys to clear out those woods in the spring," Patrick said. "Now I'm tempted to leave them as they are. And maybe we need an electric fence around the whole property."

"I don't think you need to go to that extreme based on this," said Pete. "It could have been some harmless person curious to see the estate. Before your mother bought it last spring, kids— and adults, too—sometimes came over here to look at what they called 'the ghost house.' "

"And sometimes broke into the carriage house and partied. I know," said Patrick.

I didn't mention that ten or twelve years ago I'd been one of those kids.

"That was then. This is different. Who goes wandering around in the woods in the middle of a February night in a sleet and ice storm, and just happens to peek in the windows of the place where a woman who's been getting death threats is staying?" Pete pointed out.

I didn't say anything.

Pete turned to me. "Angie, I don't want to worry you, but you got more of those nasty notes on your computer yesterday afternoon. Our computer geeks tried to trace the sender, but so far they haven't been able to. Whoever sent them is angry, and wants that embroidery and the paper you found with it."

I shuddered. So the messages hadn't stopped.

"The first messages didn't say he wanted anything other than Clem and I to die. Maybe he's getting more focused."

"That's exactly what Ethan and I are hoping. The more focused, the easier it should be to trace him. Where're the embroidery and the paper now?"

"I have them with me," I said. "In the bedroom."

"Good. They should be safe there. I'm going to make sure someone's watching this house and your house downtown tonight, Angie. Both of you, stay here. No sneaking out to see a movie in Brunswick or Boothbay."

No one smiled. If Pete was joking about our going to the movies, right now it didn't seem funny.

"Ethan's in Portland talking to some of Clem's colleagues at Channel 7. She was the golden-haired girl to the bosses there, he says, but she didn't have a lot of friends among her peers. Ethan said she might not have been the most popular girl on the block, but he doesn't think anyone she worked with had anything to do with her death. Everyone she worked with alibied one another out. They were all at the studio working the day she died."

"That's good," I said. I'd planned to talk to people at the station. Sounded as though Ethan had covered the possibility anyone there had killed Clem.

"Since someone rigged those fireworks in your car, it's seems pretty clear that, for whatever reason, whoever is doing this is focused on the embroidery and the paper, strange though that seems. If someone was just angry at Clem, why would he rig your car so you could be hurt? Why continue sending messages and threats?"

"Unless someone's trying to cover Clem's murder with some crazy story about an embroidery," Patrick put in. "But I honestly don't care what they think they're doing. I want Angie to be safe, wherever she is. Right now she's here. Are you sure you have someone to watch the house tonight?"

Patrick and I both knew the Haven Harbor police department was small. Assigning one officer to a single location would reduce their effectiveness.

"Last summer when there were problems out here I got one of our retired officers to help out. But since this time we've already had one murder, Ethan promised he'd get one of the Maine State guys over here if I thought it was necessary." Pete looked at Patrick. "I'll tell him we need someone tonight."

"Thank you, Pete," I said.

"I'm going to send pictures of the footprints to the crime lab. They might pick up something we missed," he continued. "Within an hour someone should be here to patrol the place. After I leave, close the gates again. You should both be all right for now."

Of course, Clem had been shot in her own car in the middle of the day in downtown Haven Harbor. I didn't mention that, but I suspected we were all thinking it.

"Don't worry, Angie," said Pete. "We'll get this fellow. We just need a little more time."

Time. It had been forty-eight hours since Clem died. The more time that went by, the harder it would be to get new information.

We all knew that. No one pointed it out.

CHAPTER 29

"May Spotless innocence & truth my every action guide and guard my unexperienced youth from arrogance & pride."

—In April of 1797 Betsy Davis of Providence, Rhode Island, finished this elaborate sampler that includes eight detailed people, animals, a house, trees, birds, and flowers. She was probably a student of Mary Balch, a Providence teacher who emphasized her students' use of the rococo stitch.

The afternoon was quiet. No cookies; no phone calls. I even managed to take a nap—something I hadn't done in years. But the past few days had been exhausting, and the stress wouldn't be over until the killer was found.

Patrick painted the edges of two of his paintings, and then marinated the steak he planned to broil for dinner. I'd convinced him to bake the enormous potatoes he'd bought instead of microwaving them, and was pleased to see he had both sour cream and butter in waiting.

Last night's dinner had been fun, a game. Tonight we were going to have serious food.

A state police car was parked nearby. We had protection. Would we need it tonight? Would I be able to go home tomorrow?

By five-thirty Patrick had put the potatoes in the oven and opened a bottle of burgundy. I wasn't an expert on wines, but this one seemed perfect. As Patrick added wood to the fireplace, I began to relax. "Would you mind if I turned the news on?" I asked. "I feel out of touch with the rest of the world."

"Under the circumstances, that's not necessarily a bad thing," he suggested, handing me the remote.

"Local news only," I promised. "If the rest of the world has come to an end, I don't want to know about it tonight."

"Makes sense to me," he agreed.

I didn't turn on Channel 7. That broadcast would just remind me of Clem. I skipped the stations broadcasting in French and chose Channel 5.

A fire in Grey. A multiple car pileup on the Maine Turnpike. A wheelchair basketball tournament. Temperatures might reach above freezing tomorrow. The usual local news.

Then I sat up, straight. The burgundy in my glass sloshed, spilling red drops down my red and gray plaid flannel shirt.

"What is it?" asked Patrick, looking from me to the screen and back again.

"Shush! I recognize that man."

"We're pleased to welcome to our studio this evening Mr. Seaward Holgate. As many of you know, Mr. Holgate founded the Evening Promises.com Web site, an internationally famous site that matches people and events for romance, companionship, or just for the fun of it. Thank you for joining us tonight, Mr. Holgate."

"I'm pleased to be here, back in my home state," said the man sitting on the blue couch next to the interviewer. He looked as though he was in his thirties, and was wearing a well-tailored suit. "I may live on the West Coast now, but my roots and my heart are always in the Pine Tree State."

"And today you're here to make a special announcement," the pretty young anchor continued.

"I am. While I was growing up in this wonderful state, my mother and I didn't have a lot of money, but she valued music and drama, and somehow she managed to take me to concerts and plays several times a year. My joy at attending those events gave me the idea for EveningPromises.com. I wanted everyone to have the opportunity to enjoy the arts and to share those occasions with others who also value them. I've been lucky that EveningPromises.com has become a success, and I've decided to give part of that success back to Maine. I've purchased land in Westbrook, just west of Portland, where

I'm going to build a state-of-the-art concert stage and theater, with practice halls and flexible space for music, theater, and dance practices. It will be called the Barbara Holgate Theater Complex, in honor of my dear mother, and ten percent of the seats at each performance will be donated to schools, churches, hospitals, or other nonprofit organizations, so that all Mainers, no matter what their incomes, can participate."

"That is truly exciting news, Mr. Holgate. Thank you for joining us tonight so we could share it, live, with our viewers."

"I might add, construction on the Barbara Holgate Theater Complex will begin in a few weeks, and will be providing jobs to many Mainers. I'm looking forward to watching the construction, and to making my mother's dream of making the performance arts available to all come true."

The station cut to a commercial for a Maine ski resort.

"Holgate. I heard that. He's a Holgate," said Patrick. "How do you know him?"

"I saw him at the auction," I said. "A couple and a woman who was alone were bidding against each other for some of the same items. I'd heard the couple talking during the preview; they were members of one of the consigning families. I assumed the other woman was, too, and they were trying to outbid each other for family pieces. Then that man—that Seaward Holgate—came in and outbid both of them."

"If he was a Holgate, why wouldn't he have inherited the items he was bidding on?"

"Sarah told me sometimes a family puts all of an estate up for auction. Members of the family bid against one another to determine who gets what. Items no one in the family wants, of course, are bought by other people. It's one way of settling disputes. Or giving a number of family members the chance to go home with family treasures, instead of them being left to one or two people." I thought for a moment, trying to remember all that Ruth had found out. "Wait! Senator Holgate's husband had a sister who was disinherited. I think her name was Barbara. That man—Seaward—could be her son."

"And you saw him at the auction? That would make sense. But why is that important?"

"Patrick, the day Clem was killed a tall man was asking about me at the post office. And after my car burned, a tall man was looking at samplers in Sarah's shop, and asking about the auction in Augusta and the needlepointed coat of arms. I'm wondering if all those men could be Seaward Holgate."

"You think a multimillionaire would care about an old piece of embroidery, enough to kill someone?" Patrick shook his head. "It doesn't make sense."

"Nothing makes sense," I agreed. "But I'm pretty sure Seaward Holgate is Clem's killer." I hesitated a minute. "Or, if he isn't, then he's somehow connected to what's happened. After all, it all started at that auction."

"The Holgate family had an interest in the auction, so I believe you. He was there. But why didn't he buy the coat of arms, as he did the other lots he wanted? And those other times people saw 'a tall man' in Haven Harbor? A lot of tall men live in Maine."

"I know. Maybe I'm crazy. But now I'm curious about the man."

"Seaward Holgate. He's got a strange name," Patrick commented, lifting his wineglass toward the television set, in tribute.

"Not so much in Maine, Patrick. 'Seaward' is an old Maine name. Not used too much today, true, but it was in the eighteenth and nineteenth centuries." I finished my glass of wine, and Patrick refilled it.

"I know you're anxious to solve Clem's murder, but you're stretching your imagination a little too far to think the killer might be a dot-com giant. You're the one who's always told me that a murderer has to have MOM."

"Motive, Opportunity, and Method."

"I can't see how that man would have any of those." Patrick stood. "The potatoes should be baked by now. I'm going to keep them warm, and broil the steak. You can stay here and figure out why a man with that much money would be wandering around Haven Harbor setting off fireworks in your car or tramping around the carriage house, to mention two of his lesser crimes, or you can join me in the kitchen and kibitz."

"I'd like to make one fast phone call to Ruth, all right? Then I'll join you, and promise no more talk of murders tonight."

We clinked glasses.

"It's a deal," he said. "But be careful you don't get involved in a thirty-minute discussion with Ruth about people who died hundreds of years ago."

"Promise," I said, blowing him a kiss as he headed for the kitchen. Trixi jumped up and settled herself on my lap. "Trixi, I have to make one telephone call. Then I'll be yours and Patrick's all evening." She squeaked her assent, curled up, and fell asleep. I wished I could fall asleep as quickly.

"Ruth," I said, when she answered her phone, "did you see the news tonight? The interview with Seaward Holgate?"

CHAPTER 30

"This Needlework of Mine Can Tell
When A Child Is Learned Well
That By My Elders I Was Taught
Not to Spent My Time For Naught."

—Words worked into the earliest known
sampler from Rhode Island, stitched
by ten-year-old Mary Burges in 1725.
Her sampler is similar to those made in
England at the end of the seventeenth
century, a long rectangle that included
short lines of patterns and letters
as well as a moral verse.

"Seaward Holgate?" Ruth asked. "I didn't watch the news tonight; I did a little more research for you, and then I proofread one of my manuscripts for the rest of the afternoon. My eyes find more mistakes when I read out loud, so right now my voice is as tired as my eyes. I was about to get a little sherry, scramble myself two or three eggs, and find an old movie. Tell me what I missed."

"Patrick thinks I'm crazy, Ruth."

"You're creative. So is he. Maybe you're both a little crazy. But that's not bad, and it makes for an interesting life. So what did you see on television?"

"Seaward Holgate was announcing that he's building an arts center for Maine, in Westbrook. He said he grew up here, but made money with a Web site matching people who liked to go to arts events."

"Sounds interesting," said Ruth. "Is his business called Evening Promises?"

"Yes! That's it! How did you know about it?"

"Read about it in a *People* magazine article a few years back. I wrote it into one of my books. Of course, in my book the promises were for more than seeing ballet together."

"I can imagine," I said, sipping my wine and grinning to myself. Ruth's erotica was probably not exactly what Seaward Holgate had in mind when he dreamed of publicity for his site. "Anyway, he's a Holgate. That name keeps popping up. I think I saw him at the auction in Augusta. I'm just checking—didn't you say Senator Holgate had a sister named Barbara? Because that's the name of this Seaward Holgate's mother."

"He could be Barbara's daughter. She had a son out of wedlock. But you think this philanthropist Holgate is a murderer?" Ruth sounded as skeptical as Patrick had been.

"I know—it's not likely. But he did look like the man I saw at the auction. And Pax Henry at the post office said a tall man was looking for me. And then a tall man and a shorter, older woman were at Sarah's shop yesterday, asking about the coat of arms embroidery after my car exploded."

"My eyes are too tired to do any searching tonight, but I'll see what I can find out about him tomorrow. I remember Barbara Holgate had a son, but I didn't check to see what his name was."

"Thank you, Ruth."

"Are Pete and Ethan any closer to finding out who killed Clem?"

"If they are, they haven't shared it with me. I'm caged up at Patrick's house. It's a great place, and he's a wonderful host, but I'm anxious to get on with my life."

"Of course you are."

"Two minutes to dinner!" Patrick called from the kitchen.

"Got to go, Ruth. Patrick's made dinner, and I have to go and eat."

"And appreciate the moment, Angie dear. Don't forget to appreciate today. You never know the future."

Ruth was right, but under the present circumstances, her advice sounded a little grim.

But I wasn't going to have any trouble being appreciative of a steak and baked potato and another glass of burgundy. I might sometimes feel as though I were in prison. But the food and company here couldn't be beat.

Trixi and Bette had gotten to the kitchen ahead of me.

The steak was resting, awaiting our forks and knives, the potatoes were on the table, with complements of sour cream and chives, and Patrick had also cooked frozen peas and decanted another bottle of burgundy. The kitchen table was set with an ocean-blue tablecloth and napkins and white plates. Three candles were lit in the middle of the table.

"Wow," I said, handing him my empty wineglass. "My car should blow up more often."

"You're welcome any time, my dear," he replied, eyes sparkling. "Don't people eat like this every night?"

Ruth was dining on scrambled eggs accompanied by a glass of sherry tonight. She'd been looking forward to her supper, but she would be alone. I was lucky. My evening was special because of the company as well as the food. I was almost embarrassed at the attention Patrick was paying to me, and even to my cat, as I realized he'd cut a piece of steak into tiny pieces and divided it between two dishes in the corner of the room. Trixi and Bette were both gobbling.

I could get spoiled being here. My cat already was. Another cat to antagonize and play with, enormous windows to see the world, and steak for dinner?

She'd miss all this when we got home.

I would, too.

CHAPTER 31

"Catherine of Aragon, one of the unfortunate queens of Henry VIII, was a notable needlewoman, and spent much of her short, unhappy time as Queen of England in embroidering. The 'Spanish Stitch' was introduced by her from her own country, and many examples of her skill in embroidery are to be seen in the British Museum and the various homes belonging to our old nobility."

—From *Chats on Old Lace and Needlework* by Emily Leigh Lowes, London: T. Fisher Unwin, Ltd., 1908.

Patrick finally accepted (or said he did) the possibility that the multimillionaire Seaward Holgate I'd seen on television might be the same person I'd seen bidding at the auction. But he insisted Holgate couldn't be the man who'd been in Haven Harbor the day Clem had been killed, or at Sarah's antiques store after my car had blown up.

"It's too big a coincidence, and there's no logic," he insisted. "Why would someone like that ask questions at a post office or—even less likely—kill Clem or blow up your car? It doesn't make sense."

Motive? Okay. I admitted that wasn't at all clear.

Means? Well, the man could have afforded fireworks—a whole yacht full if necessary—and could have gone wherever he wanted to.

Opportunity?

I hadn't seen the "tall man" postmaster Pax Henry had talked to, or the man who'd been at Sarah's store. Before I did anything else, I needed to know if either Pax or Sarah could identify him.

"Sarah?"

"Hi, Angie. Did you make cookies this afternoon?"

"No. Patrick didn't have any flour. But would you do me a favor?"

"Sure!"

"Look up a man named Seaward Holgate on your computer. See if you recognize him."

"Right now?"

"If you can."

"Hold on a minute. My computer isn't even turned on. I was taking the afternoon off. Cookies, hot tea, and *Casablanca*. I always cry when Ingrid Bergman flies away."

I could hear Sarah's computer turning on. "I'm putting you on speaker, Angie, so I can use both hands on the keyboard."

"Fine. I appreciate this."

"What do you want me to look for?"

"I want you to Google a man named Seaward Holgate and see if you recognize him."

"Funny name."

Sarah's fingers were hitting the keys.

"It's an old Maine name."

"I've never heard it," she said. "Okay. Seaward Holgate. He's on Wikipedia. Dot-com millionaire or billionaire, born in Maine."

"Do they have a picture of him?"

"Yes. Very corporate, suit and tie."

"And?"

"I'm trying to think where I might have seen him. I've never been to California, where he lives."

"Look at his face." I didn't know what picture Sarah was looking at, or how old it might be.

"I'm thinking. I'm thinking. He does look a little familiar. Angie, I really don't know for sure. But he does look a little like that man who was in my store the other day, the one who was with the older woman, who was interested in samplers."

Yes! "Are you sure?"

"No. But he might be that guy. Isn't Holgate one of the names you were having Ruth research? One of the families auctioning things in Augusta?"

"Yes. And I saw him at the auction. Do you remember a tall man in the back of the auction hall who bid up several of the expensive lots?"

"I wasn't paying much attention to the people. I was focused on what I wanted to buy."

"Okay. I hoped you'd remember him, too."

"Sorry, Angie. But he might have been the guy here yesterday. I was so worried about the broken window, and the snow blowing in, and getting you to the hospital, that I didn't pay much attention to that couple."

"I understand."

"How did you connect him with Seaward Holgate?"

"I saw Holgate on the evening news. He's donating an arts center to the town of Westbrook."

"Great. I wish I could help you more. But I can't be certain. I gave you his e-mail address. Why don't you write to him and ask him? That guy wanted me to let him know if I found out anything about the coat of arms embroidery. You could tell him you have it."

"What if he's the killer? I already have enough problems. I need to be more certain it was this Holgate before I do anything like that." But it was an idea.

"Are you all right, Angie? You sound upset."

"Of course I'm upset! Clem's dead; my car blew up; someone wants the embroidery I have; Tom's in the hospital. Last night a prowler walked around Patrick's house and probably looked in the windows, and I'm stuck trying to figure out how everything is connected without leaving the house!"

"How does Patrick feel about all this?"

"He thinks I'm crazy. He made us a great dinner, with wine and steak and candles, and all I could think about was Seaward Holgate. Now he's cleaning the kitchen."

"Hey, friend? Go out there and dry dishes or something. Try to relax. Patrick's trying hard to make this as easy as possible for you. Don't mess up your relationship by obsessing about someone who was more likely talking to his investors or his architects during the past couple of days than following you around Haven Harbor."

I sighed. "You're right, Sarah. I'll try. But I can't help thinking that guy is somehow connected to this whole mess."

"Hold on a minute. A whole list of articles popped up when I searched for his name. There aren't a lot of people with the name Seaward. Let me see if any of them look interesting."

"Thanks."

Sarah was silent for a few minutes. Trixi and Bette batted an orange plastic ball around the living room. It ended up under the couch, where they couldn't reach it.

"Okay, Angie? The articles on the first page are all about his business. He seems to be very successful. It's now listed on the New York Stock Exchange. He recently bought a large home near

Westbrook. That's where you said the arts center would be, right?"

"Right."

"There've been a couple of articles about him in financial publications. Look boring. I don't see anything that would connect him to embroidery or Haven Harbor."

"Okay, Sarah, thanks for checking. Go watch your movie!"

"If I can help with anything else, let me know. But do try to relax, Angie."

"I will." I fished the plastic ball out from under the couch to the delight of the cats, and took Sarah's advice to go and help Patrick in the kitchen.

I wanted to call Pax, to ask him if he'd recognize Seaward Holgate. But I'd wait until the post office opened in the morning. There was nothing else I could do tonight besides worry.

Sarah had said the man in her store looked somewhat like Holgate. I wasn't ruling my idea out yet.

CHAPTER 32

"The sisters of King Ethelstan were famous for their skill in spinning, weaving and embroidery, their father having educated them to give their entire attention to letters first, and afterwards to the distaff and needle. The queen of Edward the Confessor was well known as an expert needlewoman, and the celebrated Bayeux tapestry, worked by the wife of the Conqueror, is a grand proof of what can be done with that feminine implement, the needle."

—From *The Ladies Guide to Needle Work, Embroidery, Etc., being a Complete Guide to all Kinds of Ladies' Fancy Work* by S. Annie Frost. New York, Adams & Bishop, Publishers, 1877.

Patrick and I cleaned the kitchen and settled in to watch the Celtics play the Cavaliers. I hadn't paid much attention to sports since I'd returned to Maine, but practically everyone in the state stopped whatever he or she was doing when the Celtics or Patriots or Red Sox or Bruins— depending on the season—played. I hadn't known Patrick had become addicted to the Celtics. Living with someone, even for a short time, you learned details about their lives you hadn't known before.

Ruth called at halftime. "Angie? Hope I'm not bothering you."

"Not at all. Patrick and I are watching the Celtics."

"Right. It's halftime. The Red Sox are my team. But when the baseball season is over, the Celtics do fine. Do you have a minute? Despite my eyes, I took a few minutes to check that Holgate you told me about."

"Absolutely." I moved into the kitchen, so I wouldn't disturb Patrick's viewing when halftime ended.

"Remember I told you Senator Holgate's husband had a sister who was disowned?"

"I remember. And his sister Barbara had a son."

"Exactly. Seaward Holgate is that son. The Internet is a wonderful tool, Angie. I found one of those 'personal details about the life' articles about business tycoons published several years ago."

"Seaward Holgate certainly is a tycoon. Sarah told me his dot-com has gone public."

"This article was written before all that happened. It was about several multimillionaires who'd made their money in Silicon Valley. There were only a few paragraphs, but it said

Seaward Holgate had grown up in Maine, the son of a single mother who struggled to keep food on the table and her son in school. He'd gotten scholarships, and then had the idea for his company. He was basically a self-made man. He hadn't married; he worked all the time. The first thing he'd done when he had money was buy his mother a house."

"Interesting. So even though Seaward had wealthy cousins—or at least a wealthy uncle—he made all his money himself."

"Right. I did find second and third cousins in the Holgate family, but he's the only one in his generation who's a close relation to the senator's husband."

Maybe the women at the auction bidding on the Holgate items were the cousins. "I'd be angry if I'd grown up with nothing, and my mother worked hard, and she had a brother who was a philanthropist to the world, but didn't give me or my mother a penny."

"Agreed. Although from what you said, he's a philanthropist now, too."

"He's naming the arts center after his mother."

"Sweet of him to do that. A real tribute."

"Ruth, after I saw him on television I recognized him. I'd seen him at the auction where I'd bought the needlepoint. Since he's a Holgate, that would make sense."

"It would," Ruth agreed.

"I also wondered if he was the man Pax Henry had seen at the post office, asking for me, or the man who'd been in Sarah's store, asking about samplers. I called Sarah, and she wasn't sure, but she said it might have been him."

"Was he alone in her store?"

"No. He was with an older woman. It could have been his mother, Barbara, I guess."

"If it was him, he might be the man you're looking for. But we still don't know why he would kill Clem. Maybe he wanted the needlepoint you bought. Especially since you found papers in back of it that probably no one knew were there before you found them. But to kill for them?"

"I agree. It doesn't make a lot of sense."

"What are you going to do next?"

"I'll call Pax in the morning and see if he recognizes a picture of Seaward. And the man in Sarah's store gave her an e-mail address. I could write and ask him if he's Seaward Holgate."

"Be careful, Angie. Make sure you tell Pete and Ethan what you're doing. I don't know if Seaward Holgate is the man you're looking for, but someone killed Clem Walker and has been stalking you. Whoever it is, you don't want to fool around with him."

"I know, Ruth. I'll be careful. I promise. But if it should be Seaward Holgate, I can't let him fly back to California and disappear."

"He won't disappear, Angie. His mother is here. And if he wants that embroidery you have, he won't leave without it. Anyone who's climbed out of poverty to become wealthy is persistent. He won't give up easily."

"You're right, Ruth. But neither will I."

CHAPTER 33

"In Books or Works or healthful Play
Let my first years be past that
I may give of every day some good
Account at last."

—From large sampler stitched by Elenora
Ainslie in 1825. Elenora was born
in Roslin, near Edinburgh, Scotland,
July 26, 1816. Her family emigrated
to America, but she stayed with her
grandmother in Roslin until she was
an adult. In 1863 she married Colin
Campbell, a tailor who had also been
born in Scotland, in Louisville, Kentucky.
Although Elenora had no children, her
husband had two sons from a previous
marriage. Her sampler includes her
family home, a thistle, several trees and
flowers, and initials of many family
members and friends.

The next morning Patrick convinced me to call Pax, not to go to the post office. "In case you're right," he pointed out. "That guy went to the Haven Harbor post office once. He might do it again. Ask Pax to do what Sarah did: check that Seaward guy's picture on the Web."

"I know you're not convinced he's the man I'm looking for."

"I'm not. And Sarah couldn't identify him for sure. I know Ruth's connected him, but his last name is Holgate, so that doesn't surprise me. I'm sorry, Angie. I know you want to tie up all the ribbons and solve this case. But I can't believe anyone—much less a wealthy man—would bother to shoot a television reporter and blow up your car to get an old piece of embroidery, even if the embroidery and the paper in back of it did have something to do with his family. He could have just offered you a lot of money for it."

"I agree. But it's the only lead I have, and I have to check it out. Murders never make sense, do they?"

"Not to me. But if you find out anything more definite about this guy, promise me you'll let Pete and Ethan know. It's their job to follow up." Patrick put his arms around me. "I don't want you to get hurt."

Patrick's voice was soft, and his arms were reassuring. But I was determined.

"I'll be careful. I promise. And, of course, I'll tell the police if I find out anything definite. Right now they'd laugh at me, the way you do."

"I'm not laughing, Angie. I'm worried."

I gave him another hug and phoned the Haven Harbor post office.

"Good morning, Pax? This is Angie Curtis."

"Good to hear your voice, Angie, after all that's been happening in town. And you haven't gotten your mail for the past couple of days. Your mailbox is full. I was beginning to worry about you."

"Can you hold my mail for me, please? Just for another day or two, I hope. I'm staying somewhere else right now."

"Hope it's somewhere good, with a friend. Can't be too careful these days."

"I agree. Pax, a fast question. Last week you mentioned that someone you didn't know was asking for my address."

"I remember. Skinny fellow."

"Would you recognize him from a picture?"

Pax hesitated. "Not sure I could. Didn't pay much attention. As I recall I was sorting mail at the time. Have you got a picture for me to look at? I'd be happy to check it out."

"I don't, Pax. But I have the name of someone it might be. Sarah Byrne told me there's a picture on his Wikipedia page."

"He's a big deal, then?"

"The guy with the page is, yes. But I don't know if he's the one who was in Haven Harbor. Would you mind taking a look?"

"Can't do that right now. Got to get the mail set to be delivered. Might have time in a couple of hours, though."

"That would be fine. As soon as you can. The man's name is Seaward Holgate."

"Good old-fashioned name, that. I had a great uncle named Seaward. Passed away back in 1967 or thereabouts. Seaward Holgate. Got it written down, Angie. I'll let you know. And I'll hold your mail until you tell me different."

"Thank you, Pax." I hung up. More hours to wait.

"I take it he wasn't going to look right away," said Patrick.

"He had to organize today's mail. He'll check when he can."

"Don't be too disappointed if Pax doesn't recognize him, Angie. He saw the man days ago, for a few minutes."

"I know. I keep hoping someone else who saw him can identify him for sure. I was so positive when I saw him on television that he was the same guy I saw at the auction house."

"Which he could have been. He's a Holgate, and Holgate lots were being auctioned. But even if he was there, that doesn't mean he had anything to do with what happened in Haven Harbor later."

"True enough."

Trixi took a big jump and landed on my lap. She turned around and looked at Bette as if to dare her new friend to follow her. But Bette headed for her food dish. Trixi jumped down and joined her. They'd been sharing their food dishes.

"Auctions keep records of who consigns lots and who purchases them, right?" I asked.

"I'm no expert on auctions. But I assume so. For tax purposes, if for no other reason. When you registered to bid, did you give them your name and address?"

"Sure."

"Then they have a record of who you are, and what you bid on. I predict you'll get your own personal notice of their next auction."

I picked up the phone again.

"Who are you calling now?"

"Last week I talked to a woman at the auction house. Jessica Winter. She's the one who told me the Holgates and Goulds were the families whose possessions were being auctioned. She was a big fan of Clem's, and she called me when she heard of Clem's death on the news. Maybe I can convince her to tell me who bought the carved mahogany bed—one lot I remember that man buying."

"Wouldn't that information be confidential?"

"She gave me names last week that she shouldn't have. If she won't tell me, I'm no worse off than I was before."

Patrick frowned. "I wish you'd relax and let the police take care of this. It's their job, not yours. One of these telephone calls of yours could put you in more danger. We don't know who killed Clem, or how that person knew she'd be in Haven Harbor that day. Assuming the same person left the fireworks in your car, how did he or she know it *was* your car? And who was walking around this house while we were sleeping? I'll take a wild guess and assume that person wasn't looking for me. But how did he know you were here?"

"I don't know the answers to any of those questions. But being here? You're well-known, Patrick, because of this estate, and your mother, and now your art gallery. I'd be surprised if there was anyone in Haven Harbor who didn't know who you were and where you lived. Or even that you and I have been seeing each other. And if I'm not at my home, and not with Gram and Tom . . . where else would I be? This is a logical place for me to have gone, especially with the locked gate."

"Which, thank goodness, is now being watched by a state trooper."

"Someone is still out there?"

"If no one were there I'd have called your friend Ethan. I even checked in the middle of the night. I'm not afraid of much, Angie, but I don't like the idea that someone can wander around and look in my windows, and who knows what else? I'm glad my car is locked in the garage, or maybe whoever it is would blow it up, too, and it would take the carriage house with it."

I took Patrick's hand. It was still misshapen and scarred from last year's fire at the original carriage house. Sometimes I forgot Patrick's introduction to Haven Harbor had included that awful scene of pain and destruction less than a year ago. "Would you feel better . . . safer . . . if I went somewhere else?" He'd rebuilt not only the carriage house, but also a new life for himself. But what had happened last year was still very real to him. Every time he looked at his scarred hands and arms he was reminded.

"No! I don't want you to be somewhere else. I want you right here, with me. What I want is for Pete and Ethan and whoever they're working with to find out who's doing all these things, and lock him—or her—up. I don't want you to be in danger."

This time I was the one who reached out and held him. "It won't be much longer. I think I'm close to finding out what happened to Clem, and why someone seems to be looking for me. I need to talk to a couple more people."

"I know you, Angie. You're strong, and determined. But you scare me, too. I don't want anything to happen to you."

"Hey, I'm the one with the gun, remember?" I said. "I'll be all right. I promise."

I hoped I was telling the truth.

CHAPTER 34

"Beauty soon grows familiar to the eye
Virtue alone has charms that never die."

—Mary Hall (1789–1868) of Groton,
New Hampshire, the eldest of thirteen
children, stitched this sampler including
the dates of the births and deaths of her
siblings. Mary never married.

I gave Patrick another hug, and then called the Augusta Auction House. A man answered.

"Could I speak with Jessica Winter, please?"

"Just a minute."

I heard whoever had answered yelling, "Hey, Jessie? Phone for you. Don't take long. We need to get through this inventory before lunch."

It didn't sound like a good time for her to check something for me. But I'd called; I wasn't going to give up now.

"Hello?"

"Hi, Jessica. This is Angie Curtis. Clem Walker's friend?"

"I remember." Jessica's voice lowered. "Have the police found out who killed her yet?"

"No. But they're getting close." At least I hoped they were. "I'm helping with the investigation.

Clem was my friend, and whoever killed her has been threatening me too."

"No! Why would anyone do that?"

"I don't know. But it seems to have something to do with the embroidery I bought at the auction last week. I'm wondering if it might also have something to do with someone I saw at the auction. He bought quite a few lots. Could you check that for me? He bought a carved mahogany bed."

"Not right now," Jessica said, quietly. "My boss is on a rampage this morning. We're trying to get an auction catalog printed, and we're behind schedule. Could I call you back?"

"Sure. The name of the man I'm wondering about is Seaward Holgate."

Jessica gasped. "Him? Sure, he was here. I remember him, because he was one of the Holgates—a bunch of them were here—but he had such a weird name."

"That's all I needed to know, Jessica. Thank you. You don't need to call me back."

"But, wait! There's something else."

"Yes?" I asked.

"That Seaward Holgate? I remember him, too, because he called asking for your name and address. The name and address of the person who bought that coat of arms embroidery."

I took a deep breath. "When did he call, do you remember?"

"It was right after you called asking about the names of the consigners. We talked about your knowing Clem, and how you two were going to have lunch that day. But, then, that didn't happen."

"No, it didn't. Did you tell Seaward Holgate who I was?"

"No. I figured he'd seen you and Clem on television, like I had. So I told him you were a friend of Clem's. In fact"—she paused—"I may have told him you were going to have lunch together."

"Did you tell him where?"

"I wouldn't do that! I just said in Haven Harbor. That was all right, wasn't it?"

"Fine, Jessica. Thank you for telling me."

Only one restaurant was open in Haven Harbor this time of year. Now I knew how Seaward Holgate had known Clem would be there that day.

Her self-proclaimed biggest fan had probably caused her death.

My hands were shaking. So, Seaward Holgate, multimillionaire and Holgate family outcast, had, for whatever reason, killed Clem and was looking for me.

I was certain, even if Sarah hadn't been. Had Pax had a chance to look at his picture? I couldn't wait any longer. I called the post office again.

"Haven Harbor post office."

"Pax, this is Angie Curtis again. I know it's soon, but have you had a chance to check the picture of Seaward Holgate online yet?"

"Impatient, are you? I was getting to that, Angie. Betsy Flannery brought in six boxes she was sending to her grandkids overseas, and we got to talking. You want to hold on while I check now?"

"Please, Pax."

A couple of minutes later he was back. "Sorry, Angie. I don't know. That man who was here asking for you was just a regular fellow. The sort of person you don't look at twice. That Seaward Holgate, he's an important person. I can't say it was him. But I can't say it wasn't, either."

"Thank you for checking, Pax."

"No problem. If I can help in any way, you let me know, Angie. No one else has come looking for you in the past couple of days."

"That's good."

"Nope. One woman wanted to know where Patrick lived, though. That was funny. People stop in all the time asking about his mom. Famous actress and all that. But this woman asked about Patrick."

"What was she like, Pax?"

"No competition for you, Angie. Not a good-looker, or even young. She must've been almost as old as I am. Maybe fifty-ish? I'm wicked bad at guessing ages. Brown hair, going gray. Looked like a regular Mainer. Not a Hollywood type, or even someone from away."

"Did you tell her where Patrick lived?"

"Nah. Never do. But I suspect she could've stopped anyone on the street, and they would've told her. Plus, I was downtown the other day and saw he had a 'closed' sign on that gallery he owns that used to be Ted Lawrence's."

"Right."

"Well, right there on that sign he'd put his telephone number. I'm no computer expert, Angie, but even I know there's reverse lookup on the Internet. Anyone putting in that phone number could get Patrick's address."

I swallowed hard. "Good point, Pax. I'll mention that to Patrick. When was that woman in the post office?"

"Seems to me it was the day after they found poor Clem Walker's body down at the wharf. Real sad when that happened. Haven't seen Mr. or Mrs. Walker since then. You happen to know when services for her will be?"

"No. I haven't heard," I said. "Thank you, Pax."

"Sorry I couldn't be of more help," he said.

"You've been a big help." Probably more than he knew.

It was time to pull all this together.

325

CHAPTER 35

"All friends must part but if they love
Their Saviour god who reigns above
Their souls will meet again on high
And friendship reign beyond the sky."

—Caroline Emerson, born July 14, 1820,
stitched an elaborate floral border on her
sampler, which included the names and
birthdates of her parents and siblings. She
lived in Walpole, New Hampshire, and
was fourteen when she finished this work.
In 1838 Caroline married Silas Angier, a
farmer from Alstead, New Hampshire.

Patrick had left me to my phone calls and gone into his studio.

My mind was buzzing.

I stood, stretched, and changed the water in both Trixi's and Bette's water dishes. Not a major accomplishment, but at least I'd done something.

I debated whom to call next. I decided on Sarah.

"Good morning," she said. Her voice sounded happier than I'd expect on this cold, dark morning. "How are you and Patrick?"

"We're fine," I said, deciding not to tell her

that one reason we were fine was the Maine state troopers who rotated shifts outside Aurora. "I think I know who killed Clem and has been stalking me."

"Wow! Pete and Ethan have figured that out so quickly?"

"No. I have. But I don't have proof."

"Who do you suspect?"

"A member of the Holgate family: Seaward Holgate."

"The one you had me looking for online yesterday."

"Exactly."

"But I couldn't identify him. Did someone else?"

"No one's identified him by sight," I admitted. "I asked Pax Henry to check online, like you did, and he couldn't be sure Seaward was the man who'd asked about me at the post office.

"But I talked to that assistant at Augusta Auction House again, and she said he'd been at the auction when we were, and he called after Clem and I were on television and asked for the name and address of the person who'd bought the coat of arms embroidery." I paused. "She also told him Clem and I were having lunch together that day. In Haven Harbor."

"Where there's only one restaurant open this time of year," Sarah said, immediately understanding what that might mean.

"Yes."

"Have you told Pete or Ethan?"

"No. But I'm going to."

"And have you figured out why all this happened?"

"No," I admitted. "That's where I'm stuck. Ruth found some information online, so I know Seaward's mother was disowned by her father for having an illegitimate son—Seaward, I'm assuming, since Ruth didn't see information about any other children. But they were Holgates. That would explain why Seaward was at the auction. He bought several family pieces, bidding against other members of his family."

"But it's a big family, I assume," said Sarah. "And anyone could have bought that embroidery. I bought several. The Saco Museum bought the best one. Why wasn't he interested in those?"

"Because of the paper I found in back of the embroidery? I don't know. But even though you couldn't identify him, I think he was the one who came to your shop. The woman with him could have been his mother, Barbara."

"At the time I wondered if the pair might be a mother and son," Sarah admitted. "The woman was the one who seemed most interested in the embroideries."

"But he was the one who gave you the e-mail address, right? For you to use if you found out anything about the coat of arms."

"Yes. I haven't used it, of course. I gave it to you, and it's still on the desk in my shop."

"I want to find out for sure why he wants the embroidery. Would you send him a short note saying you have information about the embroidery, if he could meet you at your shop at three thirty this afternoon?"

"What? You want me to set up a meeting with someone you think killed Clem? Angie, you're crazy. I won't do it."

"But I'd be there, too. And if Holgate agreed to meet you, Pete and Ethan would come, too. We could record our conversation on one of our phones. If things got sticky, then we'd have the police with us."

"Isn't it illegal to record conversations without both parties giving permission?"

"In Maine it's legal if one party to the conversation knows and agrees."

"I don't have a good feeling about this, Angie. It's a little crazy. I know you've solved other murders, but you've always figured out why someone was killed. This time we have no clue."

"If I get Pete or Ethan or, preferably, both of them, to agree, will you send the e-mail?"

"I guess."

"Then I'll call Pete and let you know."

"Angie, Pete is here, with me. I'll put him on." Interesting!

"Angie? I heard Sarah's side of the conversation. You think Seaward Holgate, the rich guy who announced he's giving an arts center to Maine, killed Clem?" Pete sounded skeptical, to put it mildly.

"Listen, Pete. Seaward was an outcast of the Holgate family. He was at the auction where Sarah and I bought embroideries. And he called the auction house the day after Clem and I were on TV and asked who'd bought the coat of arms. An assistant at the auction house told him Clem and I planned to have lunch together at the Harbor Haunts that day."

"Interesting. But it doesn't mean the man is guilty of murder."

"Have you found any other suspects?"

Pete was silent. "Not at this point. We've ruled out Clem's colleagues at Channel 7. Frankly, we're stymied at this point."

"Then why not give this a try? Sarah can send Seaward Holgate an e-mail saying she knows where the embroidery that he's interested in is. He'll meet Sarah and I at the shop this afternoon and we'll try to find out why he's interested in it. You can be there . . . either posing as a customer, or, better yet, standing in the staircase to the second floor. I was there when Holgate and his mother visited Sarah's shop before, and he had no idea anyone was listening. You could record the conversation, or Sarah or I could. And if there were any problems, you'd be there."

"I don't like it. You could be putting Sarah and yourself in danger."

"Have you any other ideas on how to get him to talk? To explain his interest in the embroidery? We know he wanted it. He asked both the auctioneer's assistant and Sarah about it."

"Angie, let me talk to Ethan. The state homicide department is in charge of this case. I can't take a risk like this without his approval."

"Then call him. Or I'll call him."

"I'll do it, Angie. You get a little carried away sometimes. And you have to promise not to do anything in the meantime to put yourself or Sarah in danger. Keep in mind, if you plan on accusing this man of doing something illegal, that he has a lot of money and influence. Anyone he sued could have a major problem."

"If you're talking about his suing me, he wouldn't get much. I don't even have a car anymore."

"You have a house, and a business."

Pete was right. I'd be risking things important to me, and to others, too. But if Seaward Holgate had killed Clem, and was threatening me . . . "I still think we should do it. No one else had a motive."

"Seaward Holgate had a motive?"

"He must have had one. Even if we can't figure it out now. Maybe if we meet him and talk to him . . . Not accuse him of anything, just talk to him.

He might open up to us. Sarah and I aren't very threatening."

Pete laughed. "Sarah isn't, Angie, but I've seen you in action. You're going to have to prove to me you can handle this calmly and discretely."

"I will, Pete. I promise." He couldn't see my fingers crossed.

"I'll talk to Ethan. That's all I'll commit to right now. I'll tell Sarah not to send any e-mails until we all agree on a plan."

"You'll get back to me soon?"

"As soon as I can."

I dropped the telephone on the couch. My hands were shaking. What if Ethan wouldn't agree? No one else was doing anything.

I walked to the window and looked out at the wall in front of the estate, and the iron gate with the state police car in front of it.

Wherever Seaward Holgate was right now, he wasn't a prisoner.

I was.

I had to change that.

CHAPTER 36

"Harriet let Virtues charmes be thine
Charmes that will increase and shine
They will cheer thy winters bloom
They will shine beyond thy tomb."

—Stitched by Harriet Peverly, aged
thirteen, in Canterbury, New Hampshire,
in 1826. Unusually, she used a black
outline stitch to define the flowers and
birds and trees that border her sampler.

"You're going to do *what?*" Patrick stood in front of me, holding the spatula he'd been using to flip the blueberry pancakes he'd made for our lunch.

I dropped my phone onto the chair where I'd been sitting. And planning. "Pete is going to talk to Ethan. If he agrees, at worst, we'll be convinced Seaward Holgate has nothing to do with Clem's murder."

"It's too dangerous. If that man did kill Clem, he's threatened you and blown up your car. He's hurt Clem's family and yours. You and Sarah are putting yourself directly in the path of someone who may be seriously deranged."

I was scared. But Patrick was more scared.

"Pete and Ethan will both be there. We'll be meeting Holgate in Sarah's store in Haven Harbor, not in a remote location."

"If you're right, Holgate killed Clem in downtown Haven Harbor in the middle of the day, and it's pure luck that you—or Tom—weren't killed, too." Patrick stared at me. "I keep thinking it could have been you getting in that car. It could have been you in the hospital. Or worse."

"I have to do this, Patrick," I said, steadily, looking into his deep brown eyes. Eyes that showed his emotions when his words said something else. Now those eyes were dark with pain. "I'll be all right, Patrick. I've confronted killers before."

Not by choice, but because darkness had seemed to follow me ever since Mama had hugged me and walked away into the night and never returned. For years I'd been angry at her for leaving, and at whoever had kept her from coming back. My anger was irrational. But it was still there, in a corner of my mind.

I couldn't fight for Mama when I was a child. I'd lost her to the night. But I could fight now. It had taken seventeen years for me to find out what had happened to my mother. Years of unanswered questions and dark holes in my heart. I couldn't let that happen to anyone else's family. Not if I could do anything to stop it.

"I have a gun."

"I know. But that doesn't mean you won't be hurt."

My phone rang. "Thank you, Pete. I'll see you this afternoon." I put the phone down and turned to Patrick. "Pete and Ethan have agreed. They'll be there. Sarah will be with me. We've planned it to be as safe as we can."

"I should go with you," Patrick said.

A little batter from the spatula dripped onto the floor. I wanted to wipe it up before it stained the small antique hooked rug in the doorway to his kitchen. But I didn't.

"No, Patrick. Enough people are already involved. You'll drop me off at Sarah's at three this afternoon. Holgate will meet Sarah and I there at three-thirty. We want him to see that I'm alone, and I'm carrying the embroidery. Pete and Ethan will already be at Sarah's and have set up a recorder, and maybe a camera." I tried to smile. It was hard to reassure Patrick when I needed reassurance myself. "After it's all over I'll call, and you can come and get me."

"Are you sure this is the only way?"

"It's the only way anyone's come up with. The longer we wait, the harder it will be. Holgate might go back to California."

"And if it wasn't him?"

"Then we'll go back to the beginning and start again, asking more questions. Right now we don't have many answers, but the ones we have all lead to Holgate."

"But he doesn't have a motive."

"People kill for all sorts of reasons. You've seen it right here at Aurora, Patrick. People kill out of anger, jealousy, resentment, because of an old grudge. . . . Murder isn't logical, except in the mind of the murderer. Whoever killed Clem had a reason. Maybe this afternoon we can find out what that reason was."

CHAPTER 37

"In Memory of Samuel Gooch who died
    Dec 1 1822 at sea aged 16 years
In memory of John Gooch who died
    Sept 12 1830 aged 18 years
These lovely sons to parents dear
Did find an early grave
One in the bosom of the earth
The other in the wave
In distant climes though now they sleep
Yet when the dead shall rise
Both sea and land shall yield their trust
To meet in yonder skies."

—Memorial sampler stitched by their
younger sister, Olive Jane Gooch
(1822–1902), in Wells, Maine, 1832. In
1848 Olive married Walter Littlefield
and moved to Melrose, Massachusetts,
where they raised their two daughters.

Patrick didn't say much more. We ate his pancakes for lunch, drenched in butter and generous servings of Maine maple syrup.

We tried to chat about the weather. The Celtics. The cats.

But we were both focused on what was going to happen that afternoon.

At quarter to three I pulled on my boots, tucked my Glock into its holder under my sweatshirt, covered everything with my parka, and picked up the padded envelope protecting the embroidery and the Foundling Hospital paper.

"No gloves or mittens?" Patrick asked.

I shook my head. If I had to fire my gun, it would be easier with bare hands, but I didn't explain that. He was already worried enough.

I'd been inside too long. My breath made a small cloud in the cold, but the world was beautiful. The sun was beginning to set. Already streaks of red and orange were reflected on the snow, glinting on the ice that sparkled beneath the latest flurries. Winter sunsets were more dramatic than those in summer, as if nature were rewarding those of us who lived in darker, colder, places.

"You're the bravest, most stubborn woman I've ever known," Patrick said on our way downtown. "Just be careful, please?"

"I will," I promised. We both knew the words were hollow. I'd do what I needed to do.

"I don't want to lose you," he said, stopping his car in front of Sarah's shop.

Lights were on inside the shop, and her windows were filled with antiques again. Nothing was quite the way it had been before the explosion, but order had been restored. New snow had already covered traces of where my little red car had burned, and where Clem had died.

"I don't want to lose myself," I answered, giving Patrick a quick kiss. Before I changed my mind, I got out of his car.

CHAPTER 38

"Welcome hero to the West To the land
　thy sword hath blest
To the country of the Free Welcome
　Friend of Liberty
Grateful millions guard thy fame Age and
　Youth revere thy name
Beauty twines the wreath for thee
　Glorious Son of Liberty
Years shall speak a nation's love
　Wheresoer thy footstep move
By the choral paean met Welcome
　Lafayette."

—Stitched by Sarah Ann Minott (1814–
　　1881), age nine, in Portland, Maine,
October 1824, to celebrate the Marquis de
Lafayette's 1824–1825 tour of the United
States. Sarah included six alphabets in
her sampler and a border of strawberries.

My junior year in high school, at Gram's
urging, I'd joined the Haven Harbor High drama
club. Gram was hoping I'd make new, more
conventional friends.

I sloshed paint on scenery and found that the prop
room also served as a private place to meet boys.

343

My favorite part of staging a new play was the moment when props and actors were in place, but silent. The moment before the curtain was raised and the action began.

Sarah's store this afternoon gave me the same sensation.

It could have been a movie or stage set of any small-town antiques store. Sarah was behind the counter, making coffee. Old prints, oil paintings, and embroideries framed in Victorian gold or carved oak frames hung on the back and side walls, interrupted only by two large bookcases, one filled with flowered china cups, saucers, and teapots, and one with nineteenth-century leather-bound books and a few twentieth-century first editions. Rows of tables leading from the front of the store to the back were covered with black cloths, which showed off sparkling pieces of silver serving pieces, brass ornaments and kitchen utensils, and crystal glasses, vases, and decorative tabletop sculptures.

Children's toys, from iron banks and fire engines to dolls, tea sets, and miniature furniture the right size for a dollhouse, were on one table, near a small grouping of children's furniture: an oak desk, a stenciled rocking chair, and two wicker porch chairs, all sized for a three- or four-year-old. A quilt pieced of velvet and embroidered with names and memories hung above the furniture.

Staffordshire china figures covered one table; sparkling green and blue and orange carnival glass another; and three blown-glass baskets Sarah had once told me were "end of the day" baskets because they combined all the colors the glassmakers had been using that day were on a third.

Where were Pete and Ethan?

"Angie!" Sarah said, looking relieved to see me. "You're here. Put your coat behind the counter."

I walked toward the back of the store and took off my parka. As I handed it to her over the counter I saw a hand reach up from behind her counter and take it.

I gasped, realizing how tense I was. And then I laughed, letting out the nervous energy I hadn't realized I was holding in as I went around the counter and looked down. Pete was crouched underneath the counter where Sarah usually stashed empty bags, boxes, and wrapping materials.

No one could see him unless they, too, were in back of the counter.

" 'Afternoon, Angie," he said, grinning at my surprise.

"Is Ethan here too?" I asked, looking around.

"At your service," he said, stepping down the staircase to Sarah's apartment. He'd been standing where I had been the day I'd overheard Sarah's customers asking her about samplers.

"All set?" I confirmed.

"We put a small camera in the corner of the store to record what happens in the next hour. Plus, I'll be recording everything from the time Holgate comes into the store. If he does."

"Is there any doubt?" I asked.

"He answered my e-mail and said he'd be here," said Sarah, taking the padded envelope I'd been clutching to my chest and putting it on her counter. "We just have to wait and see. Cup of coffee?"

"Sure. Black," I said, keeping my eyes on the door. Sarah, Pete, and Ethan were more relaxed than I was. Or maybe they were acting, the way I was. Pretending that arranging to meet a possible killer in an antiques shop was an everyday occurrence.

"How did Patrick react when you told him what we were going to do?" Sarah asked, handing me a bone-china cup hand-painted with forget-me-nots and filled with dark coffee.

"He wasn't happy," I said.

She nodded. "I'm not surprised. But did he understand?"

"I hope so."

I walked toward the front of the store. "What if another customer comes in while he's here?"

"The store isn't usually open now. Pete and Ethan suggested putting a 'store closed' sign outside. But somehow that seemed too staged. I doubt if it'll be a problem. This time of day in February I don't get many drop-in customers."

I glanced at my phone. Three-fifteen. Three-twenty. No one said anything. I wandered through the store, looking at everything, but seeing nothing. A mantel clock rimmed in brass and set in black marble ticked loudly in the corner.

I'd been in Sarah's store dozens of times and never heard it before. Today the sound of the seconds ticking off echoed in my head.

Had we made the right decision? Was Seaward Holgate the man we were looking for? Was he dangerous? Were we—was I—crazy?

No answers. Only questions.

At three-thirty the clock chimed. One bell.

What if Holgate didn't come?

What would we do if he did? Sarah and I hadn't talked through every possibility. She was depending on me to guide whatever was said.

I finished my coffee and handed the empty cup back to Sarah.

In back of me, the door of her shop opened.

CHAPTER 39

"So when the morning shineth
So when the moon is bright
So when the eve declineth
So in the hush of night
So with pure mind and feeling
Fling earthly thoughts away
And in thy chamber kneeling
Do thou in secret pray."

—Harriet Robinson (1828–1894) of Exeter,
New Hampshire, worked this sampler
while she was attending the Exeter Female
Academy in 1839. In 1859 Harriet married
Abner Little Merrill, a member of a wealthy
local family. He attended Phillips Exeter
Academy and Harvard University. They
lived in Boston, but remained involved with
life in Exeter, and donated money to local
organizations, including Phillips Exeter
Academy, throughout their lives.

The man in the doorway was tall and slender, wearing a suit and tie under his overcoat. He was dressed as the Seaward Holgate I'd seen on television, not the man who'd stood at the back of the auction hall.

But he was the same man. Maybe he'd had a business meeting in Portland or Westbrook today. Maybe he was trying to impress us, or himself.

I glanced at Sarah, to see if he was also the man who'd been in her store before. She nodded slightly and went to greet him.

"I'm glad you got my e-mail. I'm Sarah Byrne. We met a few days ago."

"Yes," he acknowledged, and then looked at me. "And you're the woman I saw on television. The woman with the embroidery I'm interested in."

The conversation could go in several directions. We could stand and discuss embroidery without acknowledging that we knew this man's name. Or we could let him know his identity wasn't a secret, although so far he hadn't introduced himself.

I was too nervous to be subtle. "And you're Seaward Holgate. I saw you on television, too. You're donating an arts center to Maine."

He blinked, as though surprised I'd identified him. "That's right. I'm naming it after my mother. She introduced me to the arts." He turned to Sarah. "You met her the other day. She's also interested in old samplers and other types of embroidered work."

"And you were at the Holgate and Gould families' auction in Augusta last week," I added.

This time his reaction was stronger. He took a

step toward me. "I was. One of my cousins was auctioning items that should have come to my mother. I was buying some of them for her."

"But you didn't bid on the samplers, or any of the needlepointed items."

Seaward Holgate's eyes were dark. He hesitated before replying. I suspected he hadn't expected to have been identified. "No. I didn't realize then how important they were to my mother. But when she saw the coat of arms you'd bought displayed for anyone to see on television, she was upset."

"Why?" I asked. "Your mother knew the embroideries would be in the auction. If they were from her family, she must have been familiar with them. I'm surprised she was most interested in the embroidery in the worst condition." I pointed toward the samplers Sarah had bought at the auction that were hanging on the back wall of the shop. "The ones Sarah bought are much more valuable."

Holgate looked from me to Sarah and back again. "You probably came from families that respected one another. That respected inheritances and traditions and bloodlines."

I glanced at Sarah, who'd paled. My family was like that, in some ways. Sarah's wasn't.

I stepped toward him. "In the television interview you said you grew up poor, with a single parent. And yet Senator Holgate's husband, your uncle, is a well-known philanthropist here in Maine."

351

"You heard right. He's my mother's brother, but, after their parents disinherited her, he followed the tradition. Nothing from the Holgate family was to come to my mother, or to me. Jonathan paraded around Maine, being applauded for the money he donated to worthy causes, but he never felt his sister, who struggled to keep food on our table, was worth a dime." Holgate's face reddened. "Now I have more money than he ever had. I've bought my mother the kind of house she deserves, the kind of house she grew up in, and should have been enjoying all the years she worked at menial jobs so I could stay in school. But when she went to Jonathan and asked for some of the family furnishings, pieces she'd loved when she was growing up that he'd kept in storage, he refused. He told her he'd rather sell them to strangers than let her have them. That she'd disgraced the family by having me. Me! I was the disgrace! Jonathan inherited his money. I've earned mine, working long hours and focusing on business, not on social giving."

"So you went to the auction to buy things your mother had remembered from her childhood and had treasured."

"And that's what I did. Distant cousins bought a few pieces, so did dealers, but I got the pieces my mother remembered most fondly. It meant a lot to her." He looked from me to Sarah. "For years she'd struggled, while her brother pranced around Maine attending museum benefits and being hosted by the best classes of Mainers, because he was a Holgate. Old Maine family. Old Maine money. Old Maine roots. And all the while he ignored his sister's suffering."

"And when your mother saw the coat of arms embroidery on the television . . ."

"My mother didn't remember it. And I don't think anyone—certainly not Jonathan—knew about the paper you found in back of it. An illegitimate Holgate! It was perfect! All these years Jonathan and his parents had lorded it over my mother. She was the one who'd brought bad blood into the family. She was the slut . . . the promiscuous one. And here, you found proof. Proof that the Holgates in England had thrown away an illegitimate baby, like Mother's family had thrown her away. Why else would anyone from a powerful English family have left a child at the Foundling Hospital? I wanted that paper. I wanted to publish it, and then to frame it, to celebrate life and survival. To stuff it up the nose Jonathan's been looking down all these years. He always said 'blood will tell.' I wanted him to know his blood wasn't pure blue; perhaps it included tinges of the kitchen or the street. I wanted him to know what it felt like to have invisible branches on his family tree."

"But you didn't contact Clem Walker, or me, to tell us that. Or offer to buy the needlepoint and paper. You threatened us. You bullied us."

"I wanted to be the one to tell Jonathan about the history of his perfect bloodline. I wanted to see the expression on his face when he found out he was the descendant of a bastard like me. I wanted to frame that piece of paper and present it to one of those museums or organizations that've been fawning over Jonathan Holgate for years, and his father before him. I wanted to prove that my mother was as good as any of her ancestors, that she couldn't be ignored any longer."

"And when you heard Clem Walker and I were going to have lunch together in Haven Harbor, you had to find us. Talk to us. Convince us to give you that paper."

"I knew what Clem looked like. I'd seen her smiling on Channel 7 before. You, I didn't remember. You were only on the screen for a few seconds. So I watched for your friend. I saw her parking that sporty little car she drove at the wharf. Stupid woman. She didn't even look surprised when I knocked on her window. She opened the door. Thought I wanted her autograph! I told her what I wanted was that paper. She said she didn't have it; you had it. And she wouldn't tell me where you were. I was so angry. I got carried away. I shouldn't have done that."

"Done what?" I asked, innocently, thinking of the tape recorder and Pete under the counter.

"That sassy bitch didn't know how much that

paper meant to me. How could she? She lived a perfect little life, flirting with her audience through the television set. Expecting to be asked for her autograph wherever she went!" Holgate looked past me, toward the wharf, toward the parking lot where he'd killed Clem. "It was so easy to kill her."

"What about the needle?"

Holgate shrugged. "Not only rich women do needlepoint; Mother does it, too. She'd asked me to buy her some new needles when I went out that morning. They were in my pocket. I couldn't resist. I wanted whoever found that Walker woman to know why she'd died."

Holgate was making this too easy. He'd confessed to killing Clem. Stalking me? Blowing up my car? Legally, they came second.

Something wasn't right.

"Ms. Byrne, in your e-mail you said you had the needlepoint of the coat of arms and the paper. I'd like to see them." Holgate walked toward Sarah with assurance.

"She doesn't have them. I do," I said.

Why hadn't Pete or Ethan shown himself? What were they waiting for? The man had confessed.

"May I have them, please? That's why I came, after all."

I walked slowly toward the counter. At this point I didn't care about the needlepoint or the paper. They'd been a curiosity. A souvenir, even, of the first auction I'd attended. Now they were forever stained with Clem's blood, in my mind if not in reality. "I'll show them to you."

I picked up the envelope and pulled out both the embroidered coat of arms and the paper.

As I turned to hand them to Holgate, he grabbed Sarah, the crook of his left elbow tightening around her neck.

"What?" I said, confused for a moment.

"Put those things back in that envelope to protect them. I'm not stupid. You didn't invite me here so I could see an embroidery. You wanted me to tell you what happened to your friend. Well"—Holgate reached under his heavy coat with his right hand and pulled out a gun with a silencer—"now you know. You don't think I'm going to let either of you walk out of here, do you?"

Sarah squirmed, and kicked back, hitting his leg.

Seaward Holgate tightened his grip on Sarah. "Hey, you, stop that. You can die a lot of ways. You want to make it quick, or slow and painful? Because I don't care. All I care about is taking that paper back to my mother's house and showing her what kind of a family she came from, before I inform my dear uncle Jonathan and his famous wife, the senator. Not headlines Uncle Jonathan would like, I assure you."

I was still holding the envelope. "We haven't

done anything to you, Mr. Holgate. Please," I pleaded, "you're scaring me."

"About time," he said, holding Sarah tighter.

I had to do something. I let the envelope slip out of my hand. As it fell I bent, as if to pick it up. At the same time I pulled my gun from under my sweatshirt, turned slightly, and fired.

Holgate yelled several obscenities and dropped Sarah. I ducked in back of a nearby table and heard china and crystal breaking as his return shot ricocheted around the room.

His navy-blue pant leg was turning red from oozing blood. My shot had hit him above the knee. Holgate tried to pick up the envelope on the floor.

"Shoot again, and I'll shoot back," Pete said. "And I'm a good shot. So put your gun on the floor."

Holgate's head jerked as he turned and saw Pete coming out from behind the counter.

"I said, put the gun on the floor. Slowly," Pete said again. I stood and raised my gun, pointing · it at Holgate. He could fire at one of us, but not both of us.

He looked from Pete to me and then back again, and did as he'd been directed.

"Angie, get that gun," Pete said. "Are you all right?"

"I'm fine," I answered as I picked up Holgate's gun and put mine on Sarah's counter, out of Holgate's reach.

"Sarah? How about you?"

Sarah had been crouching behind a pine bureau on the other side of the room. She looked pale, but she stood up. "I'm okay," she answered.

"Ethan?" Pete asked.

That's when State of Maine Homicide Detective Ethan Trask came down the stairs carrying a pair of handcuffs. "I'm fine, too," he said as he put the cuffs on Seaward Holgate. "And so is the recording. Holgate, sorry to disturb your plans for the rest of the afternoon, but you're going to the emergency room with me, and then to the police station."

"I want my lawyer," said Holgate.

"You have a right to a lawyer . . ." Ethan continued the Miranda warning as he pushed the limping Holgate out the door. As Holgate's coat brushed one of Sarah's tables, something fell out of his pocket, onto the shop floor.

Pete took Holgate's gun and followed them.

Sarah and I stared at each other for a moment. I looked at the hand that had held my gun. "I shot him."

I'd carried a gun for several years. My boss at the private detective agency in Arizona had insisted I learn to shoot, and practice regularly. I was pretty darn good with a target.

And a couple of times I'd threatened someone with my Glock.

But I'd never shot anyone before.

I looked at my gun, still on the counter where I'd put it. My hand was shaking. "I shot him," I said, almost to myself.

"You did the right thing. He said he was going to kill both of us," said Sarah.

"Pete and Ethan were close by. They wouldn't have let that happen," I said. My voice was shaky.

"Something fell out of his pocket," said Sarah. She went over to the door and picked it up.

It was an open package of embroidery needles. Two were missing.

CHAPTER 40

"Teach me the measure of my days
Thou maker of my frame
I would survey life's narrow space
And learn how frail I am."

—In 1805 Phebe Bratton, born on
March 13, 1783, made this sampler in
Mrs. Armstrong's School in Lancaster,
Pennsylvania. She included a floral
border surrounding the figure of Liberty.

The next few days were a flurry of activity. Not
even another plowable snow kept any of us home
in Haven Harbor.

Sarah and I both made official statements to the
police. Back home at the rectory, Tom stubbornly
refused to rest, and, with Gram's help, was back
organizing the Congregational Church.

Trixi and I returned home, and I turned up the
heat. I hadn't been able to get really warm since
I'd fired my Glock. The police had checked it,
and it was now back in the front hall drawer,
covered with gloves and woolen hats.

I wasn't ready to pull it out again.

But I never forgot it was there.

I'd shot someone. Despite the police ruling that

I'd done it in self-defense, I wasn't ready to use it again. Having the Glock had never been a big deal. I'd had it because it was required by my job. It was power.

Now it was something else.

For the time being it would stay in the drawer.

I hadn't attended Clem's funeral, but Patrick had. He'd wanted Steve to have a friend there.

After everything calmed down, Patrick and I met Sarah and Pete at the Harbor Haunts for dinner.

We debated: sit next to the fireplace or the window? On a weekday night in February when it was snowing outside, all options were good.

We'd settled on the window. Lights in the restaurant shone on the falling snow and the white sidewalk and street outside. Inside, the room was warm and filled with friendship, and, maybe, more. But the fireplace was glowing, and the room smelled welcoming: a mixture of wood smoke and garlic and coffee and beer. It seemed natural for Sarah and Pete to be there together with Patrick and I.

Life was going on.

Patrick ordered a bottle of wine for three of us, while Pete stuck to his usual beer. We agreed to share a large bowl of mussels in garlic and white wine and two baguettes as an appetizer, and then laughed as we all chose different pasta dishes as main courses.

Pasta and February seemed to go together.

At first we made small talk as we shared the mussels and tore off chunks of bread to dip in the fragrant broth.

Then the subject on everyone's minds came up.

"How's Holgate?" Patrick asked.

"He's fine," Pete assured him. "Angie's shot didn't hit the bone. But he won't be going anywhere but jail for a while. The judge refused to grant him bail, because of his wealth and the murder and attempted murder charges. His attorney's requesting Holgate be examined by psychiatrists."

I shivered. That was the man who'd been stalking me.

"Was it him . . . all of it?" I asked. "I know he killed Clem. But the messages . . . and my car . . . and the footprints around Aurora . . ." Patrick reached over and squeezed my hand.

"He blew up your car, for sure," Pete said. "His story changes slightly with each telling, but it sounds as though he put the fireworks there late the night Clem died, while you were at Sarah's. He correctly assumed that if you hadn't taken your car by then, it would still be on the street in the morning. He came back to Haven Harbor the next day, this time with his mother. According to Gus they browsed in the bookshop, but didn't buy anything but time. Holgate made several phone calls while he was there. One was to the activator he'd hidden under snow, under your car."

"Did his mother know what he was doing?" Sarah asked.

"So far we think she's in the clear. He'd bought her a house and given her money to furnish it, and she knew about the arts center he was donating to the state and naming for her. She knew about the auction, but, as she told you, Sarah, she didn't go to the preview or the sale itself. She didn't want to be snubbed yet again by her estranged relatives. But she'd mentioned the sale to her son. That he went to the auction and bought some of the pieces she'd mentioned over the years was a total surprise to her."

"What about the woman Pax said was asking about Patrick at the post office?"

"He wasn't able to confirm that it was her. It could have been anyone. Not enough to implicate Barbara."

"And the telephone and e-mail messages?"

"All from Seaward. From a temporary cell phone."

"What about the footprints in the snow around my place?" asked Patrick.

"He wouldn't admit to them. And, truthfully, they may not be his. Might be someone else local, checking out your place. No damage was done, and the boot prints in the snow could have belonged to any large man."

"They were scary," I admitted. "Intimidating."

Pete nodded. "And you were right to call me

about them. But for the moment, there's no reason to believe you're not safe."

Outside the window a figure appeared out of the darkness. The old man was bent over, pushing his way up the hill from the harbor against the snow and wind. He was carrying a large plastic garbage bag over his shoulder, like a Santa with a sack.

Pete sighed. "Ike Hamilton shouldn't be collecting empties in this weather. I'll get him to come in and have some chowder, and drop him at the shelter after we've had our dinner. His place doesn't have enough heat in this weather."

As Pete slipped out of his chair and went to help Ike, I looked over at Sarah. "Pete's a good man. Remember, I told you."

"You didn't have to tell me," said Sarah. "I've always known that."

"Thank goodness the nightmare of the past week is over." I watched out the window as Pete took Ike's arm and guided him toward the door of the Harbor Haunts. "We're very lucky."

Sarah's Pasta Puttanesca

Pasta puttanesa (*spaghetti alla puttanesca*) originated in Naples, Italy. Legends say this Neapolitan dish was cooked by "ladies of easy virtue" who wanted a dish they could put together easily, between clients. (*Puttana* means prostitute in Italian.) But a very similar word, *puttanata,* means rubbish or leftovers or nonsense. So perhaps pasta puttanesca was thrown together for late-night customers by a chef with limited ingredients. Whichever story you prefer, this is Sarah's version.

Ingredients

6 cloves of garlic, finely chopped
4 tablespoons extra virgin olive oil
1 large yellow onion, chopped
2 ounces anchovy fillets (1 can) in oil, drained and finely chopped or crushed
1 large (28 ounces) can of Italian plum tomatoes, preferably San Marzano, chopped, with liquid
2 tablespoons thick Italian tomato paste

12 ounces of black or Kalamata olives in oil,
    drained, pitted, and chopped
3 tablespoons of capers, drained
zest and juice of one lemon
1 tablespoon dried oregano
1 tablespoon dried marjoram
1 generously packed cup of finely chopped
    Italian parsley + extra to sprinkle on top
1 pound of dried spaghetti or linguini (1 box)

Begin heating water for pasta. (Add a little olive oil to keep pasta from sticking.)

In a large saucepan or frying pan: Sauté chopped garlic in olive oil. Add chopped onion and cook for two minutes.

Add crushed anchovies and tomatoes.

Mix in tomato paste, olives, capers, lemon zest, lemon juice, oregano, and marjoram. Cook over medium heat for 10 minutes, stirring occasionally.

Add cup of parsley, and cook another minute.

Cook pasta, per instructions on box. Drain. Top with sauce, toss to coat, and sprinkle with additional parsley.

Serves 4. Also good reheated.

Note: Unlike other Italian pasta dishes, traditionally pasta puttanesca is not served with cheese.

Books are
produced in the
United States
using U.S.-based
materials

Books are printed
using a revolutionary
new process called
THINKtech™ that
lowers energy usage
by 70% and increases
overall quality

Books are
durable and
flexible
because of
Smyth-sewing

Paper is
sourced using
environmentally
responsible
foresting methods
and the
paper is acid-free

Center Point Large Print
600 Brooks Road / PO Box 1
Thorndike, ME 04986-0001 USA

(207) 568-3717

US & Canada:
1 800 929-9108
www.centerpointlargeprint.com